A LONG WAY
FROM *Clare*

A LONG WAY
FROM *Clare*

ROBERT W. SMITH

Meryton Press

OYSTERVILLE, WA

A LONG WAY FROM CLARE

ISBN: 978-1-68131-072-5

This is a work of fiction. Names, characters, places, and incidents are products of the author's imagination or are used fictitiously. Any resemblance to actual events or persons, living or dead, is entirely coincidental.

Cover design by Janet B. Taylor
Front cover image: "On the Chicago River" (1912), photo by Leroy Goble, Chicago Camera Club
Back cover image: "Cheating the Fairies" photo by A. W. Cutler,
                published in the *National Geographic Magazine* (March, 1927)
Edited by Elizabeth L. Farlin and Ellen Pickels
Book layout and design by Ellen Pickels

Published in the United States of America.

for Patrick O'Connell

Prologue

County Clare, Ireland, 1886

Footing the turf is no task for a mere wean, the lad thought, feeling a sense of pride in his manly expertise. It was grueling work, especially in the late afternoon, but he took the sore muscles and aching back as sure signs he was transitioning to adulthood.

Pa taught the boys well before the death coach arrived to claim the old fella in early spring. The lad knew how to assemble the triangular turf foots vertically and touching at the top—for maximum sunlight over the coming weeks. The boys had developed an efficient system wherein his older brother, Kevin, would haul bricks from the strands, leaving little Conor to foot them for the final drying.

The work required Conor to periodically fix the track of the sun in his mind to capture maximum sunlight for the drying. Turning east to plot a fix, Conor spotted a thick smoke trail. Deep gray like a rain cloud, it rose slowly over the ridge just beyond the bog in the direction of the family cottage. 'Twas a curious sight this fine afternoon, for there was no burning to be done around the homeplace that day.

"Kevin," he called out to his older brother, "do ye see the smoke?"

"I do, indeed, Brother. We'll leave the turf for today and be on our way now."

At the top of a ridge—beyond the dips, stone fences, and green fields—the barefoot boys could make out their cottage in the distance. A grass fire beside the stone house spewed great flames high into the dwindling light. A crowd of men scurried hastily about the place, at least two of them on horseback.

As they drew closer to the mayhem, the young lad could see their ma standing outside the cottage holding two skinny chickens. Their few sheep and the pig stood on the back of a horse-drawn wagon.

"Sure what's goin' on then, Kevin?" Conor asked in a state of mild anxiety.

"Ah, don't ye worry a'tall, Conor. They'll all be off in the shake of a stick, and we'll be back at the bog in the marnin' as usual."

They stopped in front of their home, and the boys watched as three strange men on the roof worked feverishly, dismantling the thatch and dropping great handfuls onto a burning pile near the front door.

Apparently displeased with the lack of progress, a constable on horseback shouted to the men, "Just fire the whole bloody roof."

In the blink of an eye, the entire roof was ablaze. Even at seven years of age, Conor knew something sinister was afoot. Another three or four workers huddled around the fire, resting after their stock roundup.

Seeing the boys arrive from the bog, their ma walked toward the cart with the chickens, motioning for Kevin to join her. "Stay with the pull cart, Conor." There was not a hint of panic or anger in her voice. "Everything is fine and dandy here now."

As Conor's two last living family members whispered quietly in the trampled garden amidst the chaos, a uniformed constable on horseback galloped up to the cart. "Down from there now, boy! This cart is confiscated for arrears. They're the landlord's property now. Ye'll be off this property by morning."

The voice conveyed a hostile tone and only compounded young Conor's confusion. Still, whatever these fellas were up to did not so much as raise a hair on Ma's head—and her with a temper legendary from here to Lisdoonvarna. Before Conor could give voice to his confusion, he felt Kevin's arms around his waist, lifting him to the ground.

"Ahhh, come on now, Conor," Kevin prodded. "Sure there's nothin' t' cry about. 'Tis only the constable come to collect the rent. These eejits on the roof only did us a kindness. Sure wasn't Pa planning to replace the leaky old thatch in any case? They did us a favor rippin' it out. Sure now ye can help me t'row up a new one. We'll be all right. First thing tomorrow, Ma and me will set this right with the landlord."

"Don't be daft," Conor snapped, embarrassed. "Sure I wasn't cryin'. 'Twas somethin' in me eye."

But he did cry and did not know the reason. Still, Kevin's words reassured Conor because his older brother never lied to him. This was bad but fixable. As the gang around the fire began to hoot and pass the jug, the boys' mother, Finola, held Conor tightly by the arm. "Come now, me boys. Let's go down the road to Mrs. Hennessy for a cuppa tea."

THE NEXT MORNING, KEVIN WOKE HIS YOUNGER BROTHER AT THE crack of dawn from beside the hearth on Mrs. Hennessey's floor. "Come on now, Conor. Let's get a *craic*[1] on. Sure we're off to build Ma a new cottage. And didn't I tell ye it would all work out?"

They sent Conor out to milk Mrs. Hennessey's cow as Ma and her hostess prepared a few scraps for breakfast. Kevin remained with the women. Conor was alert for signs of sadness or fear, even whispering, but the general good nature of all drove the unsettled thoughts from his young mind, and before the sun fully shed the horizon, the boys were headed to the bog to build Ma a new house. It sounded to Conor like a great *craic*.

---

1 Pronounced "crack." Slang for *fun* and *enjoyment*, but the true meaning embraces the Irish culture and means something far greater than just a good time. True *craic* requires great company and lively conversation where everyone is involved.

Within a week, the lads laid the final turf brick in Ma's new cottage—and none too soon. The last of the early summer rains could come at any moment. It was the most backbreaking task in all of Conor's seven years, and he wanted so much to be proud of the achievement. As Pa used to say, "The harvest never lies." Sweat pouring from his little body, he stood back a good ways to judge the fruits of their labor. The mud walls appeared crooked; the one-room cottage had no windows—not even a proper door. Beyond that, the grass roof leaked and seemed alive with tiny creatures.

"Sure 'tis a good house then, Kevin?" Conor was perfectly willing to be dissuaded from his initial opinion that it resembled a hastily assembled pig shed.

"Aye. Ma will love it. Nice and cozy. And look there—isn't that Galway Bay in the distance past the cliffs? What more beauty could a widow ask for in her old age?"

"I s'pose 'tis grand," Conor conceded, "but how will Ma see the water with no windows? And where will I be sleepin' in this fine house? And yourself?" The question dogged him like a thorn in that bloody dress Ma made him wear whenever he left the cottage.

Kevin put his arm around the child and patted his shoulder gently. "Sure let's take a walk down to the cliffs and chat a bit."

Conor no longer liked the Cliffs of Moher because the sight breathed life to bad memories. "Sure you know how I feel about them cliffs, Kevin."

Kevin nodded. "Aye, I know well enough, but I t'ink it's the best place to be havin' this conversation."

His brother seemed to always know best, so Conor nodded in agreement. "That's the way then. We'll be off to the cliffs."

The locals from Lisdoonvarna, Lahinch, and such cherished the cliffs as the "grandest sight in all of Ireland." Visitors would flock there in fair weather and spread their blankets to see the wild sea and the rocky beaches below as gulls played in the wind currents of the deep drop.

The brothers sat in the long, green grass that afternoon—only steps from the edge—with the sun in their faces. "Isn't it beautiful?" Kevin asked. "Do you know what's out there?"

Conor shrugged. "Sure it's water. Isn't it?"

"Oh yes, 'tis that. But beyond the water?"

"America, I s'pose."

"Sure that's right—where yer own uncle found fortune and happiness a ways back. Would ye like to go there?"

Conor chuckled, erasing Kevin's comment in mid-air with a big hand swipe. "Ah, don't be daft. Ye're havin' me on. Sure Ma would never leave Ireland, and you know it."

"Ye're a clever boy. Ma will never leave home. But she has a fine new house now, and she t'inks it best if we go ourselves—just the two of us—and make a go of it. It'll be a great craic, Little Brother, a grand voyage on a beautiful ship clear across to New York and on to Illinois."

"And what in the be-jaezaz is *El-in-oys*?"

"Easy, boy-o. Pa would roll in the grave if 'e heard you curse. Sure 'tis like a small village outside of New York, I'd say. A grand place accordin' t' your uncle, and didn't Abraham Lincoln himself build a cottage there."

"Sure is he the gombeen from the pub? The one Pa went on about with the short arms? Pa said he fled t' America one step ahead of the hounds."

"Different fella altogether, but we'll see what Ma says tonight at Mrs. Hennessey's."

"Will I wear dresses in El-in-oys, Kevin?"

Kevin scoffed. "Ah, Jaezuz, no, Conor. All that nonsense will stay here in Ireland with the *gobshites*[2] who peddle it. Ye're growing up too quickly, but ye may as well know this minute: I put no weight in all

---

2 A person of very poor judgment and unpleasant character.

that wee fairy rubbish the old women and the priest gab about. Our Pa never bought into it himself, but Ma is another story."

"Are there no fairies in America then, Kevin? Will they not kidnap me if I don't wear a dress?"

"Ye'll sooner be kidnapped by that fookin' priest. Sure Pa never blasphemed against the Church because a fella is better safe than sorry, but he had plenty to say about the bloody fairies. Sure there's no fairies any fookin' place, so there's no fairies will kidnap ye in America if ye dress like the fine boy ye are. I give ye me solemn word on that, and that's the way of it now. And if ye decide to grow up a fookin' Protestant like the rich folks in America, fair play to ye, Little Brother."

Kevin seemed to reflect quietly a minute there in the grass. Then, looking onto the vastness of Galway Bay and beyond, he patted Conor's head and added softly with a single tear in his eye, "But there's devils. There's devils, indeed, and right here in County Clare."

Chapter 1

The old locomotive sputtered and slowed to a crawl at the Clinton Station, rousing Conor from slumber. From his window, he watched as the steam slowly evaporated to reveal the passing frame of a young soldier waiting on the platform. For a fleeting second, he thought he had seen his brother.

He stood to stretch his legs as a few waiting travelers boarded with their bags. It seemed everyone on board the half-empty train was bound for Chicago today, a mixture of businessmen, couples on holiday, and one particularly dubious character escorting four very young women.

As the train began to roll again, Conor closed his eyes but soon heard a male voice beside him. "Sir, would you mind if I sat across from you and stretched out my legs toward the window? I'm hoping to catch a few winks before we hit Chicago."

"Wouldn't mind at all," he answered. "Going on leave to the big city?"

The soldier placed his bag and campaign hat in the top rack. "No, sir. I'm just finishing my leave. Hadn't seen my family in two years."

The trooper extended his hand, smiling. "I'm Charlie Damme."

"Conor Dolan. Glad to meet you."

Conor was not accustomed to being called "sir" outside of a court-room where it meant nothing, but he was delighted to have some polite company. The soldier was wearing the army's new earth-toned tunic. It was handsome enough but lacked the romantic flare of the old Cavalry Blue, the uniform Conor's brother once wore.

Conor saw his brother in uniform only once when Kevin came to Springfield on leave. "A Clare man in the US Cavalry," Uncle Willie had said. "Oh, your old Pa would be proud." The young lawyer never forgot that visit and remembered how proud he was of his older brother that day.

Conor's thoughts sped along on a pace with the cropless October fields. Wind and wandering cows raced past his window until another cloud of bovine stink invaded the car. He tried to close the window, finding the mechanism hopelessly stuck. The elderly woman behind him expressed her annoyance by coughing loudly.

"Are you traveling for business or pleasure?" the soldier asked.

Conor felt uncomfortable sharing his story with the soldier. Char-lie was charismatic, to be sure, and they would never encounter each other again. *Besides, how would I even start?* he thought. This poor soldier would never get any sleep. Just to change the subject, he said, "Business. Did you see action in the Philippines?"

Charlie nodded. "I suppose you could call it that. I was at Balangiga on the island of Samar in 1901 when the gugus massacred the Ninth Infantry Regiment."

The Balangiga Massacre had been national news a couple of years ago and triggered high profile courts martial. As Conor recalled, upwards of fifty men were slaughtered in an early morning surprise attack by the native Philippine population. Fewer than two dozen soldiers survived, so Conor was not certain how to respond.

"I guess if running for your life counts as action, I got a heap of it," Charlie added as the train rolled toward Gilman. "What is it you do, Conor?"

"I'm a lawyer."

"Well, I'll be. Didn't figure you for that. I had some experience with lawyers and such in my youth. Anyways, I think I'll just rest my eyes for a spell."

Conor retrieved a wallet from the breast pocket of his finest suit—his only suit—and removed the old photograph of his brother, Kevin Dolan, in police uniform. Conor was proud of the image, partly because his Springfield family carried on about how much he resembled a younger Kevin—but for the older brother's extra few pounds. At six feet, Kevin was the taller by a good three inches and the bigger man all around, but the resemblance around the eyes, nose, and mouth were undeniable.

In the picture, Kevin's chocolate-colored hair was neatly cropped but covered by the cumbersome police hat, much like the pipe-like headgear of a London Bobbie. It was the full, fair-skinned face of a man who enjoyed a good meal and an extra pint now and again. Their eyes, he knew for certain, were identical: deep set and blue. Not the blue of a sunlit sea or a clear sky, but a deep, serious blue like in the Stars and Stripes, a blue that might make a man think twice about taking advantage. The nose was "downright princely," their Aunt Mary would say. All in all, it was a gentle, patient face.

"Were you a police officer before you became a lawyer?" Charlie was peeking over at Kevin's picture. *It wasn't much of a nap*, thought Conor.

Conor smiled, his eyes lingering on the photograph. Of course, the image was seven or eight years old, but the resemblance was undeniable. "Oh no," he replied. "This is my brother, a Chicago police officer."

"I hope you have a nice visit," said Charlie, apparently deciding not to press. "I'm on my way to a new posting at Fort Sheridan to train infantry troops."

"You're fortunate to be so close to home.

"Yeah, it's a real break after two years in the Philippines."

"My brother served in the army years ago. He was out West—fighting Indians, I think. Afraid I don't know much about his service. I was just a child, and he never spoke of it."

"Does your brother have a family in the city?" Charlie asked.

Conor did not mind the conversation. He needed it but still hesitated to discuss his brother with a complete stranger. One could be friendly without being intimate. A stranger could unwittingly invade private spaces, unravel nerves, and expose unwanted emotions.

"No, no family," he replied. The honest answer would have been, *"I don't know."*

Sadly, he did not know much about Kevin's life in Chicago. That was Kevin's choice for a reason that remained a mystery to young Conor. If his brother did have a family in Chicago, it was a closely guarded secret for the moment. But Conor's unannounced and uninvited appearance would change all that in a heartbeat.

"Tickets, tickets" came the conductor's voice down the aisle. There were about a dozen people in the car, and they all held out their tickets except an older, rather disheveled-looking gentleman near the front who went through the motions of finding it. The conductor passed by the vagabond without a word, quietly deciding to perform an act of charity. The gesture was not lost on Conor. Punching his ticket, the trainman said, "Good day, sir. Moving to Chicago, are you, sir?"

The conductor was only trying to make conversation, but the question stumped Conor, surprised him even. "To be honest, sir, I don't know the answer to that question." The soldier was snoozing, and the kind-hearted conductor did not disturb him. Conor closed his eyes, thinking of what was and what might come next.

THE CONDUCTOR'S VOICE AGAIN BREACHED THE RHYTHM OF THE rails as the train began to slow. "Bloomington, next stop, Bloomington, Illinois. Please remove all your belongings when you leave the train."

Only two or three passengers moved.

When the conductor had passed, the soldier yawned. "How long was I asleep?"

"Oh, not long. We're in Bloomington."

"Where's Bloomington?" Charlie asked.

Conor thought the question odd since the man's homeplace was Clinton. He said, "Smack in the middle of the state. You're from Clinton, right?"

Charlie hesitated, then said, "No, not really. Uh, my father bought a farm there while I was in the Philippines." His answer seemed reasonable enough.

The scenery only changed when the train stopped along the way. Endless wheat fields, barren and ready for seeding, streaked past his window with nary a hill in sight, not even an anthill.

At Gilman, the train switched tracks and headed roughly due north. The rattling and clatter aroused the slumbering soldier.

"I hope I wasn't snoring," said the private.

Conor reached under the seat for a small basket. "No, but it's good you're awake. Would you care for some lunch? My aunt packed me a basket. Smells very much like fried chicken, and I know for a fact there are three bottles of beer."

Charlie smiled and nodded. "I'll be damned. I'm mighty grateful to you, Conor—and your aunt."

Charlie was a pleasant companion, and beer the perfect elixir for Conor's reluctant tongue. He appreciated the opportunity to share his edited life story to a captive listener. Conor told the man about his uncle from Ireland who worked on the Illinois Central railroad and ran a small blacksmith shop in Springfield, Illinois, among a growing and ascendant Irish community. The uncle was raising nine kids of his own, so after two years in the army, Kevin went to Chicago and got on the police department, sending money for years to pay Conor's board and educational expenses. Kevin himself even arranged and paid for Conor's twelve years of music lessons in Springfield. Conor seldom had the opportunity to share the company of a friendly stranger in Springfield.

"So you were born in Springfield?" Charlie asked.

Conor smiled and shook his head. "No. We were both born in County Clare, Ireland."

"But you have no accent," Charlie protested.

"I've been in Illinois a long time," Conor explained, being well aware he had shed his brogue years ago. He preferred to think of himself as American-born, although not Protestant, but he was starting to feel guilty about that lately.

As the train pulled into Kankakee for its final stop before reaching the city, Conor laughed and said to Charlie, "By the time we get to Chicago, you'll know enough about me to kill me and steal my identity."

Charlie laughed. "That's a good one, Conor," he said, "but it's an interesting story. I enjoyed hearing it, and I hope you enjoy your reunion."

"When does your train leave for Fort Sheridan?" Conor asked.

"Not 'til tomorrow. I guess I'll sleep over in Dearborn Station if I can find it tonight."

It sounded too spartan, even for a soldier. "A bench at the Dearborn Station can get pretty cold at night, I imagine."

"I've slept on worse. I don't give it a worry."

The young soldier's easy, polite manner worked to dissolve Conor's natural defenses. "I have a nice room booked at the New Southern on Thirteenth and Michigan. It's near the Illinois Central Station. You're welcome to the floor. I'd be delighted to buy you dinner."

"It's a generous offer, Conor," replied the private, "but I'd most likely oversleep and miss my morning train. I'll think about it, but most likely I'll have a meal near the station, see the sights a bit, and get some rest on a bench at the station." Conor thought Charlie might change his mind by the time they reached Chicago.

Conor's excitement grew as the changing landscape signaled their proximity to the city. North of Kankakee, weathered frame houses began to sprout from the prairie, racing past his window. He was sitting on the western-facing side of the train. As life and civilization begin to compact closer to the city, he spotted tiny streams of gray and black smoke pouring from huge stacks in the distance. The wind carried the streams up and across the distant landscape until they disappeared into the clouds. To the east, just beyond a large tract of vacant land, he could see Lake Michigan clear to the horizon.

In the city proper, the train slowed to a crawl, with grade crossings everywhere as children played, vendors peddled, and old people shuffled along on the left within feet of the tracks. The lack of safeguards surprised him. The houses squeezed to within spitting distance of the tracks in places, and Conor could see the people inside in the fleeting moments when the late afternoon sun ducked behind a building.

As the train entered a large railroad yard, Conor moved to the right side of the car, sticking his head carefully out the window as to not be decapitated. They were now on a straight two hundred-yard run into the Illinois Central Station's great archway, topped by a red-brick clock tower rising perhaps four stories into the sky.

Near the end of the working day, the station pulsated with activity. Clerks, lawyers, and merchants of all kinds in their bowlers and derbies lingered and roamed the cavernous station along the platforms, newspapers in hand, pipes on display. Nearly every man in Chicago appeared to have a bushy mustache, something Conor considered an unattractive waste of time. He could see only very few women from the window, but all were meticulously dressed and buttoned from neck to feet in the Edwardian way, hair gathered and piled directly overhead under garish hats.

Finally, the train stopped on Platform Seven, exhaling a belly of steam in a shock to Conor's ears. Charlie Damme appeared nervous, searching the platform with his eyes, end to end. "Do you see any soldiers on the platform?" Charlie asked.

"Notta one," Conor replied. "Why?"

Conor did not see the pistol at first, but Charlie Damme flashed a look of pure evil that told Conor he had one. Then he saw the barrel poking out from over Charlie's coat pocket. The deceitful soldier whispered, "Now you and me are gonna walk side by side and find a nice private place close by to swap clothes. We understandin' each other, friend?"

"I suppose we are," Conor answered stoically as a long arm swooped down from the aisle, just out of Charlie's sight, planting the cold steel of an enormous handgun across the soldier's skull. The warm blood spray spattered Conor's face and clothing as Charlie's limp form slumped slowly across the seat.

A deep voice from a big man in the aisle announced, "Your friend Charlie is wanted for murder and robbery in DeWitt County—not to mention the army wants him for desertion. We wanted to nab him away from the train but…"

"Well, I appreciate your intervention," Conor managed to say.

The cop looked like a lawyer, but the ancient Navy Colt distinguished him. The pistol lay at rest in the man's right hand as drops of blood from its violent encounter with Charlie's head oozed onto the floor. The man's associate disarmed the unfortunate soldier, ripping him from the seat and slamming him face down to the floor. Shockingly, Charlie maintained a state of semi-consciousness throughout the gruesome ordeal.

"Check the bag, Bill," said the big lawman, his knee planted firmly on Charlie's neck as he struggled to attach the iron cuffs. Looking at Conor Dolan, he said, "Lucky for you, son, we managed to board in Kankakee. If you'd left the train station with this one, today might have been your last day on earth."

A bloodied Charlie Damme, his face ground into the filthy floor, managed to laugh. "Damn, in another thirty minutes I'da been home free with a new name. And we wear the same size clothes to boot."

Conor had not moved a muscle since seeing the Colt. His heart was beating like a headless chicken's, but he managed to say, "Thank you, Officer."

The man's partner, now dragging the criminal by the collar, wiped his brow with the free hand as he spoke to Conor. "Welcome to Shi-kaw-go, sir. Do you own a gun?"

Somehow, Conor found his voice through the depths of his consternation. "I do not."

The big man tapped his shoulder holster as his words filtered through the handlebar mustache. "Were I you, I would remedy that situation, sir."

On the platform, the big cop pulled out a small notebook to take Conor's information, speaking matter-of-factly. "Name, sir?"

"Conor Dolan," he replied, handing the cop his lawyer identification.

The cop looked at Conor's identification. "Oh, a lawyer. What's the purpose of your travel?"

Conor shrugged. "I'm here to visit my brother." The cop appeared unconcerned that Charlie Damme was bleeding like a stuck pig on the platform and continued writing in his little book.

As the steam swelled and the noise surged, the big cop, nearly shouting but undeterred, said without looking up, "Says here you're from Springfield. May I ask your brother's name and address?"

The train was moving, chugging forward now. Conor needed to be on board. "Look, I have to catch that train. My brother's a cop. You might even know him. His name is Kevin Dolan. You can find me at the New Southern Hotel tonight."

He had struck a nerve. The big man looked up from the notebook, obviously startled. He hesitated, apparently trying to formulate a response. *Why? If he knows Kevin, why not say so?* "Never heard of him," the cop finally said. "Stay in town. We may need you to testify."

Chapter 2

Cold and drizzle defined the morning, but Conor figured the old black overcoat would carry him through a Chicago winter. His destination was Kevin's boardinghouse where he hoped to reunite and maybe get a room.

He did not know what to expect, and the anxiety was building. What would he say? *"Hi, Kevin. I know you always wanted me to stay away from Chicago, but I just happened to be in the neighborhood."*

Conor was, after all, a lawyer, so he knew very well that Kevin kept secrets. Kevin's infrequent visits to Springfield and his disparaging comments about Chicago in nearly every letter were all clear warnings. *Stay away from this city!* Kevin's Springfield visits had dwindled to about one every other year—just enough to pretend life was beautiful and maintain the boundary line.

Likewise, Conor's every effort over the years to extract even the most innocuous personal details from Kevin met with a brick wall of evasion or deflection. *Do you have a wife? A family? A sweetheart?* Kevin's life was always "grand," and he would soon have "a few surprises for ye, Little Brother."

The boardinghouse was less than a mile from the hotel, so he opted to walk rather than ride the trolley. No point in wasting money. Besides, it was a chance to familiarize himself with the neighborhood. He walked north on State Street for less than a mile before turning left on Polk Street. He needed to consult the map constantly.

Saloons dominated the route among plenty of dive restaurants and small stores. The resident flats were mainly second and third story apartments above the street level commerce. In the streets, without any hint of organization, men pushed carts, horses pulled carts, people rode bicycles, and kids played baseball. Pedestrians seemed to ignore near-death experiences as they dodged electric trolleys and cable cars. At the intersection of Twelfth Street, a streetcar stopped traffic in all four directions while one of the two horses patiently dropped its calling card on the old cobblestones. Conor looked north toward the Loop and saw the intersections were jammed and nearly impassable with early morning traffic of all kinds—from pedestrian to equestrian to electric. Nothing in Springfield had prepared him for the sights.

As he crossed west to Plymouth Court, an unbroken line of brothels appeared on the west side of the street stretching north over the entire block. Even this early in the morning, the vice business flourished along the street. The brothels were not confined to a given area along State Street but were clustered randomly, half a dozen on one block and a few two blocks over. He found Kevin's boardinghouse a bit further west on Polk, just before Clark.

Kevin's place on Polk looked decidedly uninviting. A sign on the door below a Star of David read "No Vacancy." He hesitated. His stomach churned. *What if Kevin is angry? What if he sees this as an intrusion?* It was even possible, he thought, that Kevin was lying in all those letters. Maybe his brother was not on the police force anymore. Conor had a hundred excuses not to knock on that door and willfully ignored them all.

A short, stocky woman of around sixty appeared, identifying herself as Mrs. Spector, the owner. She was friendly and even invited Conor into the reception area where the place showed an instant improvement. Conor found it clean, neat, and appropriately appointed like the lobby of a modest hotel. Hat already in hand, he handed the lady his card. "Good morning, ma'am. Conor Dolan. May I have a word?"

They sat in upholstered chairs before a small warming stove.

"A lawyer! Mr. Spector was an accountant, you know. He left me this building so I would always have a good living. So how can I help you, Mr....?" She glanced at the card in her hand before completing the question. When the woman looked up, her expression had changed; it was unsettled, uncomfortable. "Mr. *Dolan*?"

"Yes."

"Any relation to Kevin Dolan, the policeman who lived here?"

He smiled. "Yes. I'm his younger brother. He no longer lives here?"

The woman looked down nervously, adjusting her dress and stiffening on the sofa. "I'm sorry. I thought you knew. You should have known." It was only then that she looked up and, with great effort, directly into his eyes. Her message was clear.

Even in that moment, with the breath rushing from his body, Conor cherished the woman's kindness. "You mean my brother is dead," he declared as if the announcement had come from his own lips. It was the one thing Conor never considered. To him, Kevin was a rock—immovable, unbreakable, and invulnerable to demons like disease and execution, even old age. But his brother was not the North Star or the morning sun. The man was dead.

"I'm so sorry, Mr. Dolan, truly," the woman whispered.

"Do you know how he died, Mrs. Spector?" he asked. "Or when?"

"Maybe six weeks ago. I know he was on duty but nothing more. I don't read the papers much. Nothing but bad news. I think you should speak with the police. There was a detective here after it happened. Flynn I think his name was, from the Harrison Street Station."

"Why were the police involved?" he asked. "Was he killed?"

"Oh my goodness, nothing like that, but you'll need to talk to the police."

The woman was obviously holding back. She knew more, but Conor was not about to cause her more distress. He tried to muzzle his emotions to gather information. "Tell me, Mrs. Spector, did he have a wife or…anyone living with him, anyone I might speak with? I know that sounds strange, but we've been apart a good while. Anyone at all close to him?"

She did not hesitate. "Not a soul in his life that I knew of, Mr. Dolan, except maybe a few friends at the saloon down the street. He was polite but very private." Then her mind seemed to jump tracks. "Are you without a place to live, sir?"

Maybe he would have some luck at the saloon…later, after he had processed all this. In any case, he was bound to find friends at Kevin's police station. "For the moment, yes, ma'am. I'm in a hotel near Central Station but looking to rent a flat or a room. I'd like to live here if you have a vacancy. Otherwise, I'll look for a place nearby. It would help to live in my brother's neighborhood while I figure out what comes next."

"I'm dreadfully, sorry, but I let out the last room on the first of the month." Then the woman took a pencil and small pad from the desk, wrote an address with a note, and handed him the paper. "You must see my friend from the synagogue, Mrs. Kaplan, up on Fifth Avenue, just south of Van Buren, only a couple of blocks from here. She has a lovely three-flat with a basement. It's a bit more money, mind you. Tell her you come recommended. She will be delighted to have a young lawyer."

"Thank you, Mrs. Spector. Oh—did my brother leave any personal belongings?"

"My goodness," she exclaimed, grabbing his arm, "I nearly forgot. I have a box of things—two boxes, in fact, and a letter. I think it's addressed to you in Springfield. Strange thing, but he gave me the letter a few months before he died with instructions to mail it should he ever encounter a grave misfortune. He was very clear that I should wait three months before mailing it. I even marked the date on my calendar when he…well, when he passed. I'll get it for you now."

"Did the police see the letter?"

"I felt it wasn't their business. The letter and one small box were in *my* custody. Your brother wasn't the friendliest man by a stretch, but he placed his trust in me. I felt it was a duty."

"Thank you, ma'am." Then, before she left the room, Conor asked, "Do you know where he's buried?"

"Rosehill Cemetery, up on the North Side." she replied. "I'm certain of it from the newspapers."

With the letter in hand and the woman's promise to hold the boxes for a few days, Conor set off for Mrs. Kaplan's boardinghouse. He opened the envelope as he walked. Inside he found a lawyer's business card and nothing else. A handwritten note on the card said, "Go and see him."

Mrs. Kaplan was, indeed, receptive to his needs. For Conor, the Steinway in her parlor sealed the deal, and he had yet to see the accommodations. Her home was a three-story, stone house with a basement walk-in flat—the classic Chicago row house in a much better neighborhood than the last. Conor's "room" was her last vacancy, a basement flat with two rooms and a separate entrance in front at the basement level. The rent included two meals per day in her dining room with access to the grand piano. He even had a roommate, a stray dog huddled up in the brick stairwell. He was scrawny and yellow with floppy ears and sad eyes. Someone had left an old crate for him to sleep in.

The rent was somewhat over budget at twenty dollars per month, but Conor did not hesitate. "I won't make dinner this evening," he said, counting out the money on her table, "but I'll return this evening with my things."

His new landlady handed Conor a key. "Happy to have you, Mr. Dolan. I'm told the saloon down the block, Andy Murphy's, is a quiet place where you can get a decent sandwich. It's open late."

The corned beef was lean and ruddy like the bartender's middle-aged face. He could pass as an Irish immigrant, Conor thought, but the accent was pure Chicago. "Good sandwich," Conor managed to say while chewing.

"Glad you like it," the man said, smiling, hands on the bar. "New to the neighborhood?"

Conor smiled. "How'd you guess?"

"We have our ways here," said the bartender cryptically, holding out his hand. "I'm Andy Murphy. Call me Murph. Welcome." He took Conor's empty glass. "Next one's on me."

"Conor Dolan."

"And the one after'll be on me," came a voice with a Galway accent from down the bar.

"Conor Dolan, meet Brendan White."

After extracting the sanitized version of Conor's life story, the two men seemed genuinely pleased to have him as a neighbor. Conor's recent experience with Charlie Damme tempered the instinct to flap his jaws excessively. He made no mention of his brother.

By the end of the third beer, Brendan had completed Conor's introductory course on what Brendan called, "The Chicago Way," a short lesson in ward politics, comparing it to the social order of landlords and peasants in Ireland over the last two hundred years.

"You sound like an expert, Brendan," Conor observed.

Murph had not missed a word of the conversation and piped in with his opinion on the subject. "He is indeed. Brendan solves a boatload of problems around here. Knows every alderman and committeeman personally."

Suddenly, Brendan flashed a startled look and exclaimed to Conor,

"Jesus, Mary and Joseph, I'd say he's spotted me. Be a good lad and hold me place here for a minute."

Brendan walked over to a booth along the wall where a middle-aged man was engaged in intimate conversation with an attractive young woman. "And what are ye doin' in an ungodly place like this so far from home, Charles McLaughlin," Brendan said, "and after nine o'clock in the evenin' to boot? And ye with a poor wife and babies in the flat."

The poor man turned white, stunned.

"I come into the devil's own places the odd night on the chance one of me own flock would stray from the fold. Now I'll not be sayin' a word about this night to anyone but himself if I have your promise to spend those wages only on those who love ye and not on sinful pleasures...and I will expect to be hearing no excuses when ye make ye're next confession."

"Of course, Father," mumbled the thoroughly humiliated patron, head bowed, scurrying from the booth and finally from the saloon.

Conor was thoroughly bewildered. When Brendan returned to the bar and downed the shot, he said, "You're a priest?"

Brendan nodded. "I am that. I am, indeed, Conor. If ye'd asked, I would have told ye."

"You've done this before," Conor suggested.

"I have, indeed, but I try to avoid it. And does it shock ye?"

"I suppose it does a bit."

The priest put his hand on Conor's back and whispered, "Who but a great sinner can touch his flock with the hand of empathy? I'm no hypocrite, son, only a humble sinner who loves his people and keeps his pairsonal life separate from his work. If our Lord God does not reserve a place for such a man, who among us shall not be cast into the pit?"

"I see your point," Conor admitted, not certain he did.

Father Brendan nodded. "And Charles's family will be the better for it in the morning."

When Brendan left and Murph came over to get the empty glass,

Conor asked, "Why does he prefer Friday evenings?"

"His girlfriend has a flat in Chinatown. This place is halfway between there and home —well out of his own neighborhood—and it's rare he would see anyone he knows. Wonderful fella. That's how he gets things done. Don't ever underestimate him."

As Conor turned to leave, Murph motioned him back to the bar. Leaning over so as not to be overheard, he whispered, "Did you know the coppers are following you?"

The question unsettled him. "What? How would you know that?"

"Same way I knew you moved into the neighborhood today. It's a quiet area—no brothels or nickel flops, only working stiffs. Certain things stand out. A big detective named Schneider followed you to the boardinghouse early this afternoon and was still on your tail when you returned with your bags. Be nice to the newsboys, Conor. They know everything, and they can spread the word faster than these new telephones."

"Why would they be following me?" Conor pleaded. "And why are you only telling me now?"

Murph shrugged. "I got no use for the coppers. Only time they pay attention to me is when they come for their weekly tithe. And I'm telling you now becuz Brendan and me had to decide if we liked you first." Then he burst into a big grin.

"Well...thanks, Murph. I appreciate the tip. Father Brendan is a very unusual priest."

"He's a good man, and don't ever underestimate his influence. They say Brendan heard the mayor's confession once when the man was a young alderman, and Brendan's had a foot on his neck since that day."

Conor was more concerned with the cops and had a good idea who the detective was. He had mentioned Kevin's name to a big detective with a Navy Colt just yesterday. Why would the man deny knowing Kevin and then follow him? He had to know Kevin Dolan was dead. So why would it matter to the police that Kevin's brother was in town? There were questions to answer, and the sooner he started asking them, the better.

Chapter 3

A poor man walked into the lawyer's office at Clark and Madison early one morning, and a rich man walked out...

It would be a good beginning to a joke, Conor thought, or maybe the beginning of a new life. The late morning sun raged in a cloudless sky high above the lake, rendering the crisp breeze almost pleasant, a perfect morning, he thought, for his first stroll along the lakefront. The smokestacks were still there in the distance to the north—by the hundreds maybe—and still pushing out the black spew, but today's wind carried the soot up and away to be devoured by the clean air.

At State Street, Carson Pirie's big department store was already emptying its display windows in preparation for the lavish, Christmas presentation of the latest fashions. The elevated train overhead announced Conor's financial good fortune with a rolling thunder as he crossed the Wabash Street cobblestones on the short walk east to the lake.

Twenty-seven hundred dollars was a virtual fortune, more money than the average man would earn in several years. If necessary, he could rent a small office and hire a secretary. He thought he might even do it right away as he had seen a suitable place for rent in the neighborhood. It would anchor him to the community and open doors into Kevin's life and death that might otherwise be closed.

How had Kevin managed to save such an enormous sum? True enough that his brother lived a frugal life in a slum neighborhood, but try as he might, Conor could not reconcile the arithmetic. Kevin literally paid thousands for Conor's upbringing and education. He was concerned, to be sure, but excited and grateful at the same time.

Nearly sixteen years had passed, but he remembered the long road to Queenstown aboard an old horse or a donkey though he had no memory of how they acquired the animal. He vaguely remembered a cow as well.

Kevin never spoke of those things in his letters. They were difficult days, Conor knew, but the stress and worry had been Kevin's alone to bear, assumed willingly to minimize for his little brother the added trauma of two or three weeks in the bowels of a steel-hulled steamer. He recalled a huge, dimly lit cavern where hundreds of filthy beds lay in the open, stacked three or four high. He remembered the stale repugnant odor: a brew of oil, filthy people, and rotten food. When he complained at first, Kevin told him the smell was only someone boiling turnips. To a seven-year-old who hated turnips, it was an unpleasant but reassuring explanation.

He would discuss it all later with Rebecca, his new neighbor, and tell her the whole story—*Charlie be dammed*. She had proven to be a most delightful and trustworthy dinner companion in Mrs. Kaplan's dining room over the past weeks. Their shared passion for music and conversation fostered a true friendship. The only thing he had disclosed to her about his presence was that his brother died in Chicago a couple of months ago and he had only found out recently. But the first order of business was to visit the Harrison Street police station on the way home to find out how his brother died and why the cops were involved.

"HARRISON STREET"—AS THE LOCALS REFERRED TO THAT POLICE station— *"is as notorious in its own right as the most debauched brothels in the Southside Levee."* That was the description Conor recalled from one of Kevin's more vivid letters. His brother was not fond of the station responsible for policing the city's most vice-ridden area.

The facility also housed the municipal police courts through which droves of vagrants, prostitutes, thieves, and drunks would rotate at all hours of the day and night. Kevin even described the unique practice of housing hundreds of homeless people in the station's basement on a nightly basis. According to Kevin, the practice left the station with the permanent odor *"not unlike the smiling corpse of a rotting pig in the bog."*

"Look," said the desk sergeant. "I'm sorry about yer brudder, but you don't just get access to a report 'cuz yer family. If yer a lawyer, show me identification. We ain't got no choice wit' lawyers."

Conor gave the man his identification, at which point the surly officer decided to retrieve and duplicate the report. He took fifteen minutes at the task and, upon returning to the desk, announced, "The duplicating machine ain't workin', mister." He then placed a two-page report on the desk. "Here's the report. I gotta give you access to it, but you gotta look it over right here and take your notes. We ain't set up to nursemaid no lawyers here, buddy."

"Suicide," the report said. *Suicide...* He recorded the important facts carefully. As he turned to leave a few minutes later with his notes, Conor heard someone call his name. It was a detective coming over from the staircase, a shockingly old man of at least fifty-five, bald on top with gray around the ears and a disheveled appearance. "Mr. Dolan?" the man asked, extending a hand, "I'm Detective Sergeant Eammon Flynn. I handled your brother's case. You have my apology, sir. We

had no information about family here." The man was Irish-born, Conor could tell.

Conor took the hand. *You're a detective. Why didn't you detect? The family's not difficult to find.* "Nice to meet you. The lawyer tracked us down in Springfield." He lied. He was not about to engage in conversation about the case with this detective until he was prepared to do so. He understood now why the desk sergeant was gone so long. Still, the detective was a source of information.

"Yes," said Flynn, "good to finally make your acquaintance. Can I help you?"

"Well, I know I'll be coming to see you later. I do have a few questions."

"Sure." Flynn pointed to a bench along the wall. "Let's sit."

Kevin must have made friends here, and Eammon Flynn was a good place to start. "Tell me, Detective, did you know my brother? I mean did you know him personally?"

"I'm sorry, Mr. Dolan. I only knew him to say hello at the station. I met him several times in the Levee at crime scene investigations, but that's it."

So the case had been closed for six weeks, and Conor made no waves, filed no complaints. Why would this old detective risk stirring up the pot by seeking Conor out? Especially if he hardly knew Kevin. It must have something to do with the cops following him. "Well, could you give me some names? People to talk with about Kevin?"

"I'll see what I can do."

"And why would my brother kill himself? What did you learn? What troubles could have caused him to—"

"I'm afraid I can't add anything to the report."

"Did they find anything in Kevin's pockets? Anything at all? A billfold?"

"Nothing—but I'll double check the inventory of course. I thought that was odd as well," Flynn conceded.

"Good and thank you. I may have more questions later. I hope you won't mind."

For some reason, Conor's last remark provoked an unhappy expression on Flynn's face. "Not a'tall," he said.

That's odd, Conor thought. A logical reaction to his appearance would have been for Flynn to hide in a closet or escape out the back door; instead, Flynn's behavior suggested an agenda. He was worried about something. They did not know each other from Adam. Conor never asked to see the man by name, and the case file sat closed for months. He could have watched Conor leave and wished him good riddance, but the desk sergeant alerted Flynn for a reason. Why?

WITH THREE HOURS OF DAYLIGHT LEFT, CONOR HOPPED A SOUTH-bound Fifth Avenue trolley for a short ride to the end of the line; it opened into a spacious area of warehouses, vacant land, and railroad track with no through streets. It seemed a perfect location to either dispose of a dead body or dispatch a living one. Conor did not know much about suicide, but trekking through mud and trash seemed an unnecessary inconvenience for someone intending to kill himself. *Maybe Kevin died somewhere else, and his body drifted here.* The report was silent on that issue.

He walked along the river through tall weeds and discarded trash to the area of Fourteenth Street where the river swung back west toward Clark. A railroad track ran parallel to the river only feet from the east bank. He made a mental note to invest in a pair of Wellingtons. *According to the police sketch, they removed Kevin's body on this spot.* He stared at a thick weed bed among the rotting remains of an old dock.

Sifting through the marsh-like bank with his feet, Conor kicked up a rotten board to find a big, gray rattlesnake loosely coiled but not particularly annoyed with the intrusion. *It's a good time to head back.* After so many months, the outdoor scene would likely reveal no more secrets.

Conor paid more attention to his environment on the walk back as he considered the case for suicide. Why was there no supplemental investigation? A suicide generally merits interviews with friends, co-workers, and family to determine whether the victim was predisposed by way of financial problems, depression, personal issues, or even blackmail. The desk sergeant was unequivocal; the two-page report *cleared* the case. There were no other reports. "That's why we call this report a 'Clear and Close,'" the man had said. This Detective Flynn apparently expended minimal effort on Kevin's case. *Why?*

According to the report, the body was dressed in full uniform—on his day off. Why? When had he last reported for duty? Who was the last person to see him alive? Where? When? The report offered no answers to these and other questions that would help fix the time of death or shed light on the motive.

With darkness descending, Conor decided it would be worth a return visit after all with more facts—snakes be damned—but he would buy some Wellies first. Making his way back to Twelfth Street, he spotted a man in a gray coat and Derby hat opposite the tracks, standing and staring with both hands in his coat pockets. Conor did not approach, and the man made no attempt to leave. He was clearly issuing a warning, a threat. It was not the big cop from the train.

On his way home, Conor's mind turned back to the case. There was no evidence of either suicide or murder, but the investigation was shoddy and incomplete. Clearly, Conor's appearance had spooked someone or some group. If not murder, the circumstances suggested impropriety or a secret related to Kevin's death. In either case, Conor had unintentionally stirred the pot. It would not be long before the interested parties delivered a more forceful message because Conor fully intended to pursue his answers, whatever the risks.

Even as a child in Springfield, Conor was not easily intimidated. It was another useful life tool attributable to his brother and traceable to that harrowing journey from Ireland on the coffin ship, the one Kevin once described as "a grand voyage on a beautiful ship." Not once during the voyage did little Conor feel the sting of fear or the horror of human misery because he fell asleep in Kevin's arms each night and walked every step in Kevin's armor-plated shadow. For one hour every morning, they sent the steerage passengers up to walk the aft deck where Kevin would regale his little brother with colorful stories of cowboys and Indians or the great Irish king, Brian Boru. Conor looked forward to the walks every day.

Sounds of violence often punctuated the damp, cold darkness, followed by bodies carried from the hole in bags to the accompaniment of mournful wailing. It all happened mostly in the blackness of night but always involving others. In the safety of Kevin's arms, the darkness became a shelter for the seven-year-old boy, a tiny haven in which he became invisible there on the dirty cot under his brother's protective shield.

Thus, he never feared the darkness while growing up in Springfield but embraced it as a source of strength and invulnerability. It made him different from the other boys. He was different in other ways too as these bullies might soon learn if they pushed him. Paradoxically, he remembered the voyage as more of a great adventure than a tragic necessity, just as Kevin planned.

He suddenly realized, in all the excitement of the long day, that he had forgotten dinner. If he were late, Mrs. Kaplan would surely have her petticoat in a tangle.

Rebecca Fletcher was a widow from New York, a buyer for a New York garment manufacturing concern and seated permanently beside him by Mrs. Kaplan's arrangement. A Raven-haired matron of about forty she was, with imperious chocolate-brown eyes and toned skin that bestowed an air of mystery to her face. Though slightly on the plump side, Rebecca emitted a sensual presence, an air, despite her prudish Edwardian ensemble. The hair was balanced and pinned high atop her hatless head in rings or buns, allowing for the prominent display of an elegantly sculpted neck and flawless skin.

"We're always delighted to see you for dinner, Mr. Dolan," said Rebecca. "The company of women can become…well, let's simply say a fresh, young perspective and a modest display of whiskers is a welcome addition." It did not sound mean-spirited, just a slip of the tongue, but Mrs. Kaplan and her sister, Mrs. Goldman, may not have agreed.

Conor found Rebecca attractive. He was a novice in dealings with girls…women…but had never fancied the wallflower type, the delicate gem of Edwardian society. This Rebecca was no mere girl, and her impetuous manner bordered on flirtatious.

Dinner was family style except for the first course, chicken soup. As Mrs. Kaplan was still serving herself and Mrs. Goldman, Conor's eyes inhaled the subtle vision of Mrs. Fletcher's upper torso along with the hot chicken soup. His eyes refused commands to turn away, so he took care to be unobtrusive. Her blouse, modestly buttoned to the neck, was lace-covered down the middle and around the buttons. Still, every time she leaned over the soup bowl, Conor watched the white, lacy fabric stretch around the third button from the top, giving him just a bare hint of naked breast. The button strained under pressure each time she bent forward, and each time he was certain it would launch across the room. It seemed a question of which would give out first: the soup or the button. He was certain his admiration went unnoticed and prayed Mrs. Fletcher's affinity for soup extended to the vegetable variety and beef stock as well.

"Will you be staying in Chicago for long, Mr. Dolan, or are you only here on business?" Rebecca asked. In the parlor, she quietly addressed him as "Conor."

"Difficult to answer," he replied, but after two glasses of wine, he decided to say something. It would all come out anyway. Because a discussion of suicide and murder would quickly turn salacious, he simply announced to the diners that his brother was the cop found dead in the river several months ago. He could not bring himself to use the word "suicide," but it was clear they all made the connection.

Rebecca looked shocked. "Dolan," she said. "Of course, the newspapers."

"I'm sorry. What?"

"Nothing," she replied. "Please, go on. I'm sorry. I read about it in the papers. It was front page in all the editions the next day."

If it was front-page news, how is it this Schneider, the big detective, never heard of a cop named Kevin Dolan? "I have some things to do here. If it takes longer than expected, I may try my hand at practicing law for a time."

"Oh, do try, Mr. Dolan," Mrs. Goldman said. Mrs. Fletcher's smile told him she agreed.

He was not in love with Rebecca—not that fluttering, wispy, heart-thumping feeling he experienced with Lori Howard in Springfield years ago. Still, Rebecca was smart, confident, and beautiful; but most of all, she conveyed a real sense of affection for Conor, and the pain he could see in her eyes made her all the more attractive. Besides, it was wonderful just to talk with someone who wanted to listen.

After dinner, Conor and Rebecca retired to the parlor as was becoming their custom.

He settled at the piano and began to play Chopin from memory. Mrs. Fletcher seemed to warm a bit more and sat beside him on the piano bench.

"Chopin's 'Love Prelude,'" she declared. "You haven't played that before."

"I'm full of surprises," he said.

As the piece settled to a soft tempo, she asked him coyly, "Were you looking at my…ankles during dinner, Conor?" The question caught Conor off guard, but his fingers held steady on the keyboard.

"No, Rebecca. I'd never be that rude." She was obviously not insulted and Conor concluded no harm was done. Innocent flirtation was an acceptable, Edwardian vice.

And so he played and they talked. He had learned that Mrs. Fletcher's husband and two-year-old child both died of cholera three years ago. Her work had become her life.

Conor had lost his brother, not a wife and child, and the loss still dominated his life. He wondered how a woman like Mrs. Fletcher, approaching midlife but still alive and vibrant, could carry on in the wake of such unspeakable tragedy. She was not morbid or weepy in raising the subject, only matter-of-fact. How must she feel in the mornings—to wake up alone in a boardinghouse with nothing of her own? To Conor, she was a mesmerizing, enchanting character, but he determined never to speak of her loss again without an invitation.

Rebecca must come from another world—a world of big houses, fine clothes, and important friends. Yet there was something earthly and enticingly sensible about the woman that defied her debutante history and elevated Conor's humble immigrant experience to a common, plain one. He was comfortable in her presence and felt alive in her company.

They took a brandy on the green velvet sofa, and Rebecca made a startling admission, albeit in a near whisper. "Everything I told you is true, Conor, except for one thing: I'm not in the garment industry, and I don't live in New York. I'm a Pinkerton detective working on an investigation for Scotland Yard. To disclose my true identity and purpose would threaten my investigation, maybe worse. Do you understand?"

It was a great deal of information packed into a couple of sentences, and Conor had to think about it for a minute. He also thought about Charlie Damme. "No," he said honestly. "I don't think so. I can understand your reasoning, but you're a…spy?"

"In a way, I suppose I am, but I'm not working against the United States or anything like that. Are you upset with me?" she asked, her hand on his arm.

Was he upset with her? He was going mad from thinking about her, and now she had confessed to deceiving him. He wondered whether anyone in this town told the truth. "I don't know, but what would Scotland Yard be investigating in Chicago?"

She hesitated a moment, then put her hand on his. "I can't tell you at the moment, Conor, but that may change after I speak with my superiors. I'm sorry to say my investigation may be related to your brother."

Chapter 4

Knowing he would be in Chicago awhile, Conor spent much of the last week visiting Kevin's grave and renting a suitable office, the same storefront he noticed in the neighborhood earlier. Now he was open for business and finally had time to explore Kevin's beat, the notorious Levee District, especially since he had no cases of his own. As he began to close up the office, a visitor entered. "Good morning, Mr. Dolan," said the little man in a squeaky voice. Conor noticed the man did not remove his Fiddler's cap but thought him a new client. *Finally.*

"Ah, good morning, sir," he said, offering a hand. "How may I help you?"

"I be Boris," said the little man, "helper for precinct captain."

The man went on to welcome Conor to the First Ward and the Nineteenth Precinct in a heavy Russian accent. By then, his friend, Father Brendan, had explained that the First Ward is shaped like a reverse numeral 7, following the river from the lake west and straight down the South Branch to Twelfth Street. It was the biggest and most powerful ward in the city. He had also described it as the most corrupt of the fifty wards. "Kind of like the wettest section of the ocean" was how Brendan had described it, although Conor still did not understand the metaphor.

Boris explained, in his own way, that his precinct captain and the alderman had been expecting a visit from Conor; they were disappointed. He pointed out that the precinct had two lawyers already and they both contributed generously to the alderman's campaign fund and did favors for the bosses.

It was a shakedown, Conor knew, and he should have given more consideration to the possibility. "Sorry, Boris," he said. "I'm new to Chicago, and frankly, I don't have any clients yet, so I'm hardly in a position to respond at the moment." *When caught off guard, stall*, he thought.

Boris kind of nodded and shrugged his shoulders. "Okay," he said, "I fix. We talk later."

Just like that, Boris was gone. Conor recalled his initial conversation with Father Brendan and the short course on Chicago politics. *This Boris must be a ward heeler*, he figured, the guy who carries out the dirty deeds of his alderman while shielding the alderman from liability or scrutiny—a layer of insulation, if you will. Conor figured he could deal with Boris later, and he put a little sign on the door, indicating he would return at three o'clock in the afternoon.

IT WAS A WARM, DAMP MORNING FOR LATE FALL WITH NO TRACE of a breeze. The black and gray smoke from the stacks north of the river hovered over the city like a blanket, fouling the air and smothering the sidewalks, windows, and carriages with a fine black silt. Nothing escaped it, not even the squeaky-clean streets and fine mansions of Astor Street and Prairie Avenue. The difference was that the wealthy could make the grime disappear quickly so as not to damage the illusion.

Near Plymouth Court, a narrow street housing several upscale restaurants, Conor spotted the yellow dog begging for a late breakfast in the alley behind a row of fine restaurants. He had finally realized last week that the animal was missing his front right leg. The dog was limping badly that morning, something Conor had not noticed before, and it mused him. The animal had a knack for turning up around lunch or dinnertime for a good meal. The exaggerated limp was probably his methodology.

Conor boarded a Wabash Street L train and exited at Eighteenth Street, down the staircase, through the station's decorative arched entranceway, and onto the potted cobblestones of Eighteenth Street, rutted and neglected along the old streetcar rails. The dirt alley, running back under and parallel to the elevated tracks, teemed with filthy urchins playing baseball amid trash of all sorts. Laundry, drying on back porch lines stacked up three stories, was already streaked with the black waste of industry. The wives and mothers would simply start over again, fully expecting the occasional filth storm.

A makeshift sign pointing west said "Levee"—likely erected for the drunks and perverts who might otherwise turn the wrong way and thus deprive the Levee landlords of their booty. At Dearborn Street, Conor turned south, crossing an invisible boundary into another world, a decaying city of sin. Along Eighteenth Street, he passed a row of decrepit frame houses, obviously in defiance of post-fire building codes. These were some of the real "nickel flops" his brother wrote about. A crude sign just off the sidewalk read "Bed Bug Row," announcing cheap rooms available to the down-and-out after being fleeced in the Levee. They would all be filled to the rafters with transients just prior to the next election.

This was Kevin's world, the capitol city of debauchery. One after another, the lecherous establishments lined the long-neglected South Dearborn Street. An old horse-drawn streetcar sat at a dead stop on the rails, a prone human body blocking its way across the iron tracks. The driver swore like a sailor while trying to pull the body from his path.

Conor strolled the unbroken line of brothels, saloons, gambling houses, and peep shows: Five-Cent Poker, Southside Jim's, Madame Shima's. Finally, he passed the Midget Club, complete with two pint-sized ladies outside, shivering in scanty outfits—twin Thumbelinas with generous accoutrement, their faces decorated with enough layers of powder and rouge to mortify Hans Christian Andersen.

Prostitutes, procurers, and hustlers assaulted Conor at every step with promises of carnal pleasure or riches—and it was still morning. Posters and photos of salacious bodies—mostly female—plastered the windows and street signs amid loitering perverts, making the walk slow and tedious. Conor silently rejoiced that there was no one in Chicago to recognize him strolling through the successor neighborhood to Sodom and Gomorrah and give voice to slanderous rumor.

Only a two-block walk from the station, the Levee District might have been located on a different planet from Lake Shore Drive or Lincoln Park. Nothing in Conor's young life prepared him for the experience of Chicago's brutal dichotomy and demographic extremes. At Nineteenth Street, he turned west and back north again on Armour. Nothing changed.

This was a city of irreconcilable extremes and antagonistic realities between affluence and poverty, vice and virtue, good and evil, and even clean and dirty. The names only became more vulgar as he walked: Bucket of Blood, Blind Pig, even a brothel called 10 to 13-Year-Olds with children sitting in the window.

How could his brother have spent his life here? If he had, how could all this still exist? Conor wanted to puke, knowing he could not in this lifetime make inquiries about his brother inside such places, so he cruised the degenerate vice buffet before spotting a small, benign-looking saloon called Jim Finley's Dive, just around the corner from Ike the Jew's Place. Jim had posted no agents on the sidewalk and no lewd images outside, so Conor popped inside to rest his feet and enjoy a beer and a sandwich. Jim's looked like a good place to start his inquiry.

"Good afternoon, sir," said the muscular bartender through his meticulously trimmed handlebar mustache. The man's hair was thickly greased and packed down, almost as if he could lift it from his head and hang it from a coat rack at the end of a long day. Jim was drying a beer glass in the dim light with his filthy white apron. By the looks of the few, broken-down patrons, Jim's place catered to the less well-to-do crowd, the old men with enough money for a beer but a nickel short of a blowjob, as they say. What thrills they managed came from the windows and the lewd posters along the street.

"I'll have a Schlitz and a corned beef sandwich," Conor announced. "Are you Jim?"

The bartender gave him a funny look and said, "I ain't Jim, and my guess is you ain't from Shi-kaw-go."

"What gave me away?" Conor asked.

"Nobody from town would be in here asking for a Schlitz."

"Why's that?"

The bartender seemed to think for a spell, then said, "Well, most of the Levee establishments carry only Wacker and Birk brands. If you like lager, I got Perfecto."

"Why most and not all?" Conor asked.

"Mister, I guess some people are just special. You get used to that here."

"Perfecto sounds good," Conor replied, "but why would these places carry only one brand? That's unusual."

The bartender laughed. "I think you might be from the moon, but let's just say when certain influential ward people invest in a business—like, say, da beer business—they encourage support from da local establishments. Where you from?"

Conor sipped the glass of Perfecto. It was not bad. "Springfield," he answered. "I'm here trying to gather information on my brother. He worked in this district and died recently."

"Sorry to hear that," said the bartender, sounding sincere. "Was he a pimp, or did he own a place here?" The man seemed not to recognize the irony of his question, and Conor let it pass. *Might as well get to the point.* "Neither. He was a cop. This was his beat. Name was Kevin Dolan."

The bartender bristled, and his mustache twitched. "Mister, you're welcome to eat and drink here so long as you can pay, but we ain't got no further business between us. That'll be sixty cents." With that, the man turned his back and posted up at the end of the bar, returning only to deliver the sandwich and collect the money.

THE L CAR WAS FULL TO STANDING ROOM ON THE NORTHBOUND return trip. Conor noticed a man in a gray coat boarding the next car down. It was the third time he had seen the man since exiting at Twelfth Street earlier. This chap had apparently been following him all day. Enough is enough, he thought. As Conor approached to confront his shadow, the fellow scurried off the car, disappearing down the stairway like a cockroach.

Was it the police again? He thought briefly about Rebecca's secret investigation and thought about mentioning it to her later. It was a sure bet that his shadow was recording his every move.

On the walk back to the office, he noticed the wind had picked up, blowing the toxic overcast out over the lake. Women were sweeping the sidewalks and pulling in the filthy laundry. The people here seemed to never be discouraged or dissuaded despite nature or the hazardous consequences of their own civilization.

Conor's problems were mounting. The demands for graft were piling up, and he was likely now on Clan na Gael's radar. First, he would need to decide what to do about the damn politicians. If he pulled up stake and moved, it would only be the same problem in a new location.

If he started paying these people, where would it stop? Even the local beat cop had stopped at the office to secure a promise of bribery. Eventually, one of them would come to him with money in a reverse scenario, expecting him to break the law or betray a client in the service of ward politics. That would never happen, but it could still be a slippery slope. He kept telling himself that paying an extortion demand was less morally corrupt than making one, but he knew corruption did not operate on a sliding scale. If he could not make it in sole practice without becoming a criminal, he would simply get a job and let someone else deal with the ethics—or go back to Springfield.

On the other hand, as Brendan made clear, this was the *de facto* mode of governance in Chicago. All the wards embraced this system, and somehow, the system had fueled economic growth and job creation at a pace unmatched in the nation's history. Was there a way to walk a line? *This apparent conundrum will require consultation with the good priest Brendan White.* He seemed to have the number of these cops and politicians. Maybe there was a way to manage it.

Conor was back at the office at three o'clock sharp where he found a skinny kid of about sixteen, scruffy-looking, disheveled, and wearing an old newsboy cap. "May I assist you, young man?" Conor asked, unlocking the door.

"Yeah," answered the youngster. "I need a lawyer. Boris, da Heeler, sent me ova' here. I got lifted ova' at da Dearborn Station boostin' a wallet. Needed a little extra to get me tru da week. Boris said it would only cost me the five bucks I posted for bail, and I should see you right away. My brudder caught a case last week. I'll get him out by Friday. I ain't got no money now, but I'll grab a few wallets by then and reach for him. Boris said it's better to just post the whole bail amount than mess with a bondsman. They ain't honest."

"I see. Come on in," said Conor, opening the door. He knew how the bail bond system worked, and now he had a pretty good idea how it worked for the politicians as well.

On serious cases with higher bail bonds, a bondsman would charge 10 percent of the bail amount and post 90 percent with his own money. At the end of the case, the bondsman kept the client's 10 percent for his fee, like 10 percent interest on a loan. If a defendant posted his entire bail amount, cutting out the bondsman, the lawyer could have that full amount assigned to him as a fee, to be paid when the case was closed.

Boris the Heeler was obviously telling Conor he would feed petty cases down the pipeline for a cut of the bail money. Conor's educated guess was that Boris used the same system with the bondsmen, who would split his 10 percent fee with the local alderman. There was apparently nothing these insatiable politicians would not monetize.

It would not hurt to talk to the kid. He could always decline to take the bail money. Besides, he needed to get some cases. "Have a seat, son." Conor said, hanging his coat on the rack. "We'll talk it over. What's your name?"

"Lefty Hawk."

Following the conversation, Conor knew he would have a talk with Father Brendan—and soon—because *Shi-kaw-go* was creeping up on him.

Chapter 5

A week later, the young lawyer was getting used to the smell inside the Harrison Street Station. Until recently, he thought that impossible. This was his first appearance in the array of second-floor courtrooms, but the whole building carried the same odor. The four main rooms housed Prostitution Court, Vagrancy Court, Petty Crimes Court, and Gambling Court, respectively. Another room was dedicated to the least serious felony preliminary hearings, cases deemed not serious enough to warrant the grand jury process.

Conor's client that morning was Lefty Hawk, who just yesterday posted bail for his brother, Red Hawk. Lefty was on time and waiting at the courtroom door when Conor arrived. He was a nice enough kid, one of the "newsboys" of the downtown Loop streets and an eminent character in his own right as Conor's research had disclosed. Lefty was a good talker and, surprisingly, a good listener.

The kid had spruced up his appearance as Conor suggested. He still sported the woolen P-cap, but he had ditched the overalls in favor of a sparkling clean, collarless, button-down shirt with calf-length, brown knickerbockers. So long as he did not smile, revealing two missing front teeth, Lefty looked like a college student. Conor snatched the cap from the kid's head in a friendly way and handed it to him. Lefty's hair was closely cropped, a function of street life, he figured. Short hair means fewer bugs. These kids were known to live together in packs—little families of fifteen or twenty—moving between abandoned building. The numbers helped with security and moral support. They were a tough lot.

"If you live in the streets," Conor asked, "where do you keep the clean, starched shirts?"

Left smiled. "Oh, da shirt? I got dat from da Chinese laundry on LaSalle. Made a deal wit' da Chinaman. I gotta bring it back after court. Same wit' da pants."

"And what exactly is it you do for the Chinaman in return?" Conor asked. Then his brain kicked in. "Wait! Don't answer that. The less I know, the better." They took a seat on the wood bench along the wall. "Now just keep your mouth shut in the courtroom. I'll do the talking. If the judge asks you a direct question, count to five before you open your trap. That gives me a chance to intercede."

The newsboys were homeless street hustlers whose primary business was to hawk newspapers. They would buy bundles of the daily locals and push them all over the downtown area, day in and day out, sometimes well into the night with the evening editions. When broke, they were known to grift or pick pockets to make ends meet. There were no off days, no holidays, and no wages. They were independent businessmen. If they wanted to eat, they had to make a profit—or develop a side business.

Young Lefty was no ordinary criminal. The kid was a legend among the newsboys and a bona fide Chicago celebrity of sorts. A few years ago, a sixteen or seventeen-year-old Lefty Higginbottom defied William Randolph Hearst and ended up a local hero—for a few months anyway.

The Chicago Newspaper War became a major story in 1900 when Hearst moved into town with his *American* to compete with the *Daily*

News and the *Tribune*. Unknown to the man himself, the Hearst people used gangs to intimidate the newsstand owners into reducing their orders of the competing papers. Then they even intimidated the newsboys and forced them to buy more papers than they could sell. With a zero-return policy, the newsboys ended up going into debt. True or not, that was the way the papers reported it and Conor heard it.

The kids hawked papers late into the night, every night, and still lost money. Somehow, this Lefty Higginbottom kid got three hundred newsboys to refuse papers and strike. They marched to the newspaper office and blocked the exit for two days until the paper relented. The cops were so impressed with Lefty's hutzpah that they refused to arrest the kids. The *American*, at the time, had no alternative distribution system, so Lefty's brazen leadership had them over a barrel, and the paper caved in to the newsboys' demands. The newspapers dubbed the kid "Lefty Hawk" and it stuck.

The courtroom that morning was jam-packed. Conor counted fifty-one cases on the petty crimes call alone. Inside the courtroom, it looked more like five hundred.

The Police Court used county prosecutors, and the system was mainly used for misdemeanor offenses punishable by county jail time or fines. Felony preliminary hearings were transferred to the Cook County Criminal Court on Hubbard Street upon a finding of probable cause.

Conor sat on the lawyers' bench up front, waiting for the case to be called. Thankfully, they called the lawyers' cases first.

"People versus Lefty Higgenbottom: theft from person," the court clerk bellowed.

As Conor approached the bench with Lefty in tow, Conor thought the judge looked amused to see the man. Not a good sign. "Lefty Hawk. I think you should move closer to the police station. You'd save money on carfare. And how is your brother, Red Hawk, these days?"

Lefty did not count to five. "Oh he's fine, Judge," the newsboy answered. "You'll be seein' him next week."

Looking at Conor, the judge seemed to reflect a minute, then said, "Counselor—Mr. Dolan, is it?"

"Yes, Your Honor."

"Mr. Dolan, you must be new in town. Our friend Lefty couldn't get a local lawyer to help him. On the last court appearance, I gave him a final continuance for a lawyer or be ready to proceed to trial without one. According to the charge here, Mr. Hawk picked the pocket of our Second Ward Alderman, Eugene Tully, inside the Carson's Department Store. Good luck trying to get a plea offer. The prosecutor will provide you with the report." Looking at Lefty, he added, "Sorry, son. A day in the sun can't last past sundown. Good luck. Welcome to Cook County, Mr. Dolan. See my clerk for a trial date."

Conor knew he still had much to learn as he stepped over to the clerk. The man pretended not to notice him, but Conor played his game. The clerk was sending Conor a message: *This is my space. I'm in charge.*

Finally, the man looked up, feigning surprise, "Oh, sorry," he said. "I didn't see you. Your trial date for jury is January 11." As Conor turned to leave, he heard a whisper. "Oh, Mr. Dolan, since you're new here, I should probably fill you in on the protocols. There is no actual rule that lawyer cases are called first. It's kind of a courtesy I provide to lawyers. The regular lawyers generally see me, say once a month? You know, to show their gratitude. That sound all right to you?" It was technically a question, practically a threat, and definitely a solicitation for a bribe.

Your first morning in court could have gone better, Conor told himself, wondering how much he could make as a full-time bartender. He would be spending a week in January trying a petty jury case for a five-dollar fee, then give 10 percent to the alderman.

AT CONOR'S SUGGESTION, HE AND REBECCA MET AT THE RESTAU-rant rather than walk there together. Kevin's lawyer had personally recommended Gianelli's for Italian food, Conor's favorite. Rebecca arrived five minutes late, wearing a beautiful Edwardian coat, a light purple cut just at the ankle over the tops of lace-up high leather shoes. A wide, black fur collar with matching cuffs rendered a look of pure elegance under a simple, all black, ribboned hat.

She smiled as the waiter assisted with her chair and coat. "Being a wealthy man does have its advantages, Conor. What a delightful restaurant. I just adore the checkered tablecloths."

"Thanks for coming," said Conor, waiting for her to be seated first. "I only hope I haven't scandalized you, Rebecca. The last thing I'd do is compromise your integrity. Those women do talk."

She almost laughed, but she was not laughing *at* him. He knew that. "Dear Conor," she said, "We've both been scandalized since the night of our first dinner at Mrs. Kaplan's. As for your invitation, I'm thrilled you could tear yourself away from that…dog."

Conor could not suppress a smile. "Actually, this is his favorite restaurant," he teased. "I saw him begging here in the alley one day. He loves the Ossobuco. There is no tastier bone." He could tell something was weighing on her and added, "Looks like you have something to tell me."

"My assignment—it's an undercover investigation of the Clan na Gael. You're Irish. Have you heard of the organization?"

"Every Irishman has." The disclosure surprised him. The Clan na Gael was generally regarded to be a secret society of alcoholic eejits, headquartered in New York with a major chapter in Chicago, and dedicated to the establishment of a united and independent Ireland. They were Irish Republicans, if you will, whose mission was to support the Irish Republican Brotherhood in Ireland, both financially and with violence when necessary and required. Its local membership alone was alleged to be in the tens of thousands.

What do you know about them?" she asked.

"As far as I know, it's more of a drinking club where blustery old Irishmen gather to drink beer, sing songs of the old sod, and tell lies. Back in the late 1880s, they engaged in that London dynamite campaign. According to the papers, the whole thing was a fiasco—incompetence start to finish. They even tried to bomb the Tower of London but were captured or killed."

"That's what they'd like you to believe," Rebecca said, "but innocent people died in that dynamite campaign. Besides, dynamite is even more dangerous in the hands of fools."

The waiter appeared to pour their wine and take the orders. His timing could not have been worse, Conor thought, annoyed.

Privacy restored, he said, "The Clan hierarchy turned on one another in the early 90s. I read all about the murder of Dr. Cronin in the papers, even followed some of the later trials. Without the Chicago papers, people in Springfield would have nothing interesting to read about. Politics gets boring quickly. It was big news, but the papers focused on the murders not the Clan itself. I learned later their infighting nearly did them in."

"Well, they're at it again," she quipped. "I assume you're familiar with Parnell and Irish Home Rule?"

"Yes, of course." He knew that Parnell had come within a hog's breath of bringing Home Rule to Ireland through his longstanding political campaign and peaceful, parliamentary negotiations, even siphoning away key support from the violent Irish Republican Brotherhood, effectively silencing the IRB for years. After his movement collapsed, the Republican movement in Ireland essentially went quiet, trying to reorganize.

"Right," she said, "but the Clan na Gael in Chicago wouldn't accept a strategy of non-violence and advocated for continued bombings." Rebecca stiffened and finally delivered her real message. "Let me tell you directly: multiple informants have identified Kevin Dolan, your brother, as a mid-level Clan leader and recruiter in Chicago."

Her disclosure was disorienting, and it came as the waiter delivered their salads. Kevin had never mentioned the Clan na Gael in any of his letters or in person and never even expressed an interest in Irish

Republicanism. Still, he thought, it might help explain the large sum of money he bequeathed to Conor. How much should he share with this woman? Who was she really and what about the lessons of Charlie Damme?

"I can't believe that," he protested. "I knew my brother better than that. He didn't give a damn about the Irish Republicans."

"You told me yourself that you only saw him a few times over the years. Why do you think that was the case?"

He began to feel like she was attacking Kevin and resented having to defend his brother. "Why should I believe any of this?"

"I can only share my information with you. You'll have to decide for yourself what it's worth, but I saw your brother entering a Clan meeting with my own eyes."

"Tell me what you know about his death," Conor demanded.

"Probably no more than you do. We have the same questions and none of the answers. Maybe we can work together."

On the walk home, Rebecca led him on a detour, but he said nothing. This woman was full of surprises. Conor told her about his dead-end investigation and about being followed. Then Rebecca dropped a clue of her own. The Pinkertons had once followed Kevin to a flat west of the river. The resident was a woman named Maureen Brogan. They never saw the two together in public, but Rebecca was reluctant to approach the woman herself for fear of tipping off the Clan. She thought Conor's relationship to the dead policeman would give him a reason to visit the girl and give him cover with the Clan, protecting her investigation. Conor agreed that he was the perfect person to talk with this Maureen.

As much as Conor fought to keep his guard up, his judgment of Rebecca had already taken shape. He trusted her. In any case, his upcoming visit to Maureen Brogan would settle the issue either way. "Why is Scotland Yard interested in my brother?"

"Conor, you have a right to know what you're involved in. We believe Chicago's police chief is also a member of the Clan na Gael's ruling Triangle and that Detective Flynn is an active Clan member as well. I personally saw the chief going into a Clan meeting with your brother. We think the Clan, or a rogue element of the Clan, is planning to assassinate a visiting British dignitary."

They crossed Fifth Avenue, barely missing a passing streetcar as he processed this barrage of bad news. The signs were all pointing in this direction since he arrived in Chicago, but there it was from Rebecca's mouth. During Conor's entire lifetime, Kevin had not once spoken in favor of the Irish Republicans or expressed hatred of the Crown.

Is the police chief of a major American city actually a sworn member of the secret Irish nationalist society? It just kept feeling more and more like a world created by Jules Verne. Every government employee was entitled to have a personal life—hobbies, outside interests, even political views—but sworn allegiance to a foreign group conducting a murderous bombing campaign on British soil? It did not require a law-school course on conflict of interest to conclude this was an ominous development.

They came to a small, brick house less than a mile from the boardinghouse. It looked familiar to Conor. Rebecca stopped. "My agency maintains a flat here for meetings and as a kind of safe house. We have good Tennessee whiskey inside. It's vacant at the moment." She took his arm. "Would you like to go in?"

He wanted to say "of course" but forced the words, "Don't you think that would be improper, Rebecca?"

She squeezed his arm and smiled wickedly. "Improper schmopper. Have you ever been with a woman, Conor?"

He thought briefly about Lori Howard and their summer evenings in the park and realized the ambiguity of Rebecca's question. Conor was fairly certain the answer was *yes*, but he had never been able to shake a couple of technical questions regarding that calculation. He put his arm around her and smiled as they climbed the staircase to carnal knowledge. "If you're not certain, dear Conor, I'll ask you again in a couple of hours."

Lying quietly in the dark, Rebecca touched his cheek. "Have you ever known any Jews before, Conor?"

"I suppose only you and Mrs. Kaplan. Well, there's Mrs. Goldman, but I don't spend much time looking at her ankles. Why would you ask? Are Jews different in some way?" He kind of smirked. "I mean do they taste better or something?"

She pulled herself up in the bed and hit him with a pillow. "I'm serious."

He had to think for a second. "Well," he began, "We didn't exactly have hordes of Jews running around Ireland, and the Catholic Church wasn't fond of them. They liked to tell us, 'The Jews murdered Jesus.' But, after what happened to my family in Ireland, I don't give much weight to anything the Church says, so I'd say I never thought much about Jews."

It was an honest, spontaneous answer, he thought, and it seemed to satisfy her, but he could not help himself, so he added, "Would you like me better if I had a long beard?"

She laughed out loud, to the point of covering her mouth, but her mood turned somber as the laugh subsided. She leaned over, kissing him on the lips. "You must promise me to be more careful, Conor."

"Tell me, Rebecca: Was my brother murdered?"

"I don't know…but that's enough spy talk for tonight. Now that you're an expert in lovemaking, why don't we really give Mrs. Kaplan and her sister something to talk about? Let's spend the rest of the night here and go back for breakfast."

He was worried about Rebecca. They were good for each other. Still, Conor worried about damaging her reputation, even about damaging Rebecca herself. He would inevitably hurt her one day. As much as he cared for her, he was not in love with her and could never marry her. It took all his fortitude to finally say, "Rebecca, I have to tell you something. I really care about you deeply, but…"

He could almost feel her smile there in the dark. She put her palm on his chest and said, "Oh, lovely Conor. You're so adorable," and he thought she was fighting back tears. *Can this woman read my mind?*

You made her cry after all. This woman seemed always one step ahead of him, or maybe Conor Dolan was just a willing actor in her play. She knew the beginning and the middle. Why should she not already know the end? "I'm sorry," he said.

"You are a mensch, Conor," she whispered, "a clueless one—but a mensch all the same. Promise me you will be careful."

Chapter 6

The new information from Rebecca last night cried out for another visit to Detective Eammon Flynn, but this time Conor arranged to arrive just before lunch, between the chaotic morning court calls and the slightly less chaotic afternoon calls, to avoid the daily crush of troubled humanity. His main objective was to explore for a link between Clan na Gael and Kevin's death or at least make sure the Clan na Gael knew he was coming. Rebecca would not be pleased.

He had learned so much more about Rebecca in the last twenty-four hours, each discovery more fascinating than the last. But he took no joy from the new information about his brother. It was piling up faster than green grass through a goose.

It was a cold morning with the wind whipping straight off the lake down Harrison Street into his face and threatening to blow his seven-dollar homburg clear to Iowa. It would get much worse before spring, he knew. He might have been wrong about the old overcoat. He would need to invest in a new one before long, but the station was only a few blocks from his office.

He thought about Kevin's letters filled with noble thoughts and dreams of Conor's future, all becoming more paradoxical against the backdrop of this terrible, magnificent, and complicated city, not to mention the growing evidence about Kevin and the Clan. Was Kevin involved in the corruption of the city and the deviance of the Levee? Why were people reluctant to speak of him? Was he a part of it? Was he involved with the Clan murders? Was he actually a killer? Most importantly, was *he* murdered? When he thought about Kevin's letters and the precious time the two had spent together on Kevin's visits to Springfield, the doubts about Kevin shamed him.

DETECTIVE FLYNN WAS NOTICEABLY LESS FRIENDLY THIS TIME, SO Conor started with specifics. Why was the file lacking an autopsy? Why were there no supplemental investigative reports? Why were no friends or witnesses listed or interviewed? Why were Kevin's finances not investigated? Why was his room not searched, especially since his service revolver was still missing? More importantly, did Kevin fail to appear for work at some point before they found his body?

"I'd like to see the shift attendance records," he demanded. "It seems to me they might help fix the date of death, and there is no mention in the report of when he last reported for duty."

"It wasn't necessary," Flynn replied. "As I recall, he missed only one shift, hardly enough to send out a search party. The two days before that he was off duty. Look, I'm tryin' to cooperate, but ye are making it very fookin' difficult."

"So that means he couldn't have been dead more than three days," Conor observed, ignoring the attitude. "We know he didn't report for duty the day his body was found, so why was he dressed in his uniform?"

Conor had touched a big nerve. "Look, who in the fookin' name of Jaezuz do you think you are?" The detective's brogue got thicker, the angrier he became. "I investigate over fifty murders every year—meself. You t'ink I can recall every detail of every case? You t'ink I can't tell the difference between a murder and a suicide? If ye want to see internal police records, get a fookin' subpoena, Counselor." The way he said "Counselor" made it sound like a dirty word.

Conor then threw his best pitch. "Were you aware that my brother was a member of the Clan na Gael?" he asked directly.

Flynn sat back in his chair for nearly a full minute, staring at Conor as he would a man who had just beaten his dog. Finally, he called across the cavernous, second-floor room to one of the half-dozen men doing what detectives do. "Frank, will ye come over here for a minute? I'll need a witness for this interview." As Frank pulled up a chair, Flynn added, "I'm not certain Counselor Dolan here understands which one of us is the detective."

Pointedly, Flynn ignored Conor's question about Clan na Gael. Had this detective been truly interested in Kevin's fate, in his own investigation, that question would have raised alarm bells or at least stirred enough interest to explore the subject further. Flynn had no intention of discussing Clan na Gael and that fact alone condemned him in Conor's eyes. But he decided to keep pushing.

"Then let me try a different question," Conor pushed. "Have you been following me around town or having one of your cops do the job?"

Flynn's tone threatened imminent violence now. "Look, Dolan, I told ye ye're brother killed himself. 'Tis not uncommon here for cops to do that. It's a stressful job."

"I don't believe that," Conor replied defiantly, "and I don't think you do either."

"And why is that, Mister Dolan?"

"Because you don't like it when I ask about the Clan na Gael. So let me ask it a different way. Are you a member of the Clan?"

Flynn rose from the chair and growled, "We're done here, Dolan. Ye got any more questions, put 'em in writing, and give 'em to me captain. Now get outta my house."

ON THE WALK TO MRS. SPECTOR'S BOARDINGHOUSE TO COLLECT Kevin's belongings, Conor reflected on the encounter. The Clan na Gael question lit a fuse under Detective Flynn, but it had not surprised the man. The reaction told Conor that the Clan was definitely woven into this quilt somewhere and that Flynn was determined that fact should not come to light. Rebecca was right. If the chief of police was a Clan leader and Kevin a member, Flynn likely was as well. All these facts tipped the odds heavily toward a conclusion that Kevin's death was in some way connected to a dispute within the Clan na Gael.

The small box of Kevin's belongings was sealed and waiting in Mrs. Spector's foyer. He had come twice before but missed her both times. This time he sent a note first. She showed him a second box with some uniform shirts, a police tunic, and a thick sweater. Conor immediately donned the sweater under his overcoat and tucked the small box under his arm, instructing Mrs. Spector to donate the clothing to St. Vincent DePaul, or whatever Jewish organization she might know.

As he left, she handed Conor a list of a few names and addresses, including a saloon just down the street. "I spoke with the other residents and gave the matter more thought. We managed to put together a list of a few names, people your brother was friendly with." She shrugged and added, "It's not a long list, I'm afraid."

It occurred to him that this woman saw his brother nearly every day for a long while. She would know something of his ways and his character, and Mrs. Spector had no horse in the race. He wanted her to simply talk about Kevin. "Mrs. Spector, why do you think it is that my brother had few friends? What was it about him that caused that? I promise you won't upset me. You see, I didn't know my brother very well, as it turns out so…"

Mrs. Spector sighed. "All right then, Mr. Dolan. I think people were afraid of your brother, afraid of upsetting him. I'm sorry to say it, but he was an angry man, quick to assume insult and ill intent.

He seemed always in a hurry and never showed a flicker of interest in another person's welfare as far as I could tell. But he paid his rent on time and was never violent with me or my tenants."

It was far from a glowing endorsement of Kevin's character, but he knew it was objective and honest.

He cruised the neighborhood, looking to match faces with the three names and locations on her note, but the list proved useless. One man had died, one moved to New York, and the third just disappeared.

Along the way, Conor continued to discover how Chicago works. The constant struggle for the streets fascinated him. Carriages, cabs, horse-drawn streetcars, cable cars, and trains all shared the streets with the local inhabitants who used them for gatherings of all kinds: kids playing games, sports, impromptu markets with vendors and peddlers, even half-frozen musical performers playing for tips. There were licensed carts peddling near-expired groceries including slightly overripe fruit at bargain prices. He had learned from Brendan that the hungry politicians would sell the space on the public streets to railroads, commuter lines, utility companies, anyone with a dollar— or next to nothing in some cases—and pocket the money. Travel by public transportation could be so slow that walking was faster.

The saloon was also a bust. Everyone was hesitant to talk about Kevin, even bartenders, and "nobody knew nuttin'" about the Clan. The dead cop was not popular. Conor pieced together enough information to support a conclusion that Kevin was widely considered dishonest and corrupt. Nobody wanted to talk about him or the Clan, so he decided to head for his office.

Downing the last of his beer, Conor started for the door when he heard a voice from the bar. "So ye hail from Clare, do ye?" the voice asked with a Clare accent.

He was an older fellow, a working man as opposed to a transient, nursing a beer at the end of the bar. Conor rested his hat on the bar beside the man. "Would you care for a whiskey to wash that down, sir?" Conor signaled the bartender for two shots. It was always Jameson unless another preference was stated.

"I would now," said the man. "I'm grateful to ye, sir. Seamus Gibbons is me name, and ye'd be the brother of Kevin Dolan."

"That's right. Conor. Pleased to know you, Seamus, and how did you know my brother?"

Seamus tipped back his wool cap and considered his answer carefully. "Well, ye might say I was his only friend in the neighborhood. Those who didn't fear Kevin didn't know him, and those who did stayed well clear."

"And how is it that Kevin was so friendly toward you?"

"I'm a Clare man," Seamus announced proudly, "from Lahinch, not far from your own homeplace of Liscannor. Sure I knew your father, Emmett, the Lord have mercy on his soul, and your poor ma, Finola. We would both haul our wool to Lisdoonvarna for the auctions."

Conor was suddenly breathless. "When did you come over here? Do you know anything of my mother?"

Seamus made a point of glancing over at his empty whiskey glass, and Conor signaled the bartender for two more. "Sure I do not, nor had I heard of poor Emmett's passing until Kevin himself infarmed me of it."

"What can you tell me about my brother? It seems Kevin had no other friends. The people who will talk about him say terrible things."

Seamus downed the full shot, placing the empty ceremoniously on the bar. "I'll take no more drink from ye, Conor. T'ank you. As for Kevin, it was a troubled, unhappy man he was. He loved to converse about the old country but only in the most general tearms. He would not discuss pairsonal or family history other than me own interactions wit' chore dear family. Aye, and he hated the English, to be sure, but I will say no more on that subject."

"Seamus, did he have anyone else here? Anyone at all?"

"He did mention a woman, now, as I recall. There was a child, a wee'an I t'ink."

"A baby? He had a woman…and a baby? Was her name Maureen Brogan?"

Seamus raised his hand in a gesture of caution. "Easy now, Conor. I wouldn't go rushing to conclusions. Sure I've no clue if the child was his own, and he never mentioned the woman's name."

On the walk back to the office, he had plenty to think about. If there was a woman out there with Kevin's baby, the child was his nephew. Rebecca had the address. It had to be the same woman. If Kevin had a child, why would he kill himself?

As for the box of Kevin's belongings, a little voice told him it might be wise to secure it somewhere in the office until he examined the items carefully.

From the sidewalk, Conor noticed a man seated in front of his office in the cold. The squatter brought his own chair. "Why are you here?" Conor asked.

"I'm on da job," said the squatter. "Boris told me stay right here all day every day and don't let nobody in dis office except fer da guy what works here."

Over the last few days, several new walk-in clients had appeared, one a shooting that promised a handsome fee. Unfortunately, all the clients were referred by either the Russian ward heeler or a helpful beat officer. Boris checked in yesterday, hoping for a dusting, but Conor stalled him again, claiming—truthfully—that he still had not been paid on any of the cases. Boris was polite but disappointed. Conor needed to figure out how to handle all these parasites. Losing his temper was not one of his productive options.

Conor put his key in the lock. "Well, the guy that works here is me so… Look, just go away, please, or I'll call the police."

The guy smiled. "Oh, you mean Tommy Higgins? The beat cop? I can get him for you. He's just down the street."

"I'm sure you could," said Conor, exasperated. But he realized that he was just fending off the inevitable. Better to surrender now than after bitterness and bad feelings kicked in. "Wait—if you can find Boris, send him over. Tell him I'm ready to work this out."

He put the box from Mrs. Spector on his desk and opened it, examining the items one by one. A common pocketknife, a carefully bundled pile of old letters, three faded photographs without frames, a packet of postcards, and a total of three dollars and seventy cents. Rounding out the contents was an old announcement of sailing for the vessel that carried the young Dolan brothers on their arduous journey across the water. Inside the announcement was a folded piece of common writing paper. On it was written the lyrics to an old Irish Folk song, "Galway Bay." It was a relatively old Irish ballad dating back to the 1870s. The tune was among Conor's earliest memories, and he recalled with fondness the image of the boys' father, Emmett, sitting by the hearthstone in the evening, the tune whistling from his wooden flute. Their mother would sometimes sing the haunting lyrics as tears flowed from her tired eyes and weather-beaten cheeks.

The sailing announcement itself bestowed new life upon old memories. It had been some sixteen years since their long voyage from Ireland. Conor still remembered the voyage and the Port of Queenstown, but Kevin had never spoken of those things in his letters. They were difficult days, Conor knew, but the stress and worry was Kevin's alone to bear—assumed willingly—to minimize for his little brother the added trauma of two weeks on a "coffin ship."

RETURNING EVERYTHING TO THE BOX, HE TOOK GREAT CARE TO store it under a loose floorboard beside the stove alongside a significant amount of cash. He would need to read the letters and reexamine every item in that box carefully as his investigation progressed.

Recent developments all conflicted with his personal memories of Kevin. He still believed his brother was a hero but was no longer oblivious to facts. Disillusionment threatened him as witnesses painted an increasingly unflattering portrait of Kevin. *"Drank too much." "Shook down all the businesses on his beat."* Beyond that, it appeared Kevin was a violent Irish Republican. Conor's chances of proving Rebecca wrong were diminishing.

Whatever the answers, Kevin had essentially sacrificed his own happiness, deferred his life, to give Conor the gift of opportunity. Conor decided then and there that he would not dishonor Kevin's efforts by becoming a bartender. He had worked hard to become a lawyer, and he liked it. If Father Brendan White could find a pathway through this quagmire of corruption and vice, humanity intact, then so could Conor Dolan.

It took the man outside less than fifteen minutes to find Boris the Heeler. The Russian arrived, walking two paces behind the captain of the Nineteenth Precinct, introduced to Conor as Vincenzo Ruffulo. A short, cheerful man, Vincenzo arrived armed with a broad, friendly grin and a basket of freshly baked cannoli. "I'm-a welcome you to the neighborhood," bellowed the short man, speaking mainly with his left hand. "My wife-a she send-a to you a gift, eh? You like Italiano cuisine? Pasticcino?"

"I do, indeed, sir. Thank your wife for me."

Vincenzo offered his hand and all but hugged Conor like a baby. "We be good-a friends. You need-a something, you call-a Vincenzo. I ring-a da bell sometime for da big-a boss. We take-a care you real good, Mista Dolan."

With that, Vincenzo was gone, leaving the details of the graft to his faithful ward heeler. When Boris had finally left, Conor had to marvel at the intricacy of their operation. Boris would keep an eye on his client portfolio and obtain updates from the court clerks on all bail bond payouts assigned to Conor as fees. Essentially, the ward politicians would monitor his gross receipts and skim 10 percent from the top. Boris started at fifteen.

One of the services Boris pedaled in his inventory of corruption services was fixing criminal cases. For that noble service, the alderman would get half the fee for all cases except for murder. For murders, no guarantee was offered, but a successful fix would cost 70 percent of the lawyer's fee.

On this point Conor was clear. He would not participate in fixing cases, tampering with juries, or suborning perjury. Also, they could take their extortion money, but he would have no part in doing favors for the bosses. Finally, Conor would retain the right to do free legal work for the poor without interference. They made a tentative deal on the spot with the understanding that Vincenzo himself would return with a face-to-face agreement to Conor's conditions.

These politicians, Conor thought, had perfected a system of corruption so pervasive and organized that it operated like a large corporation. Conor had to marvel at the level of sophistication. As Boris was leaving, it occurred to Conor that he might as well solve all his corruption problems in one sweep. "If you see Tommy Higgins, the beat cop, please ask him to come see me."

"Da," said Boris. "I see kheem across street now."

Conor wondered whether it was technically possible to be only partially corrupt or whether it worked more like pregnancy. He hoped Brendan would approve of his deal with the devil.

Chapter 7

Boarding a westbound streetcar on Harrison, Conor soon passed Grand Central Station only to find the drawbridge up as a cargo barge lumbered its way through a narrow point in the river. Past the bridge, he exited directly at Clinton Street and found the house with no trouble. Maureen Brogan's building looked similar to his own although her Little Italy area was without the homeless vagrants and rundown buildings common in the Nineteenth Precinct. The Irish and Italians had largely moved west across the river by the end of the century, north and south of here, replaced by Jews from Poland and Russia and by other Europeans. Mrs. Kaplan had carefully explained the demographics.

The landlady was decidedly unfriendly. "Why do you want to see her?" The woman asked with no regard for etiquette or manners. "She's recently widowed—if that policeman was ever her husband. He was only here half the time."

Conor was quickly losing his tolerance for fools. "That's between the lady and me," he snapped. "My name is Conor Dolan. Here is my card. Now, if you'd be kind enough to announce me...?"

"Very well, but you'll see her in the parlor. I'll not have any goings-on in my house."

Maureen Brogan appeared shocked upon entering the parlor. "You're Kevin's brother," she declared.

The woman was neatly if humbly dressed in a plain white top—buttoned in front with long sleeves and puffed up shoulders—and a heavy, broadcloth skirt. She was maybe twenty-one, not unattractive but gaunt, her red hair turned up unceremoniously and over into a thick braid stretching to near the small of her back. Poor lighting in the modest parlor concealed her eye color. He thought it might be gray—that last light shade before powder blue. The girl had obviously been living hand-to-mouth.

"I am," he answered, the homburg under his arm.

"Ye're younger, of course," she said, "but the resemblance is uncanny. Sit, please. I can only stay a few minutes. My baby is upstairs."

He wanted to blurt out, *Is the child my nephew?*

The girl sat forward on the sofa across from his chair. "How may I assist you, Mr. Conor Dolan?"

"I'm here to settle my brother's affairs, Miss Brogan," he explained. "I just wanted to introduce myself. I'm told you and Kevin were...friends."

The woman breathed deeply in a contemplative way, maybe even annoyed. "Friends, indeed," she said nervously. "Mr. Dolan, I would offer ye tea, but Mrs. Carson here would not approve." She flashed a wicked look at the old landlady listening from the kitchen door and said loudly, "Still, the next time I've a visitor, male or female, I will accept the visit in my own room."

Then she looked back at Conor, all business, and asked, "How did ye find me, and what do ye want?"

Conor reached into his breast pocket and held out an envelope. "I settled my brother's affairs, and he left you a small sum of money. I'm here to deliver it."

She opened it straightaway, removing the $200 bank draft. The girl clearly had to restrain the joy and excitement fighting for release. Conor guessed she was likely only days from being evicted. Still, she said, "Sure your brother didn't leave me any *mooney*, Mr. Dolan, and I am not in the habit of taking mooney from strange men." Curiously, she did not hand back the draft. "But a child doesn't understand pride, and unfartunately, everyone understands hunger."

"I wasn't aware there was a child until now," he said. "I mean…"

She was apparently not about to offer information on the child's parentage, and she let the question float in the air.

He could not help but wonder how she had earned money to feed the baby and pay the rent these last months. It was likely the girl had been reduced to nefarious practices. That would explain the landlady's attitude. Conor felt ashamed. "The money was Kevin's," he assured her. "Keep it, please. I know he would want you to have it."

She stood up from the sofa, indicating the meeting had ended. "I thank you, Mr. Dolan, for your generosity. Good day, sir."

He needed a drink after the awkward encounter and remembered this was Friday evening. He might catch Brendan at Andy Murphy's Bar.

HE AND BRENDAN WERE PASSING WORDS AT THE BAR, DISCUSS-ing Conor's new arrangement with the precinct captain, when the three-legged dog hobbled in behind a patron and lay down beside Conor.

"Is he yours?" Brendan asked.

"He's nobody's. I guess you could say we're friends."

Murph put a small bowl of beer on the bar for the dog. He smiled and said, "It's on the house." The dog lapped it up the moment Conor placed it on the floor.

"Brendan, what can you tell me about the Clan na Gael?" Conor asked in a hushed tone.

Brendan's elbows came off the bar and he turned toward Conor. "Just a load of drunken big mouths these days. Since their great bombing campaign failed a few years ago, they only meet to brag and drink away from their wives. Now, why would the likes of ye be interested in that scruffy lot?"

"That's exactly what I thought," Conor replied. Just maybe, Brendan White—priest, politician, philosopher, and fornicator—did not have the answer. Conor recounted his story of the spy, the Clan, and the "not quite a maiden" for Brendan. Murphy came over and filled their glasses just as Conor was considering whether to include the facts of his scandalous relationship with Rebecca. He decided it might sound vulgar or braggadocios even without the use of names. Brendan was still a priest. The friendly bartender was obviously tuned in and straining to eavesdrop, but a look from Conor sent the street-savvy Murphy to tend his other patrons.

Brendan flashed him a look of astonishment. "Sure you've been a busy lad, Conor."

As Conor decided to spare Rebecca's reputation, a scruffy-looking fellow on his way to the door stopped to drunkenly curse the mangy dog. The latter paid him no mind. Miffed at receiving no reaction, the scoundrel kicked the dog violently in the rear end.

Almost before the animal could react, Conor planted his right fist squarely into the man's jaw, promptly ending the disturbance, with the dog little more than annoyed and his attacker muttering nonsense from the dirty floor.

Murph was over the bar in a flash, dragging the groggy trouble-maker to the street by his collar. "Now that's the kind of fight I like. One punch and no damage to the establishment."

Returning to his beer, Conor said quietly, "I just can't tolerate a man who will mistreat a dog."

"So I gather," said Brendan. "Would ye care to elaborate?"

Conor downed three fingers from the glass and decided to share an old memory with Brendan. "My pa gave me a short-haired collie pup from the old dog's last litter—you know, to take care of until he could be trained for the sheep. I was a wee tyke of about six and called the pup Boy. The dog and I were close for a few months. It was a common thing."

"I remember only too well," said Brendan. "I raised a few of me own as a boy back home."

Conor felt bad about losing his temper like that in the bar. So why was he wasting Brendan's time on a dumb story from twenty years ago? He was sounding like a whiner, he decided. "It's just a child's memory, not even worth recounting."

But Brendan prodded him. "Aw, go ahead with the story now ye started it."

"Well, when the time was right, Pa would take the dogs to the fields every day to learn about working sheep, but Boy refused to work. His tail was always up and wagging like a child who just can't bring himself to do homework. No matter what method or tricks Pa tried, Boy only wanted to play. One morning, Pa announced with regret he would take Boy to town and sell him. It broke my heart.

"I was only six but not daft. Who would buy a useless dog? So I followed him, staying out of sight, as he led Boy down the road toward the Cliffs of Moher overlooking Galway Bay. The cliffs were only a short walk from our farm. He was throwing a bone along the way and the pup would fetch. Near the edge of the cliffs, Pa gave a mighty heave and the bone soared high over the bay to the rocks below, followed playfully by my trusting little collie. The poor thing yelped helplessly all the way down."

Brendan nodded. "Sure such things were common in the old country then," he pointed out. "Necessary even, but did ye confront your old pa?"

"Neither of us ever spoke of it. I told my brother the same night, and he said much the same as you. Kevin understood Pa's grief, but I didn't—not then. In Ireland at that time, you didn't eat if you didn't work—dogs included. It was no easy thing for my father to do. I see now that he did it for his family. Kevin said we would only make it worse by confronting him."

"'Tis a sad story indeed." Brendan sat quietly for a minute, maybe thinking of a way to lighten the mood. Then he said, "Sure that eejit you poonched made me lose me thought. Did you know, Conor, there are seventy-two t'ousand Irish-born people in Chicago?"

"And…?"

"Sure it sounds like a proper overload of souls, but it's not, not really when ye consider they are mostly all Catholics on the lookout for a church steeple or a good saloon. I'm sayin' it's a small world, and they tend to congregate…so I've been t'inkin' over your story about the Clan and that young Irish lass."

"You're being cute, Brendan. Out with it."

"Sure is her name Maureen Brogan by chance?"

ON HIS WALK HOME, CONOR THOUGHT ABOUT THE COINCIDENCE and about what Brendan had told him. Brendan knew the girl's whole story. He had once provided shelter to her on an emergency referral from the Hull House. Her child was not Conor's nephew. Maureen left Ireland alone and pregnant and ashamed at nineteen. The putative father was supposed to join her on the departing dock but abandoned her. She arrived at Ellis Island alone in 1901 and was one of the first groups to see the Statue of Liberty. She had told Brendan she thought it was laughing at her.

According to Brendan, a representative of a relief agency in New York spotted the girl pregnant on the dock. They put her up temporarily in their facility until the baby was born. It was pure luck as the dock was always crawling with pimps and procurers on the prowl for troubled girls.

They got her a job cooking right there at the settlement house because she would not give up the baby. She had an aunt in Chicago, so they got her a train ticket and took her to the station in Hoboken where she got a ticket to Chicago.

"So she found the aunt?" Conor asked.

"Never found a trace of her, but thank God, she'd found Hull House. One night, she and the child showed up at my church with a social worker, like Mary with the Baby Jesus. I took her into the church basement for a few nights, then found her a room and leveraged a month's rent from the landlord."

"Do you know how she met my brother?"

Brendan shook his head. "I'm sorry, Lad. I never saw her again after I put her in the hotel. I gave her enough for passage home to Ireland, but apparently I didn't do enough."

It was an astonishing coincidence, and the story painted Maureen Brogan in a new light. It did not matter how she had met Kevin, so why did he keep thinking about it? Kevin had acted decently in telling the landlady they were married. That counted for something.

Conor downed the last few drops of beer and headed for the coat rack with the dog at his heels. "Well, Brendan, that's a basket of questions answered in one night. I'll see you next week. Good-night, Murph."

As Conor turned to cut through a vacant lot a few doors from the bar, he felt a vicious thump on the back of his head and was on his back, looking up in the dark at two masked men with clubs. He rolled into a ball to protect his ribs and head, but they kept kicking and beating him until someone started yelling from a back porch.

Before disappearing down the alley, one of them whispered in his ear, "Leave the girl be, and let it go. No more questions about the dead cop." The words were delivered in a Dublin accent, something young Conor could still identify after all these years.

Dazed and roughed up, Conor made his way back to the boardinghouse. He needed help so went straight to Mrs. Kaplan's upstairs where his appearance caused quite a stir only a couple of hours into the Sabbath. Mrs. Goldman nearly fainted, and Mrs. Kaplan was determined to call the police. With Rebecca's help, he managed to keep her away from the telephone.

With the other women calmed down, Rebecca tended to his injuries at the kitchen table. He explained to the women that his assailants were only hungry kids and were long gone by now. Rebecca would know better. When Mrs. Kaplan went to bed, he told Rebecca about the assault and about young Maureen Brogan, including what he had learned from Brendan earlier.

"You'll have a big bump on your head by morning," she said, rinsing away the soap with a clean cloth, "but there's no bleeding, just an abrasion. You'd better see a doctor just the same."

"I'll see the physician in the office next door to mine. He's a nice young fellow. Just moved in himself."

"And you shouldn't go back to see Maureen Brogan again," she warned. "It's too dangerous. Whatever is going on, the girl may be part of it. I never should have involved you."

Rebecca meant well, and she knew her business, but she never met Maureen Brogan. Conor had. They had sat and talked, and Conor came to a different opinion of Maureen. It was the same principle used in evaluating credibility in courtroom witnesses: seeing the witness, watching reactions and body language, and looking them squarely in the eyes. It was all part of the calculation and more meaningful than mere words.

Whatever else the young woman was, Conor figured, she was serious and sincere, any moral deficiency notwithstanding. He was hoping the Charlie Damme experience had sharpened his judgment.

"Well, I *am* involved," he reminded Rebecca. "That's why I'm in Chicago. I am involved, and now I'd like to know who assaulted me. It had to be either the Clan or the cops, but I don't think this Maureen Brogan is part of it."

"Maybe it was the Clan *and* the cops simultaneously," Rebecca suggested. Then she explained that informers recently reported infighting within the Clan. It was more likely than ever that the dispute was linked to Kevin's death because it seemed to have subsided since his body was recovered, and the Dublin accent of Conor's attacker only strengthened that conclusion.

According to Rebecca, some Clan leaders were less than enamored with the halt to the bombing campaign, disappointed with the subsiding of IRB violence in Ireland, and decided to act on their own. "Let the girl be, Conor. You may be getting in too deep."

"No, I'm going back. She knows more. Maybe not everything, but more." He was betting Maureen was not involved in whatever criminality was afoot, but Rebecca was holding back. That much was clear. There was more going on. "I think it's time you told me precisely what you're investigating, Rebecca."

She finished washing her hands and sat across from him at the table. "More monitoring than investigating until today."

"Until today?"

That's when she told him about the Prince of Wales's scheduled visit to Chicago in late December. Rebecca's mission was to make sure the visit went well and to monitor Irish Republican activity, although she had no specific evidence of a plot. Still, based on these recent rumblings, she feared the Clan—or some faction thereof,—might be planning to assassinate the royal prince during the visit and thought the chief of police may be a principal in the plot. That meant he might have had Kevin killed for opposing the assassination. Her fear was that Conor was getting too close to exposing the chief's involvement and blowing up her surveillance operation in the process.

It sounded like madness to Conor. The assassination of the future King of England on American soil could literally wreak havoc on key international alliances and maybe even cause a war in Ireland—or a slaughter. Private American financial aid to Irish Republican causes was a sensitive topic in Britain. Growing diplomatic and economic ties between Britain and the United States helped keep Germany in check lately, and the British were known to be using the alliance to push hard for the US Government to crack down on support to the IRB.

The assassination alone would be enough to rock the world, but what would happen when the investigation implicated Chicago's own chief of police as a Clan na Gael assassin? And it might not stop with the chief of the Chicago police. If the Clan had penetrated that far up into city government, it could go higher.

Conor could think of a simple solution. "Why doesn't Scotland Yard simply cancel the trip?"

It was apparent to Conor that Rebecca was finally bringing him on board—fully. The Prince of Wales, she explained, would not cancel his visit based on Pinkerton's speculation, and the foreign intelligence section of Scotland Yard gave no credence to a potential threat since Irish nationalist violence had subsided all over the world. Besides, Scotland Yard, in its collective arrogance, considered the Clan na Gael a pack of inept buffoons. The Yard's chutzpah was staggering and foolhardy, but they would be generous in assigning blame to Americans should there be an attempt.

As for Kevin Dolan, Rebecca opined, "We think your brother was a well-placed and loyal Clan member threatening to blow the whistle on the rogue elements."

Finally, something good about Kevin! Conor did not give a damn about the Prince of Wales, but he had an opportunity to help his dead brother. They could not report their suspicions to the police, obviously, because the chief himself might be a conspirator. *Even the Chicago mayor could be involved.* So he would team up with Rebecca and do the job.

Rebecca removed a small revolver from her skirt and placed it on the table. "Take it," she ordered. "It may save your life."

He shook his head. "I wouldn't know what to do with it. Now, if you have a shotgun that will fit in my pocket..."

"You're hopeless," she declared.

Maybe so, he thought, but one thing was certain now. Conor's visit to Chicago had transformed into an investigation of Kevin's death. His answers lay somewhere within the secrets of Clan na Gael. Conor was on a mission.

Chapter 8

With all the excitement over the weekend, Conor almost forgot about meeting a prospective client on Monday morning. He promised Father Brendan he would speak with the woman, but it was a murder case and required a more experienced lawyer. Nellie Finley was residing at the Hull House facility on Halsted Street where she was on bail for the alleged murder of her one-month-old baby. All Conor knew from Brendan was that the girl had thrown herself off a bridge with the baby in her arms. Before meeting her, he would see the doctor next door about his thumping headache and the lump on his noggin.

"I wouldn't worry too much," said Dr. Camp, concluding his physical examination of the wounds. "You can get off the table and put your shirt and tie back on."

Camp was a muscular fellow of about thirty with short black hair; he was clean-shaven with thick eyebrows and chocolate-brown eyes. Conor figured him to be of Italian descent, maybe even Spanish. Non-Irish ethnic families would often shorten their names to blend in. Camp might have been Campinella or Campineros when his parents arrived from Europe or wherever.

The doctor sat down at his desk and began making notes on the file. "A headache is normal after a blow like that, but if it persists after tomorrow or you start to get blurry vision or dizziness, come back immediately. That would indicate a concussion and might require bed rest. Otherwise, try to take it easy for a few days and you'll be fine."

"Thank you, Doctor," Conor said, straightening his tie. "Are you all alone here? I see no nurse."

"Oh, I've only been here a couple of weeks. Moved in several days before you. I'm just starting in private practice. Can't afford a nurse just yet."

That reminded Conor about the business end of a doctor visit. He reached into his coat for the billfold. "What do I owe you, sir?"

The doctor looked up from his desk and waived him off. "It won't be much. I'll slip an invoice under your door next week."

On his way out of the office, Conor held the door for a pair of delivery men—Negroes—carrying a large crate into the doctor's office from an old horse cart, then started west on his walk over to Hull House.

Hull House was a widely known and respected institution dedicated to improving the lives of immigrants both generally and individually, regardless of language or country of origin. Hull House was more than a relief agency. It tracked poverty and homelessness scientifically and methodically, tracing the movement of immigrant communities and advocating relentlessly for social reform. It did not—and had never—catered to pretrial felony defendants, let alone for a murder. Father Brendan somehow raised the woman's bail money and persuaded Hull House to accept her into one of its resident programs. After all, she was hardly a dangerous criminal.

The People v. Nellie Finley was a tragic and sympathetic case to say the least, and it would be certain to attract its share of sensational newspaper attention. With all the papers in this city, the dailies scoured the town for something salacious to write about—the more scandalous, the better. Morning, afternoon, and evening editions had the newsboys blanketing the city all hours of the day and into the night with whatever would sell papers. A down-and-out mother jumping off a bridge and killing her own baby would have their tongues hanging out. Publicity was not necessarily a bad thing for a girl in Nellie's position. Chicago was home to a powerful reform movement led by some of its most respected citizens, notably Jane Addams.

Conor was reluctant to even interview a potential client in such a serious case, but Brendan twisted his arm—not for himself but for this young Irish girl he came to know through his work with Hull House. In any case, Conor thought there would be no harm in talking with the girl as a favor to Father Brendan White, Patron Saint of Lost Souls. Maybe he could at least match the girl with a suitable defense lawyer. He already knew several highly skilled criminal lawyers in the city.

The social worker was prepared and waiting for his visit. They adjourned to a small office off the foyer of the three-story building. Following introductions, the social worker, Miss Potter, laid the ground rules. Conor was expecting a stern schoolmarm type with hair in a bun and a scowl on her lips, but Miss Potter was quite un-social-worker-like in both manner and appearance, evidenced by a full view of her ankles in black stockings below a scandalously short, mid-calf skirt.

Nearly all women, he knew, opted for some form of Edwardian pompadour hairstyle piled and rolled high atop the head, sometimes even with a hidden hair pad to increase the volume. Slim and around twenty-one, Miss Potter was the notable exception. Her hair was short in the extreme, efficient, falling straight down over her ears and curling gently forward in a crescent pattern toward the cheeks. Her voice was soft but confident. Conor pegged the woman as a suffragette.

She placed a file in front of Conor on the desk. "Mr. Dolan, this is a rather unusual situation for us as we don't normally admit criminal court defendants, especially not those charged with serious crimes. Still, this is an exceptional case. We won't presume, of course, to become involved in Miss Finley's defense but will be willing to assist so far as we're able should you desire. We're always pressed for resources, but we do have a dedicated reserve of professionals to call on. We've put together Nellie's history as best we could through records and interviews. Nellie doesn't talk much herself. Everything will be available to you should you decide to represent her. You may examine the file in this room now, of course."

Conor cradled his homburg in the stark, wooden chair. "Thank you, Miss Potter, but I would appreciate anything you could tell me about the girl herself to begin with."

You got facts out of a file, but sometimes impressions and opinions could be equally important. He had learned that much in his brief career. Miss Potter, after all, was a trained observer and social worker, not just some do-gooder handing out meals on a street corner.

"We prefer to call our residents by their names, Mr. Dolan; however, I understand you're unfamiliar with our particular quirks here." Her voice was mellow and friendly. She seemed like a nice person, and he was comfortable in her presence. He sensed his question weighed on her. "Of course, Miss Potter," he said.

The social worker stood and walked over to the window facing Halsted Street. In the background, the street outside teemed with life, commerce, the prancing of working horses, and the clatter of streetcars. A heavyset woman was passing on the sidewalk with a cart of groceries and a small child in tow.

"They don't all end up like Nellie," Miss Potter said wistfully. "They're by and large industrious, hardy people determined to thrive in their adopted country, but…sometimes it all goes wrong for one reason or another, mostly through no fault of their own. I think that was Nellie. She never found help until it was too late, and that, unfortunately, is a common pattern.

"Something terrible happened to that girl, something so horrific that she couldn't live with it and wanted to save her child from the same fate." Then Miss Potter seemed to snap back into business mode, turning back to the desk. "I know you're here to help, so I'll tell you what little we know. We know she came alone to New York from Queenstown in steerage in 1900. The only identification she carried was her immigrant inspection card. She came here out of shame to make a new life. I get the sense that the human predators from the Levee never got their claws into her. But someone did, Mr. Dolan. Someone certainly did. That's who I'd be looking for."

"Then she hasn't communicated with you at all?"

"Nellie goes in and out. She knows her baby is dead and that she's responsible. She can respond to simple questions most of the time, but her memory is blocked somehow. She knows the baby's name yet can't tell us her mother's name or the location of her home in Ireland. She mumbles sometimes about a 'dark angel' on the bridge, but there was an eyewitness to the incident—two in fact. She was alone with the child and simply jumped."

"How did she not drown in the river?" Conor asked.

He could see tears forming in Miss Potter's eyes. "Nellie simply had the great misfortune of being rescued by Good Samaritans who saw her jump and spotted her floundering. The men were working on a boat or something just under the bridge. It was a small miracle. A large miracle would have saved the baby as well, but…well, you know…"

Conor leafed through the file. "I see nothing here about her employment history, nothing to piece together a picture of her life over the last three years. If she remains in her current state…"

Miss Potter sighed. "Believe me: I understand. The only thing we know is that she gave birth at Cook County Hospital. You'll see the child's birth certificate there. The father is 'unknown,' and she checked into the hospital using a seedy hotel as her address of residence. She told Father White earlier that the baby's father abandoned her on the dock in Ireland."

The file was essentially useless, eight or ten pages of nothing. With eyewitnesses to her jump from the bridge, Nellie Finley's defense would be about mitigation and insanity rather that guilt or innocence. And with no insight into her personal history or background, defending the girl would be an impossible task.

"It's not much to go on," Conor said, "but she had to live somewhere over the three years and would not have survived without employment. Has she undergone any treatment here?"

"That's what we think. These women often make the voyage with pre-arranged domestic employment. As for treatment, Nellie's only been with us for two weeks, and our attorney advised us that any notes or conversations may subject our chosen psychiatrist to subpoena by the prosecution. He suggested we wait and speak with Nellie's counsel. We thought she might open up a bit in a safe atmosphere with her immediate needs met, but that hasn't happened yet."

"I agree. There is a privilege but it's not absolute, so the key to helping her is finding a way to unlock the secrets of her life over the last three years. But frankly, I have to wonder why she wouldn't have left the child with some church or agency before trying to kill herself."

The question seemed to touch a nerve in Miss Potter. "You're not a woman, and you don't think as a woman. We don't vote yet, but we're entitled to basic rights and dignity. There are far too many Nellie Finleys in this city, and many of them are decaying unjustly in prison if not already in Potter's Field. Despite the horrific nature of the charges, Nellie was simply a mother out of options, at the end of her rope, and sick of watching her baby suffer. Why in the world would she believe the child would fare better in this hellish world without her? That's what she thought. In short, Mr. Dolan, Nellie did it *for* the baby, not *to* her." Miss Potter rose, headed toward the door, and added, "In any case, you'll decide for yourself. I'll bring her down here now, and you may use this room."

As she was about to leave, Conor spoke. "May I ask one question before you do, Miss Potter?"

"Of course."

"I'm just curious. How do these poor unfortunates end up at Father White's door?"

"If I knew, I couldn't tell you, but I don't know. I can only say that Father White is a remarkable person and a valued resource and colleague, well known in our social services community. He's always out there looking for the most desperate souls on the streets. I can assure you there is no shortage, and most of them are women. Likely, someone at the hospital contacted him."

"Why is that necessary?" he asked. "Surely there are some temporary shelter accommodations made in such cases."

"City shelters like the police stations and City Hall are only available to men, Mr. Dolan, and a nationwide social net for these poor souls may never come at all, so the prisons and asylums house the thousands of poor and insane women whose only real crime is poverty. Homeless men can at least get a bowl of soup at night and a space on the floor at City Hall. The large majority of the women are from Ireland. Remember, it's only a few years ago that the state assumed responsibility for the hopelessly insane, and honestly, those poor souls might be better cared for in prisons.

"Can you imagine being a young girl alone and spending the night in such circumstance? Or with a child? They turn to the brothels in order to live or they find their way here. There are very few options. Father White is one of the people who seek them out before it's too late. When our resources are exhausted, we call on people like him for help as well. Nellie Finley was simply too late."

"Then you know nothing about her life over the last three years? Did the police not investigate?"

She pointed to the file. "You know everything I know."

THE YOUNG, RAIL-THIN IRISHWOMAN WAS NEATLY DRESSED AND groomed but emotionless and rote, like a child's doll, as Miss Potter escorted her into the room for the introduction. With the social worker gone, Conor took the chair beside Nellie rather than the one behind the desk. She sat nervously, leaning forward with her palms rubbing back and forth on her knees. The girl did not look him in the eye. "Nellie, do you know why I am here?"

Nellie did not look up, and he had to repeat the question. Finally, she said, "They told me you're a lawyer."

"That's right," he said gently, "I might be your lawyer if you want my help. Nellie, please tell me, do you know what a lawyer is? Do you know why you need a lawyer?"

This time she looked up, and her eyes were pure glass, two colorless objects through which light and form pass unrecorded. "I killed my baby. Her name was Elizabeth."

He tried the same question a different way. "Nellie, they took you to the courthouse, and you saw a judge. Do you know what happens in that courtroom?"

Then she surprised him, looking right into his eyes. "Aye, that's where they'll punish me."

"And do you remember where you came from, Nellie? You came here from Ireland. Tell me about your homeplace, your mother."

She smiled, and for a moment it seemed to Conor like the girl's mind had just returned from a long holiday, but she said emphatically, "I don't know. Sure I must have come from somewhere."

Conor was no psychiatrist, but he was confident that Nellie's symptoms were primarily related to memory rather than processing, and that wasn't all bad. The skittishness, he speculated, would likely be the remnants of prolonged trauma.

She was a long way from being able to enter a voluntary guilty plea to a serious felony, but at least she knew the basic function of the justice system and the reason she was in court. He decided not to push the girl in their initial meeting. If he took the case, they would go slowly. More questions might only stress her, but at some point, maybe soon, he could find himself in front of a judge, recounting all the steps he had taken to communicate with Nellie to evaluate her ability to assist in her defense.

For the next thirty minutes, they talked about nothing in particular. His focus was to establish a line of communication. Did she have a favorite color? A dog? Had she ever seen the ocean? He read portions of the file to her, hoping something might spark a memory. He tried talking about Ireland, even about the Catholic Church. Finally, sensing Nellie was exhausted from his interrogation, Conor opened the door and waited for Miss Potter to appear.

"I'll see her to her room and then we can talk if you like, Mr. Dolan."

"Yes," he said. "I think we should."

Of course, there would be no getting this girl off, he thought, but the case had been grossly under investigated. There had to be some mitigating circumstances in her life sufficient to help her avoid a death penalty or a life in the hell of prison or the asylum.

Even the known facts of the case, scant as they were, supported an argument that Nellie was overcharged. Manslaughter, maybe— but murder? It just seemed barbaric. If ever there could be a case of presumed insanity, this was it. But a defense, including a proper investigation of her background and an expert psychiatrist, would cost money, a lot of money. Without resources, Nellie was effectively at the mercy of the Cook County State's Attorney.

Unless Nellie Finley somehow regained the ability to recall and communicate, insanity was the only possible defense even if resources were available. And how would he find a humanitarian psychiatrist to work for free? It was a perfect example of why the prisons were filled with poor immigrants. Being rich and insane would have offered Nellie Finley at least some hope of a life.

Miss Potter did not mince words, but closed the door, and said, "May I ask what you think?"

Conor shrugged. "I think what you already know. She's in a world of trouble."

"But surely you agree that Nellie is insane," she prodded.

Conor sat back down in the chair, and the social worker followed suit. "Mad as a hatter, but it's not that simple. She needs an expert opinion. In lay terms, she needs to present expert testimony that her insanity prevented her from knowing the difference between right and wrong, or that her insanity compelled her to act wrong wrongfully. In practical terms, all that costs money, lots of money."

"I see," said the woman, obviously disappointed. "Then you won't be representing her?"

"I didn't say that. I need to consider it for a day or two and make a few inquiries. When does she go for her arraignment?"

"She goes to the main Hubbard Street Courthouse next Wednesday, right behind the jail."

Conor thought about the situation on the short walk to the trolley. An insanity opinion could provide more than simply a defense to the crime. It could also be used as a pretrial tool to delay the trial or avoid trial completely. He could claim, with expert help, that Nellie was unfit to stand trial by reason of insanity. He could even claim both. Maybe he could delay the trial for a year or more, hoping that Hull House might achieve a breakthrough with Nellie. Lucid and communicating, she could fill in the empty history.

But what then? Insanity would still be her only chance. She would be able to provide the psychiatrist with mountains of background information that might help the expert in evaluating her case—*might* being the key word. The case was as close as Conor had ever come to a legal conundrum.

THE NELLIE FINLEY INTERVIEW UNSETTLED HIM, BUT HE HAD A good understanding of Miss Potter's bleak assessment as he boarded the eastbound trolley. Of course, the girl needed a lawyer. Murder of a child was a capital offense, but on the surface, it appeared that no right-thinking person would convict Nellie Finley of capital murder.

Still, the lawyer in him knew better.

Conor thought about the process. He would need to do research at the county library on the defense of diminished mental capacity, also called insanity, but even an inexperienced lawyer knew the fundamentals involved here. To be successful, the insanity defense required some evidence that the defendant, because of mental disease or incapacity, either did not know right from wrong or suffered from some irresistible impulse to commit the wrongful act. It was a murky and quickly developing area of law, most because of medical and scientific advancement. But whatever the current case law on the subject, Nellie Finley, the human being, seemed beyond help. Whatever horrors had ravaged her life had left little of Nellie Finley behind.

Without a doubt, he would need an alienist—psychiatrist, they called themselves now—to examine her. First, the expert would examine the entire record of the case and Nellie's history, so a thorough investigation would be necessary now to uncover information about her background. Then the psychiatrist would have to prepare the report, detailing his findings and opinion. It would cost hundreds before the psychiatrist even got to court.

Conor looked out the window and realized he had just missed his stop at LaSalle Street; he would be forced to go on to Dearborn. The late fall air was brutally cold, so he hopped a Dearborn car heading for Harrison Street.

He thought again about the separate issue of Nellie's mental fitness to stand trial. In her present state, the girl was flatly unable to assist in her defense. She could not articulate the facts of the case or her history. He could help with her understanding of the legal process, even to the point where she could get through a plea; her mind was still functioning, and that was the key. It was her *memory* that was missing.

He decided that delaying Nellie's trial until she was mentally "fit" would be against the girl's interest. She would rot in the Northern Illinois Asylum for the Insane in Elgin until she died or the court declared her fit for trial. The net result might well be a de facto life sentence in an asylum.

It was only in the last three years that the state had assumed some responsibility for the mentally ill, but the implementation of the policy was far less noble than the concept. Conor had read plenty about the Illinois asylums. They were human dumps that did not treat people. No psychotherapy, no "moral treatment" as the alienists called it, and sometimes no drugs at all—or too many drugs for the wrong reasons. Many former inmates who had suffered both considered asylums, especially the one in Elgin, to be more inhumane and dehumanizing than prisons.

The only thing Nellie could do in the current situation would be to negotiate a plea agreement. That would guarantee years in prison. But if she could hire an expert and get an insanity opinion, the prosecutor might be pushed into reducing the charge to manslaughter—even better. *Yes, better to take a chance on the insanity defense alone.* But it was all academic without the money to hire an expert and conduct a proper investigation.

Then he thought about the bail money and his fee for the case. Conor did not want to know how Father Brendan had raised $300, but it might be enough to pay an alienist to examine her, go through the record, and testify at trial, providing the man would wait to get his fee. Conor was confident that a psychiatrist would be unlikely to work on a credit basis, but it was worth a try. Without solutions, he would simply have to pass on Nellie's case.

Chapter 9

Conor's initial visit with Maureen Brogan, his brother's "friend," was bothering him in light of this Nellie Finley murder business. He might have seemed rude or insensitive during their meeting. The two women had much in common and might yet suffer similar fates, but chance and random acts of kindness had intervened to give Maureen Brogan at least a fighting chance.

That bright Sunday morning in early November was cold but looked perfect for a final outdoor excursion before winter, so he decided to call on Maureen and the toddler. For some reason, it occurred to him that Nellie Finley's court date was in just ten days.

On the trolley ride across the South Branch, he thought that Maureen and Nellie might have come from the same county back home. Both girls spoke in a thick brogue, common in the west of Ireland: Mayo, Galway, or his own homeplace, County Clare. No trace at all of the mumbling, incoherent gibberish of the Kerrymen in the South of Ireland. *What family did they leave to make the long journey? Did they have similar dreams of a life here? Or were they simply escapees following the instinct to survive another day? They might even have arrived on the same ship.*

He envisioned the worker from the relief agency, standing on the dock in New York and hoping to rescue girls such as these from the horrors that might follow. He would catch some in his safety net, but most would slip through. The unfortunate ones leave the dock without ever knowing their best opportunity had passed. The two women might both have passed him on the dock. The pregnant one, Maureen, could have caught his attention, allowing poor Nellie Finley to swim through his net.

Then he remembered Miss Potter's suggestion that maybe Nellie Finley was not in distress when she landed more than two years ago. Someone might have met her at the dock: a relative, a friend, or the representative of an employment agency. It was possible the girl secured employment while still in Ireland and her travel was arranged in advance.

Friends, relatives, or employers commonly made such arrangements. Nellie might have been one of those seemingly fortunate ones with a pre-paid passage all the way to her new employer in Chicago and a less obvious version of the same nightmare. Maybe she even turned down the offer of help at the dock, oblivious to the horrors awaiting her in Chicago.

Conor waited in the foyer this time while the cranky landlady ascended the stairs to advise Maureen of his arrival. He was finally beginning to understand that this city operates on a sliding scale of morality. Those who fail to understand the social and political reality in this heavenly place end up face down in the river or in the ground. The survivors do whatever it takes. It did not matter what Maureen had to do to survive. She was taking care of the child, and he had eased her burden a bit with his brother's bequest. For how long was another matter, but someone else could sit in judgment of her.

This time the woman escorted him to Maureen's room, a decent-sized place down the hall from the second-floor toilet closet. The landlady huffed, announcing the negotiated ground rules while she glared at Conor. "The young lady will leave the door open while the gentleman states his business."

The toddler was playing with a blanket on the wood floor. The child was handsome with rust-colored hair and a glint in his eye. "How old is the boy?" he asked.

"He's two and a half," Maureen replied.

"What's his name?"

"Patrick. What is it ye require, Mr. Dolan?"

He had forgotten to remove his hat and quickly adjusted. "I was simply curious," he began uncomfortably. "Has little Patrick ever ridden on the elevated train or been to the zoo?"

He thought she might have been looking at a two-headed monster. "Don't be daft," she said dismissively. "He's never ridden on any train or streetcar or cable car. It costs mooney."

Conor had not thought about that. He had given her $200, but she might be planning to live on that money for a long time. "That changes today," he announced confidently.

"You've been drinking, Mr. Dolan, and it's ten o'clock in the morning. Go off witch ye now. I'll say no, thank you."

And he wondered whether her attitude might have something to do with the money he gave her. She might even be thinking Conor expected some sort of quid pro quo. *Not good.* "I haven't been drinking, and why would you not go? Look, I was abrupt with you the first time we met, possibly even rude. Think of it as my way of apologizing."

She looked embarrassed but explained that "A fine Chicago day in November can turn colder than a well digger's arse in the blink of an eye. Sure, Patrick has no winter coat, and neither have I."

So she did not consider him a threat to her safety after all. That was a good start, he figured. "I can fix that," he declared. "I'll be back shortly."

He had forgotten it was Sunday but managed to find a small, secondhand clothing store on Des Plaines Avenue, run by a friendly

Jewish couple. While choosing the coats, he spotted an old baby stroller, seemingly in good condition. He was back at Maureen's within the hour.

"Not the most fashionable items," he said, "but no one will freeze today."

THEIR NORTHBOUND TROLLEY STALLED FOR A BIG BARGE CROSSING under the Clark Street pivot bridge, mesmerizing little Patrick. *What was the final factor? What was the last calamity or misfortune that caused young Nellie Finley to hurl herself and her baby from a bridge? Did she think about it in advance? If so, for how long? Or was it spontaneous? Aside from all the legal mumbo jumbo, what was Nellie Finley really like just before she jumped from that bridge?*

He had thought about it for hours last night when he should have been asleep—not willingly, but more like that nagging problem that just will not let you drift off. He would never give voice to this theory lest people think him mad, but in a sense, he thought jumping from that bridge with the child might have been a rational decision, maybe even a courageous act of mercy killing for a baby who would never know the torture of death by starvation. In any case, until he could learn more about Nellie Finley, the questions would haunt him. And what kept this Maureen Brogan from doing the same?

LINCOLN PARK TEEMED WITH LIFE, COLOR, FAMILIES, AND ALL THE magnificent things Maureen and the child had likely never seen. It gave Conor a good feeling. The great boathouse on the lagoon was shuttered for the season, but in his imagination, Conor could see the rowboats filling the lagoon with lovers, children, and happiness—if only for the day.

Still, Nellie Finley would give him no respite today. Mental disease, Conor knew, had become fashionable among the well-to-do in this new century. Neurasthenia, they called it, the form of insanity that caused great artists to destroy their paintings or successful lawyers to cheat their clients. It was all supposedly generated by "excess nervousness," a by-product of success, causing the unfortunate patient to self-destruct or commit crimes. The alienists treated the insanity with something called "moral therapy." It all sounded like old-country cow dung to Conor, an excuse for greed, self-indulgence, or alcoholism of the rich.

By that definition, Nellie Finley was the antithesis of insane. The woman jumped off a bridge with her baby in her arms to save him from the suffering of slowly freezing or starving to death. What act could be a greater manifestation of a sound mind? Even an extreme form of courage. *Excess nervousness?*

Besides, Nellie Finley was poor. For the down-and-out people of Chicago, insanity was anything but a badge of honor to be admired like a war wound. To be poor and insane was to be forgotten and warehoused in a prison or an asylum without proper treatment, medication, or even food.

He felt a poke in the arm. "Mr. Dolan," Maureen said excitedly, pointing. "Look, there's the zoo. Maybe Patrick could see a bear or a bison." She was having fun, he thought, and it filled him with joy.

At the bison exhibit, Maureen seemed to open up rather abruptly. "Sure I've been reporting on ye to the Clan na Gael," she confessed nonchalantly out of the blue as though she was giving him the time. "'Tis a fair bet yeer man will come see me tonight for a fresh report."

It was a mouthful of information, not to mention a fistful of possible consequences. "And what man would that be?" he asked.

"Sure the detective, Flynn is his name, but 'tis not police business he's after detecting. He's Clan na Gael, and he works directly for a local section leader, our own chief of the Chicago police."

The disclosure stunned Conor, not because the information surprised him—it did not—but because Maureen Brogan had knowledge of it and just confirmed it. If the Clan was this worried about Conor's snooping around, then he and Rebecca were getting dangerously close to something big, and Maureen was involved up to her neck. It was pretty clear this girl was changing sides, so she must have figured Conor was her best chance to stay alive now. He could hardly blame her. She would do whatever was necessary to survive, maybe even change sides again, he thought.

So why was he still so concerned about how she had met his brother? He thought about asking the question straight out but dismissed the idea as heartless, even mean. Maybe he was afraid of the answer, hoping she would say they met at Mass but knowing she would not, afraid of how he might react, what he might think. For young immigrant women, this was often not the city of happy endings and welcoming arms. At least, it was clear the child was not Kevin's.

The two grizzlies were kept apart from the black bears, the habitat divided by a thick wall. A deep pit kept the brown monsters from getting too close to patrons. Patrick looked unimpressed and wanted only to go back and pet the bison.

"What do you know about the police chief and Flynn?" Conor asked as Patrick struggled to escape the stroller.

Maureen lifted the child into her arms. "Sure I don't know the chief personally, but Kevin did. Twenty t'ousand dollars went missing from Clan funds, and it caused a fuss. There's a split in the Clan. A small faction refused to renounce violence when ordered by the IRB in Ireland. The Clan proper believes that faction is planning something violent and stole that money to finance the operation." Maureen went on to explain that she saw a message about the dispute in the course of her courier duties. Kevin, when confronted, gave her that explanation before his death. He told her he sided with the peaceful Clan majority.

"Then it's possible those rogue actors killed Kevin because of the dispute." Conor suggested.

"To be sure. The chief and his dog, Flynn. Sure there were others in it with them."

The cold air and rhythm of the stroller along the gravel path settled little Patrick into a deep sleep as the wonders of Lincoln Park led them to a line of food vendors where they stopped for lunch on a park bench.

"What was my brother like?" Conor asked. Who better to ask? Whatever her motives or the circumstances of their association, this woman practically lived with Kevin. Conor figured Kevin took over her rent payments in exchange for…well…there was no reason to consider that now.

Maureen fidgeted nervously. "He kept us from starving, Mr. Dolan. What was it you wanted me to say?"

He was not very good at this. "Please, call me Conor," he began, hoping to deescalate. "I'm not probing for scandal, Maureen." He assumed a liberty with her Christian name. "I haven't known my brother since I was eight years of age—not really. Most of our relationship has been built on letters."

That's unfartunate," she conceded. Patrick was suddenly awake and expressing his hunger emphatically. Maureen unwrapped a few small pieces of fruit packed for the occasion.

She leaned back on the bench and folded her arms. "As you wish, Conor," she began before unloading. "Sure your brother was a bully, a drinker, and meaner than a rabid dog. He struck me on several occasions to the point that I lost a tooth once. Still, whatever Kevin was, he helped keep my baby alive and was never cruel to the child."

Three weeks ago, her words would have upended Conor's world, but not today. This woman was Kevin's mistress and knew the man far better than Conor ever did. He wanted to understand her, to sympathize. Her every decision had been one of necessity, not choice. Still, he could find no words to comfort her, only the involuntary silence of judgment and disapproval, but Maureen was having none of it.

"If ye expect me to cry and beg forgiveness, be on your way now," she scolded. "Sure I've no apologies to make to you or your priest friend or anyone else." She stood defiantly, heading down the path toward the exit behind the stroller.

He caught up with her quickly, and for a few minutes, neither of them spoke. "I'm sorry," he finally said.

"All right, then—shall we see the greenhouse before heading back?"

"I think it's that way," he said, pointing, "at the far end of the park."

So his brother's death was related to the Clan na Gael. Conor had no feelings about the Clan one way or the other. Every Irishman knew about the Clan and Dr. Cronin's murder and the trials that followed a few years ago.

That entire incident had exposed the Clan na Gael as an organization more adept at infighting than working for Irish independence. Murder was their purpose for existence, and internal, violent conflict within the group was legendary in Chicago. But, for die-hard Irish Republicans, it was the only game in town. Conor never expected Kevin would be one of them. His brother was clearly stricken by the fever of Irish Republicanism. How was it that Kevin managed to suppress such strong feelings in his many letters? And why?

What about Maureen herself? Did she secretly harbor her own passion for Irish independence? More likely fear of starvation motivated her, and she had admitted to spying on Conor. But what was to say she would not go right on doing it? Look at the things she had done already for herself and the baby. He would discuss it all with Rebecca later.

Chapter 10

Rebecca arrived at his office shortly after lunch the next afternoon as arranged; Conor was reluctant to discuss his news anywhere in Mrs. Kaplan's house.

Despite their intimate relationship and real friendship, a strange awkwardness came over him as Rebecca walked in the door, and he could not decide how to greet her. Taking her into his arms seemed inappropriate despite the affection he felt. A handshake would be ridiculous. Inside the Agency flat, he and Rebecca had created their own reality it seemed, a sensuous reality existing only within its confines, but a genuine mutual affection was undeniable. Meeting in a restaurant somehow avoided the complicated social interaction, and he wished they had made a different arrangement that day. He put his hands on her shoulders and kissed her on the cheek.

Rebecca listened attentively to the new information he had obtained from Maureen. Confirmation of a dispute within the Clan over an upcoming, unauthorized operation confirmed her working theory. A Clan faction, led by the chief, was planning to assassinate the Prince of Wales. But when he disclosed that Maureen Brogan was working as a messenger for the Clan na Gael and reporting on Conor's activities, Rebecca nearly leapt from the chair.

"This is what we've been looking for," she exclaimed excitedly. "It means she's opening up to you, Conor, but she has to know more. Of course, we must be careful, be certain that she's really chosen sides now."

Conor did not like the sound of that. "Wait a second. I'm not spying on her for the Pinkertons. That's not what's going on."

"Then what *is* going on?" Rebecca snapped. "I've seen the girl. She's attractive. Do you like her?"

That did not sound like Rebecca at all. It sounded like jealousy despite everything she had said. "What does that mean? I have my own agenda here, but she *does* know more than she's telling us."

"Telling *you*," she retorted, "and it appears you *do* have your own agenda."

He really did not know what to make of this new Rebecca. On the surface, it appeared to be jealously, but he knew it was more. He knew her better than that. She was genuinely afraid for him but duty-bound to keep him on the tip of the spear.

Conor was about to suggest that they visit Maureen together and come completely clean with the girl, when a tall, well-dressed stranger walked into the office, and Rebecca took her cue, nodding to the visitor on her way out.

"Mr. Dolan," the man said with just a hint of an Irish accent. There were plenty of Irish-born Americans trying to hide it for some reason. "I'm Alderman O'Sullivan. Just dropped in to welcome you to the ward and thank you for your support. I'm also your Committeeman on the Cook County Board."

What does he want now? Conor thought. This was a decidedly bad time for a shakedown.

Conor pointed to a client chair. "Thank you, Mr. O'Sullivan. Please sit down. Let me take your hat and coat."

Conor settled in behind his desk for what was certain to be further extortion. This would be the last straw. He would willingly run his office from a peddlers' cart if these thieves tried to take one more dime. "If you're here about my conversations with your friend Boris—"

"Actually, there is another reason for my visit."

Here we go. Might as well let him finish. "And what's that?"

"I've been speaking with Father White about a young Irish girl he's trying to help, Nellie Finley. I understand he's enlisted your help as well."

Brendan had not mentioned a word about involving the alderman, but the priest's brain worked like that of a chess player: calculating, plotting, and strategizing. By the time Brendan told you what he was thinking, his brain had moved far beyond his explanation. Was he trying to put the fix in for Nellie Finley? The priest knew how Conor felt about that, so he dismissed the idea out of hand. No matter, he thought, because Brendan's angle was about to become clear.

"I spoke with the girl," Conor admitted. "There are complications. May I ask what your interest is?" He would not suck much blood out of this turnip, but 10 percent of the fee did not seem enough to warrant a visit from the alderman himself in the first place.

"Father White says she may need a psychiatrist to testify, and of course, the girl is indigent. I may be able to help."

Conor held out a decorative box. "Cigar?"

The alderman had Conor's full attention and politely waved off the offer. "Well, in the event you need a psychiatrist, I can put you in touch with an experienced local man who might be able to help." Then he reached over and handed Conor a business card. "His name is Martinovsky. He has all the qualifications you need and will not ask for a fee. We help each other now and then. But if he asks for money, slap him hard, and come see me right away."

What's his angle? If it's not about the fee, and the psychiatrist comes free of charge, what does he want? He must be afraid of something. The only apparent explanation was that Nellie Finley had something on him, something embarrassing or incriminating. Or the priest did.

This politician apparently did not appreciate the extent of poor Nellie's mental dysfunction. Whatever vile secrets she kept might die with her. The best way to deal with the man was straight talk, Conor figured. He wished Brendan had tipped him off.

"Look. Mr. O'Sullivan, I'm prepared to live with our agreement, but I decline to become involved in anything else. I don't want—"

O'Sullivan held out his palm and calmly interrupted. "Please, Mr. Dolan, before you go any further, let me finish. When the case is over, I'd like you to give the bail money to Hull House for young Nellie. Just give me a fair bill for your services, and I'll pay 90 percent of it. That girl is no murderess. She's as much a victim as her poor dead baby, the Lord have mercy on her soul. In any event, Dr. Martinovsky is kind of between offices, but he can see you tonight. Here or your flat."

"What if I don't win the case?" Conor asked.

"You'll win, just so you do your work properly. Just take a bench trial and do a good job. The rest will work out. You've no need to be involved."

Conor knew from the lawyers how politicians like to fix serious felony cases. Of the four sitting, felony-court judges of the Cook County Circuit Court, at least one full-circuit judge in the rotation would always be nearing reelection and close to retirement, making him acutely susceptible to any shenanigans related to political expedience. The chief judge always helped with a favorable assignment rotation.

So what was going on here? Was the alderman planning to trigger the corrupt apparatus of his shadow government for the sole purpose of altruism? It made no sense and defied logic. Still, it did not change Conor's position on the subject.

"I'm not quite certain what's going on, but I'll talk to your psychiatrist. That said, I won't be a part of any fix, and I don't want any judge shopping. If I take the case and if your man thinks she's insane, we'll take the judge we draw and try the case to a jury, if there must be a trial."

Then the alderman surprised him. "Mr. Dolan, have you read much

Shakespeare?"

"No. Music is my passion, Mr. O'Sullivan."

"I'm a devotee of the man, myself. My favorite line is from Hamlet: 'There is nothing either good or bad but thinking makes it so.' I understand your devotion to morality and ethics, Mr. Dolan, though some may call your attitude self-righteous, even annoying, I don't judge you for it, and I ask only the same consideration from you. You see, sometimes, although it may surprise you, I have no motive other than to lend a hand to a needy soul. Perhaps, simply ask yourself, *'What is the best way to help this poor unfortunate girl?'* In any event, I would very much like to work with you in the future whenever there is an injustice in need of your talents, and I promise to respect your limits."

This city just keeps getting more complicated. Conor had been expecting the First Ward Alderman to be a three-horned toad. But he was not. He was flawed to high heaven but basically decent, and that only made Conor's life more difficult. He even felt guilty about thinking that Father Brendan was extorting the man or leveraging some incriminating information. *What a city.*

On the walk home, he stopped to buy some cigars for the office. O'Sullivan had nearly taken the last one. Conor rarely smoked himself, but clients appreciated the gesture. The shop was Italian owned, and Conor had some difficulty conveying his specific request. Before leaving the store, he decided to light up on the walk home. He figured it might aid the thought process.

So he would prevail on Rebecca for advice before making his decision. But Nellie Finley was not the only thing on his mind. This business with the Clan na Gael and the Prince of Wales had opened a can of worms that threatened to consume him, Rebecca, and Maureen Brogan like a tidal wave.

Unlike his brother, Conor had never been radicalized into the IRB or any other Irish Republican society. Conor was ten years younger when they emigrated and saw himself as American. He could not understand why the Irish appeared to be the only immigrant community to carry the old baggage of Republicanism to America and feed it like a lazy old dog. He saw a kind of hypocrisy in fighting a war against England from the safety of Illinois. Things were quiet in Ireland as the Republicans regrouped and strategized following the failure of Home Rule and the downfall of Parnell. But Conor knew the struggle would never die of its own will.

At Jackson Boulevard, he stopped into the post office to mail a letter to his aunt and uncle in Springfield. He felt bad about not writing sooner. They would be worried but not too worried. He came out of the post office to find the dog waiting for him. By then, the animal was familiar with Conor's route home and sometimes met him on the way. O'Sullivan's comments were gnawing at him like this dog with a rib bone. The alderman had touched a nerve with his Shakespearian quote and his suggestion of self-righteousness. Decent or not, the man was arrogant and an expert in fighting with the spoken word.

The silver lining of this nightmare was that his brother had been working to stop the Clan plot. Kevin surely saw that a royal assassination on American soil would be disastrous to the strategic relationship between Britain and America, finally strengthening after a century and a half of war and acrimony. No matter how you sliced it up, killing the prince on American soil, even attempting the act, would constitute treason against the United States. He would have none of that. Conor decided that his own mission was on a parallel course with Rebecca's.

As Rebecca explained, the Prince of Wales, heir to the throne of his father, Edward VII, was coming to Chicago with his family and a sprinkling of fancy lords and dukes and such. The Clan faction was hoping to reignite the armed fight for a united Ireland and to destroy the trans-Atlantic alliance. Conor had no love for the British, but he would help the Crown by finding his brother's killers and completing Kevin's final mission.

It was a far cry from lawyering, but a simple visit to reconnect with his brother had now become a mission to follow the trail of Kevin's life—to hell if necessary—and discover all the facts about his death.

DR. FYODOR MARTINOVSKY ARRIVED AT EIGHT O'CLOCK IN THE evening, only thirty minutes after Hull House delivered the file on Nellie Finley. He received the doctor in Mrs. Kaplan's parlor where they had coffee and made small talk. The psychiatrist looked the part: bifocaled, white-haired, a full beard, short, slightly gregarious, and possibly intoxicated.

The doctor was seated on the red sofa, leaning forward with his empty cup and saucer. "Will you join me in a Hennessy, Doctor?" Conor asked. The cognac was Conor's own contribution to Mrs. Kaplan's liquor cabinet.

It required effort, but the doctor just managed to maintain a professional demeanor. "Ah," he said, "Eef you are dreenkink, I suppose I veel join you, but only one dreenk. Do you khaf wotka?" It so happened that the landlady's bar was well stocked.

Martinovsky, the conversation revealed, was Russian, had studied in Vienna and gone on to practice medicine and later psychiatry in his native Moscow before immigrating to America with his wife in 1881. His wife had passed away several years earlier, and the doctor now limited his practice to "consulting" and, on occasion, testifying in criminal cases. The man checked off all the points on Conor's notepad. Martinovsky was, by all indications, the classic "psychiatrist for sale." But he might be sufficient for Conor's purpose.

Conor was not looking for Sigmund Freud. He knew that psychiatry was a quickly developing field of medicine. He just needed a qualified expert to review the records, interview the client, form an opinion as to whether Nellie Finley met the legal definition of "insane" at the time of the offense, and write a coherent report. Conor would worry about the witness's credibility and drinking habits later. He might even be able to avoid a battle of the experts at trial with a favorable negotiated agreement to a reduced charge.

During the doctor's second vodka, Conor briefed him on the case and on Nellie's history, what little he knew of it, and they reviewed the reports, medical records, and other documents. Conor promised to have the file duplicated and delivered to the doctor's residence the next day.

The file, Conor knew, was woefully lacking in the kind of information a psychiatrist would need to conduct a meaningful inquiry, yet the alienist never raised doubts during the meeting. Martinovsky spoke generically about the plight of young immigrant women in the city and seemed to fill in the blanks in Nellie's life with broad strokes of generality, assumptions without foundation, even platitudes.

"Loss of memory," he explained, "is often the subconscious mind protecting a vooman from reliving zee trauma of sexual and physical abuse. Zees is wery common, you see." And so it went for the next half hour.

With the doctor gone, Conor gave the file a more careful look. It included the police report indicating that Nellie was "homeless," witness statements, medical records from her hospitalization, even the child's birth certificate issued at Cook County Hospital and identifying the five-week-old child's father as "unknown." There was nothing at all in the file about her life prior to the bridge incident, and Martinovsky's lack of concern for that fact was troubling. Still, the investigation was ongoing, and the psychiatrist was certainly qualified, at least on paper. On balance, Conor figured this was a horse he could ride.

Chapter 11

Rebecca liked the idea that they visit Maureen Brogan together within the week and suggested they pack up a Sunday dinner for her and Patrick. It was a thoughtful gesture that Conor should have considered on his own, he knew, but he sent a note to Maureen via delivery service, announcing the intended visit and its purpose.

There was a very nice family restaurant on Fifth Avenue where Conor picked up the meal with a sufficient load of ice to preserve it overnight. Mrs. Kaplan threw in a big plate of homemade rugelach, a traditional Jewish pastry. Conor thought he was growing on the landlady, but Rebecca thought Mrs. Kaplan was simply addicted to the sex scandal and that she and her sister passed their afternoons exchanging tidbits of salacious gossip.

ON THE TROLLEY TO MAUREEN BROGAN'S, THE AROMA OF LAMB shanks on his lap was distracting, but he told Rebecca the story of Nellie Finley and her poor dead child. Conor just *happened* to bring the Finley file. The story intrigued Rebecca from start to finish, and her deductive reasoning skill somehow did not surprise Conor.

"There are resources and records that would help paint the picture of this girl's life since 1900," she said, "even before. The police made no attempt to obtain them. They might contain valuable mitigation."

"Exactly what I thought," Conor added.

Rebecca articulated her train of thought. "We know from her immigrant inspection card that Nellie arrived in New York in June of 1900, but she ended up in Chicago. That's common, especially if a woman has relatives waiting for her or she has secured employment through an agency. It's doubtful Nellie Finley has relatives because she would have gone to them. There are domestic agencies that link wealthy Chicagoans with qualified girls in Ireland. The employer pays for the steamer ticket and transportation to Chicago. To the wealthy, it's a way of decreasing the chance of employing *spoiled goods*. The young woman ends up paying for everything in the end. They take the expenses and the Agency commission from her paltry salary."

Conor had not thought about all that, but it made perfect sense. If Nellie went through an employment agency, it would be their business to compile history on her family, references, and contacts. They would have complete information on her Chicago employer as well, and all of it subject to subpoena…and all of that would cost money. "She appears to have a psychiatric expert willing to work for free, but that's only part of it. I don't need to tell you that big investigations cost money. I have no resources, Rebecca, so I may not be able to take the case."

They hopped off the Harrison St. Trolley in Little Italy with their box of food. Maureen Brogan's boardinghouse was only one block south on Jefferson. Rebecca took his arm as they negotiated some ice on the sidewalk. She squeezed it and said, "You *should* take the case. It could garner a lot of publicity and be a boost for your career. As for investigation resources, I'll talk to my office. You've been a huge help on the Clan thing, and it's the most lucrative contract in our Chicago office. I think we owe it to you."

Well, if you're going to be a lawyer, be a lawyer, he told himself. He had never even been in the gallery for a murder trial, never mind trying one by himself. The worst he could do would be to lose. He could think of a dozen stupid platitudes to recite, but it all came down to one question: *Do you want to be a criminal lawyer, or do you want to be the guy who sits in the second chair every time you try a serious case?*

Making a legal career in Chicago was never the objective of this journey. He had come to see his brother and to know the man who ushered him safely through hell and so much more. But he was beginning to feel at home here, strange as it sounded to him. He liked the city, and sticking around had become a distinct possibility, so why squander a good opportunity?

Besides, Conor Dolan was uniquely positioned now to help Nellie Finley. "Yes, we could do this, Rebecca. If you can figure out her story, we'd give them one hell of a fight, and I like our odds of helping her."

Professionally speaking, the stars were lined up perfectly for him on this case. He had a just cause and a sympathetic client. He had the services of the finest investigators in the world, and he had a qualified psychiatrist willing to work for free and, for some reason, itching to render an insanity opinion for the defense. As they reached the front door of Maureen's place, he said, "I'll take the case."

"Good. We'll start with employment agencies that deal with Irish labor. There are less than a dozen of them. If Nellie contracted with one of them, we'll be in business. I'll clear it and put my people on it tomorrow. We have other options as well. God knows you're doing enough for the Agency."

"All right, but I'm still leery about this Russian psychiatrist. He just seems too eager to help but disinterested in Nellie Finley's history and background."

He would be in court with Nellie Finley a week from Wednesday, the day before Thanksgiving. If they could paint a complete picture of Nellie Finley the human being, he would have a weapon to at least arouse the court's mercy, if not to set her free.

MAUREEN WAS DELIGHTED WITH THE VISIT AND THRILLED WITH the dinner even though Rebecca seemed to keep her distance. It occurred to Conor that Maureen's stress was lessened by two hundred bucks in the bank and a ready-made Sunday feast. Still, he could not shake her similarities to Nellie Finley, wasting away mindlessly in Hull House and possibly on her way either to prison or to a filthy warehouse for the insane in Elgin. What had these women and so many others like them done to warrant being treated worse than cattle or pets? Why could they not simply have stayed in their homes with their families and grown up to live simple, happy lives in their own country? He wondered whether Kevin had considered the question and whether the answer had factored into his social and political views.

They shared the details of their investigation with the young woman, and Maureen reluctantly agreed to help. She and Rebecca occupied the two small chairs at the kitchen table, the only seating in the room. Conor remained standing rather than seating himself on the small bed. Rebecca asked her about the protocols and procedures for delivering messages and packages. Maureen said someone would slip a postcard under her door as an instruction to meet a contact over in Grant Park the next morning, the same postcard and the same park bench every time. Kevin showed Maureen the bench some time back.

"Think back, Maureen," Rebecca said. "Did you ever break from that protocol? I mean did anyone ever deviate from that procedure?"

"Never," she answered confidently, continuously bouncing the child on her knee. "But sure there was one odd thing about me last delivery," she added. "'Twas always the same postcard and always the same man I would meet in the park, an old fella with a cane, he was, except for the last delivery."

"Go ahead," Rebecca prodded.

"'Twas a different fella altogether, but the same post card, mind ye. A young lad, he was. I'd never laid eyes on him. I wouldn't tell you his name if I knew it. He gave me the pouch with an address. Aside from that, it was all very narmal."

Young Patrick suddenly decided it was time for exercise and began struggling to get loose while expressing his boredom in a pair of blood curdling screams. Maureen put him on the floor, and he jumped up, scampering around the room.

"What was in the pouch?" Conor asked.

She hesitated, and Conor sensed some internal conflict. "I'm not an informer," she declared. "Sure Kevin never forced me to help the Clan. I do it because I hate the bloody British, and Kevin himself spoke openly of his opposition to the plot."

"We understand," Rebecca prodded. "But the pouch?"

"Mooney, and a good deal of it, to be sure, I'd say, and a sealed envelope. Sure the fella emptied the pouch and give it back. I still have it."

"Do you remember the address?" Rebecca asked.

"Not exactly. 'Twas was on Hoyne Avenue. Sure I could show ye the house."

"Was Kevin still alive when you made that delivery?" Rebecca asked.

The baby went for the stove, and she scooped him up, returning to the chair; he was not pleased. Rebecca repeated her question.

Conor was about to ask the same question because the answer might redefine the game. "I'd have to t'ink a minute now," Maureen began. "Actually, I don't know if he was alive. Sure the postcard came under the door before they found his remains in the river, the Lord have mercy on his soul. So I suppose he was still missing at that time."

"Can you describe the illustration on the postcard?" asked Conor.

"A photograph of some fine Chicago buildings, The Columbian Exposition, I'd say 'twas, the same as always."

Rebecca flashed a look of concern. "You know what that means? It means the breakaway faction behind the assassination includes people other than the chief and Detective Flynn. Who knows how many are involved? Severing the head may not kill the snake." She looked directly at Maureen and issued a warning. "The Clan may be watching your flat. Report our visit and don't lie to them about us being here. We were looking for information, and you told us nothing. All right?"

"Dat's it then, but don't be after gettin' the wrong idea," Maureen scolded. "I'll help ye save his royal fookin' highness but that's it. Those eejits plannin' t' blow him up would trigger a terrible retribution on the Irish people."

Conor had questions of his own about what this new information meant, so he addressed both women. "Think for a second. We know someone stole twenty thousand from the Clan. We know Maureen delivered a large sum of money to a man on Hoyne Avenue. Who left the postcard for her? What was the money for? If we know who the man is and can learn something about him, we should be able to find out what the money was for and who gave it to him."

If that money was connected to a rogue Clan operation, as Conor assumed, the rogue operators had tried to recreate the Clan's normal communications protocol. That could only have been to fool Maureen into thinking her mission was routine Clan business. Their reason for involving Maureen was obvious: to insulate themselves from the man on Hoyne Avenue.

That information pretty much confirmed Maureen's story, and the rogue plotters would no longer have had to worry about Kevin thwarting their plans because he was missing and likely dead already. Maybe they knew Kevin was dead because they had already murdered him. *The evidence is adding up in Kevin's favor.* The Hoyne Avenue man was the key.

Conor could tell from her expression that Rebecca was on the same track as she spoke to Maureen. "I'll have to ask you to show us that house on Hoyne Avenue this afternoon."

"But little Patrick…" Maureen protested. "It's snowing outside."

"It will be all right," Rebecca assured her. "You can bring him. I'll make special arrangements."

Before leaving the boardinghouse, Rebecca approached the cranky landlady. "If you have a phone, I will happily pay to make a call."

The woman nodded. "All right. Back of the hall on the first floor. That will be ten cents."

"You can *buy* a telephone for two dollars," Conor whispered.

After her call, Rebecca stood watch inside the front door with Conor seated in the foyer beside Maureen and little Patrick. Within twenty minutes, she announced, "Our transportation is here."

He was surprised to see a new 1903 Model A Ford touring car—for official use, Rebecca explained, by detectives in the local office, one of only three thousand such vehicles in circulation by the fall of 1903. It was doubtful, Conor thought, that the Agency could name a more important current investigation than this one.

The automobile was all black with a soft top and spacious seating area in the back behind the driver. It was a most impressive mode of transportation, and Conor wondered whether he would ever be able to own one. He guessed the color scheme was chosen to avoid attention. Fat chance of that in Chicago in 1903, but Rebecca was no fool. No one could follow them without having an automobile of his own. Even less chance of that.

"So we're off to this house up on Hoyne Avenue?" Conor asked, trying to figure out how to open the door.

"That's the plan," Rebecca replied. They seated Maureen between them with the child on her lap and covered in a thick blanket. "The driver will take us all directly home as soon as we know the house. Once we find it and know the neighborhood, Conor and I can make a plan and come back in the morning. I'll arrange to have the place watched round the clock. County records will tell us the owner's name, but our man might be a tenant. Besides, the name alone won't help us. We need a connection, Conor."

"Is the driver on our side?" Conor asked facetiously.

"I'm sorry. I forgot to introduce you." She tapped the driver on the shoulder. "Conor Dolan, meet Victor Harris. The chauffeur hat goes with the car. Victor is a Pinkerton. He's my contact on this investigation—my partner, you could say. Victor relays messages from the Agency, and I only contact the Agency through Victor. It's standard protocol on this type of assignment."

The two men shook hands. "Glad to know you, Victor." Victor was a big man with a broad smile, a handsome "Negro" in a private chauffeur uniform. Conor could not think of more innocuous packaging for an undercover Pinkerton packing a pistol.

"The same to you, Mr. Dolan," said Victor. "I've heard quite a bit about you."

"Conor," he replied.

"You two will get along well," Rebecca observed. "You both attended the University of Illinois in Urbana. Victor was chasing train robbers on horseback in Colorado until six months ago. I convinced the Agency he would be a better fit here."

"Huh," Victor grumbled. "You mean a better fit on an automobile seat than in a damn saddle. I won't even ride on a horse-drawn streetcar. Strictly a city boy. Don't believe what you read in those Western novels, Conor. It's cold, wet, and dirty with smelly animals and bad food. Rebecca rescued me."

"So how did you know each other?" Conor asked.

"Urbana," Rebecca said, "the University. Where else?" Victor laughed.

"You're full of surprises, Rebecca Fletcher," Conor observed. "So we all have something in common. Just what else do you know about me that I didn't tell you?"

She smiled maliciously. "Did you have something particular in mind?"

On Clark, the automobile had to dodge crowded streetcars, trolleys, peddlers, shoppers and children. Nearly everyone scurried to be near the shiny new horseless carriage. Chicago Avenue westbound was less congested with a following wind, providing a more comfortable ride. Maureen pointed out the house nearly immediately on the east side of

Hoyne, one of the new, brick, one-story bungalows crowded between traditional, two-storied rectangles.

The west side of the street had a mixture of saloons, retail shops, a small shipping company, and a grocery store on the corner at Rice Avenue, most with flats on the second story. All but the grocery store offered good observation of the bungalow. Tomorrow, Rebecca explained, Victor would interview the merchants. It was likely the shop owners knew their neighbors. If, not, Victor would make an arrangement with the trucking company to use their building for surveillance.

It sounded like a good plan, but as the automobile idled in front of the trucking company, a man emerged from the house, dressed in overalls and a big coat and carrying a lunch pail.

The man's appearance took the group by surprise. "Is that the man?" Rebecca asked hurriedly.

"It looks like him," Maureen answered. "He was thin like that and sure he had the same kind of hat."

As the man headed toward Chicago Avenue and a likely trolley trip, Rebecca spoke to Victor. "Follow him. Stay back. He can't see us. Hell's bells, I wish we didn't have this big calling card of a vehicle." Then she seemed to have an epiphany and was out of the car in a flash. "I'll follow him on the streetcars. The rest of you go home. Conor, I'll see you in the morning."

"Be careful," he said.

REBECCA DID NOT RETURN FOR DINNER, AND CONOR FEARED THE worst. She could be dead or kidnapped. The Hoyne Avenue man was on his way to work when she decided to follow him. Why else would he have a lunch pail? In any event, he had no baggage, and every indication pointed to a local commute of some kind. The city just was not big enough to keep her following the man late into the night. So where was she?

Down in Conor's flat after dinner, before bedtime, the three-legged dog came in from the cold with a huge T-bone he had grifted from one of the fancy restaurants up north. Conor put a bowl on the floor and poured in some of his beer for the dog. Neither of them liked drinking alone.

Under the oil lamp at the small table, Conor started to review his notes after carefully adding a narrative describing today's developments. Addressing the dog, he said, "We should have enough here, fella, to figure this out. Let's just go through everything from the beginning..."

Maureen's delivery to the Hoyne Avenue man was a break in the case. It had all merged into one case now: Kevin, the Clan na Gael, and the royal prince. His brother was still listed as missing on the day Maureen dropped the money, not confirmed dead. His body was not recovered until the next day, but the medical evidence clearly established that death occurred two days earlier. None of it made sense unless the two Clan na Gael cops killed him.

In any event, it meant Maureen was telling the truth about not knowing whether Kevin was involved with a breakaway faction. Who sent the money to the man on Hoyne Avenue? What was the money for? And who was the man on Hoyne Avenue? Did the Clan kill Kevin to foil a violent plot? Did the plotters themselves kill him? Or did Conor's brother take his own life after all?

Rebecca finally appeared at Conor's office before noon the next day, obviously still exhausted from her nocturnal sleuthing. She even looked a bit unkempt, very much unlike Rebecca. Conor poured her a cup of coffee at the small table near the window looking out onto someone's stone foundation.

"Don't take this the wrong way, but I've seen you looking better."

"I need some sleep," she admitted, "but it was time well spent."

"So where do we stand?"

"We can't eliminate the possibility that your brother was involved in some very bad business, up to his ears, but the picture is becoming clearer."

Rebecca went on to recount her last afternoon and evening. She followed the Hoyne Avenue man on trolleys and cable cars to his job at a huge, modern warehouse on Jackson Boulevard, just east of Halsted. The building housed the main administrative offices and operations center for the Illinois Telephone and Telegraph Company, the owner/operator of the new Chicago Freight Tunnels. The place was named Tunnel Station No. 1. She worked into the wee hours with her agency and others on the telephone, gathering as much history as possible on the new tunnel system.

The system was originally conceived to house massive telephone conduits running beneath the city's entire downtown area, but the company, seeing opportunity, decided to install a small-gage railroad throughout the tunnels as well, intended for easy freight transportation, an efficient means of avoiding clogged city streets.

Rebecca was well briefed. Construction of the system, she explained, began in 1899. By 1903, over twenty miles of a proposed sixty miles of tunnel was completed and in limited use for both telephone conduits and a small-gauge railroad. Its freight cars were ten feet long by five feet wide and high, running in a seven-by-six-foot tunnel—no room for a man to sidestep the small, box-shaped engine except at the intersections.

There were four main stations for freight drop-off. Large, important concerns like the post office, major railroad stations, and large department stores would eventually have their own private entrance with an elevator.

When she was finished, Conor asked the obvious question. "Interesting, but how does all that connect to our case?"

She unfolded a paper titled *Royal Itinerary*, placing it on the table. An item for December 20 was circled. It read "Grand Opening, Chicago Freight Tunnels." Then she looked up from the document and said, "Mr. Hoyne Avenue works for the tunnel company. He drives a train in the tunnels, even supervises the scheduling."

Things were becoming frighteningly clear to the young lawyer. The question of what the money was for had just been answered. Conor's first question: "Do we know whether the royal party plans to ride the train?"

"Would you go to the theater and not stay for the performance?" Rebecca replied.

"Right...and the Clan was once known for planting dynamite bombs. I can't think of a more inviting target than a little underground railroad."

Their suspicions were no longer conjecture. Someone—some group— of bad actors was going to attempt an assassination of the heir to the British throne during the grand opening of the tunnel system. They now knew the day, the time, and the place, but the *who* and the *how* were still mysteries.

Rebecca explained that, although construction would continue for several more years, London's interest in building a similar system and the visit were catalysts for the premature inauguration ceremony. The prince was coming for a firsthand look along with his immediate family and three high-ranking transportation officials on their way to spend Christmas in Florida. The royal party would surely enter the actual tunnels and ride the train, but the itinerary lacked details about the prince's role in the ceremony. Still, in general terms, Rebecca and Conor now knew roughly where and when the assassination attempt would take place.

The pieces were falling into place, Conor thought. "So whoever is left in this rogue faction is still planning to carry out the assassination."

"It seems that way," Rebecca confirmed, "and we have only a few weeks left."

As a lawyer, Conor saw the weakness of their circumstantial case. The Hoyne Avenue man had not done anything wrong yet, and their whole case rested on Maureen Brogan's statement that she delivered money to Hoyne Avenue. She did not even know the amount. They had nothing solid. Going to the Chicago Police was out of the question, regardless of the evidence. If they walked into the police station to report this, they would leave in pieces.

Surely, they had enough evidence to have Scotland Yard cancel the prince's trip to Chicago, or at least cancel the tunnel appearance, Conor thought. They could quietly tour the tunnel on a different day if the prince insisted. It would be the best possible outcome.

Rebecca had quietly come to the same conclusion. "First thing I will do is put all this together and recommend they cancel the tunnel appearance."

Chapter 12

Nellie's Finley's arraignment that Wednesday morning was Conor's first appearance in the storied Criminal Courthouse, built on the site of the original facility where the Haymarket defendants were tried and four of them hanged in the courtyard less than fifteen years ago.

Conor hired a carriage and arrived at Hull House promptly at nine o'clock. The social worker and Nellie appeared at the front door as he was coming up the walk. Nellie was plainly but appropriately dressed and covered from the top of her shoes to the top of her neck, her hair brushed back and into a bun. She wore no face paint or powder under a plain blue bonnet.

The carriage was enclosed, offering welcome shelter from the wind if not the chill. The women sat across from Conor in the carriage where Nellie stared out the window at nothing in particular. Her face was stoic and expressionless as if death was making a joke to prove that life required more than a pulse and warm breath.

"Good morning, Nellie," Conor said.

The words did not find Nellie because she was not with them in the moment. Conor hoped her mind was far away in a happier time and place. She was a pretty girl, even now, but only in the way that an artist's first sketch of a great painting can be considered a masterpiece. The sketch can hardly be compared to the final painting. It is merely an idea of potential beauty that may or may not be realized.

Did she like to run in the green fields of Ireland? Did she play music or dance? Had she seen the Cliffs of Moher? He imagined the radiant smile on her mouth and lips when something pleased or amused her, exposing a dimple on the left cheek. She had apparently been in love. Was it shame that prevented her from going home when her companion betrayed her at the dock? Was it poverty? What a profound injustice to drive young people from their own shores to the mercy of strange, foreign lands, he thought.

Conor said to Miss Potter, "Any changes since we spoke last? The judge may address her, and I prefer not to be surprised."

The woman shrugged. "She eats well enough, but still no memories. Wherever her mind is, Mr. Dolan, I hope there's no pain."

THE NEW CRIMINAL COURTHOUSE'S INTERIOR WAS ORNATE, IF not opulent, with two levels of rooms opening into a marble-tiled common space under a soaring, sculpted ceiling. The first floor housed administrative offices with a ring of courtrooms above surrounding the second story balcony.

The judge in courtroom 201 was James Buck. A youngish man for a senior judge, his youth was disguised by a prominently fright-ful, salt-and-pepper-colored beard and a shiny bald island atop the surrounding hair. The case had come to Buck through the random assignment system, or so Conor had been told. But he knew Buck had four years left on his term, and the judge on the "political hot seat"—the most susceptible to political pressure—presided in the next courtroom down the balcony, his reelection scheduled for November of 1904. O'Sullivan had apparently kept his promise not to interfere.

Nellie Finley was seated beside Conor at the defense table, and her case was called first by the court clerk, likely at Buck's instruction since this clerk was not on Conor's payroll.

Buck was reading the indictment silently as Conor approached, guiding Nellie by the arm. The judge peered down from his throne. "Mr. Dolan, is it?"

"Yes, Your Honor."

Buck then proceeded with the formalities. "Your client is charged with one count of murder. Do you waive a formal reading of the indictment?"

"I do, Your Honor, and she pleads not guilty."

"The plea is entered," Buck declared. Conor breathed a sigh of relief. Buck had to know plenty about this case already. It dominated the latest editions. Fortunately, this judge had no interest in a dog and pony show. There was no requirement that he address the defendant directly, and Buck had opted for quick and low-key.

Then the judge turned to his clerk. "Give me a February jury date." The clerk checked his book, scribbled a note, and handed it up. "Your trial date will be February 2, 1904, Mr. Dolan. I'll give you the one-month interim date for filing of motions and enter an order for reciprocal discovery." Then Buck seemed to relax a bit, leaned forward, and motioned both counsels to the bench. Looking over at the stenographer, he said in a low voice, "This is off the record." He whispered to Conor directly. "A little bird told me you will be pursuing an insanity defense and a negotiated agreement. You are under no obligation to disclose at this point, but can you indicate to the court off the record whether this is the case? Do you have an insanity opinion?"

Conor figured Buck was just hoping the case was on track for a quick resolution. This case had all the hallmarks of a cause célèbre for the reformers and the suffragettes. Politically, there was no upside in presiding over a socially prickly murder case like this one. But Conor would not be rushed. "Your Honor, we will make that decision at the appropriate time, but there is one more issue we wish to address today on the record."

Buck leaned back to his ready position, signaling to the reporter that they were back on the record. Good judges did not take offense at a lawyer holding his line. "Very well."

Conor tendered two documents to the prosecutor who examined them and handed them back. "Thank you, Counsel. I've seen these."

Then Conor handed them up to Buck. "Your Honor," he said, "I ask leave to file an original subpoena duces tecum and proof of service."

Buck looked at the documents and called out to the gallery. "Is there a representative of Top Irish Maids and Nannies in the courtroom?"

A young woman stepped forward holding an envelope. She identified herself and held the envelope up for the judge. "Here are the documents, sir."

Buck held up the envelope and addressed Conor. "What's this about and what's the relevance?"

Conor explained that Pinkerton had officially requested the records as the representative of Nellie Finley's defense counsel and the employment agency refused to surrender them. Conor had reason to believe they may reveal mitigating evidence about Nellie's background and circumstances. He nearly blurted out that Nellie was not capable of communicating at present but caught himself in time. That disclosure would have opened a can of worms he was not ready to dig into. Conor explained that the records would have vital info about Nellie's family in Ireland and, more importantly, disclose the details of her employment in Chicago. All of that could lead the defense to witnesses and mitigating evidence.

The judge looked over at the prosecutor. "Sounds reasonable. Is the State objecting?"

"No, Your Honor," replied the prosecutor.

"Very well." He handed the envelope down to Conor. "You are instructed to provide mimeograph copies to the prosecution. No need for the Court to examine the documents in the absence of objection."

Everything went according to plan for once, he thought. Judge Buck could easily have started a ruckus by attempting to ask Nellie basic questions or by questioning Conor regarding his opinion of her current mental capacity: *"Are you satisfied with her ability to cooperate in her defense, Mr. Dolan?"* There would be no acceptable answer. If he said *yes,* he might contradict himself later. If he said *no,* he would be committed to a losing strategy.

Rebecca had discovered four possible employment agencies, and the other three fully cooperated but recorded no dealings with Nellie Finley. Top Irish Maids' refusal to cooperate was a good indication they were barking up the right tree.

In the envelope, Conor discovered a treasure trove of letters to the Agency from Nellie and statements from her older sister and mother, including personal details about Nellie and her love of learning, good work habits, and bubbly personality.

The girl hailed from a rural area in County Mayo, and she was living with an aunt in the town of Westport after the family lost its tenancy. Nellie's father fell from the roof and was paralyzed, leaving the couple paupers. Nellie's sister—then married with children and living in Connemara—took the younger sister in until her own poverty intervened. Unemployed and without prospects, the sixteen-year-old Nellie was forced to emigrate and contacted Irish Maids through a locally based employment service in Galway City.

Most importantly, the file named her new employer, a wealthy Chicago industrialist with a big mansion on Astor Street, the same street as Pullman and Armour and Robert Todd Lincoln. His name was Charles Bennett III.

Rebecca knew the name well enough. Bennett was the second-generation owner of a large manufacturing plant north of the river in the industrial area. The business began by manufacturing train parts during the war, accumulating a large fortune for the family. Bennett had recently expanded into telephone equipment, and business was booming nationwide.

The correspondence from Bennett to Irish Maids was most enlightening, focusing primarily on his prospective nanny's appearance and age. It seemed important to Bennett that the girl be young and from a rural family environment with a strong religious background.

From his correspondence, a picture emerged. Bennett expressed great disappointment at the absence of a current photograph and requested a detailed physical description, a request that should have set off alarm bells in the ear of any right-thinking mother or father. But Conor understood the realities of poverty and desperation. Sometimes a bad choice was simply the only choice available. He could not help but wonder how many other young Irishwomen had followed Top Irish Maids to their doom. To Conor, it had the revolting feel of a sexual procurement service for the wealthy.

He said to Rebecca, "Don't you think Bennett's correspondence should have raised eyebrows at this employment agency?"

"I do," Rebecca replied, "but it's not surprising. There are disreputable employment agencies favored by the white slavers, the brothel owners in the levees, even pimps with assets and big operations. These agencies essentially hoodwink the Irish girls into thinking they're moving into a safe and solid situation. They charge the most money."

"Still," Conor argued, "I suppose we shouldn't put the cart ahead of the horse. It's possible this Bennett is perfectly innocent, but at least we have a place to start."

"It's more than that," Rebecca countered. "It's enough to reconstruct this poor girl's life. The answers are in there somewhere, and we'll find them."

This particular agency, according to the notes, arranged Nellie's long voyage to Chicago in normal order, third class, thus allowing the girl to avoid steerage. Their representative provided her with train tickets from Hoboken to Chicago and a boardinghouse reservation for her one-night stay in New York, better conditions than offered to most domestics, Rebecca explained. Rich men would not tolerate damaged goods.

"Disgusting, if true," said Conor, "but Bennett is a well-known industrialist. Would he be so bold?"

She flashed a skeptical look. "You think there are no pervert industrialists? How about we take this party up to Astor Street and shake up the lords of industry?"

It would take the rest of the day to get way up to Astor Street and back on the "L" and streetcars, so Rebecca offered to hire a horse carriage for the trip. She knew a company equipped with the small, New York–style hansom cab, a maneuverable, one-horse vehicle capable of weaving in and out of street congestion.

It would have been a delightful drive up Lincoln Park Boulevard and Lake Shore Drive on a summer day, but this biting cold and bitter wind more suited their depressing task. Only a canvas side cover protected the pair from the assault of lake spray along Lake Shore Drive as waves crashed the seawall in an unceasing rhythm. Conor was thankful for the cab's extra blankets.

Their hastily conceived plan was simply to ring the doorbell or front gate device and request to speak with Mr. Charles Bennett III. Neither of them was naïve enough to expect an immediate audience, but that conclusion was factored into Rebecca's plan. She called it, "seeding the ground."

Tipping Bennett off had no downside. They had no probable cause at that point to accuse Bennett of crimes, but better to have him worried and off guard if he had something to hide.

Still, Conor had to wonder. The Finley case filled the papers lately, even sparking a controversial editorial from one of the major dailies on the institutional evils facing immigrant women in Chicago and the disproportionate number of Irishwomen populating the prison system. The title was clearly intended to sell papers: "The Irish in Chicago: A Criminal Race?" Still, the editorial was pointed and thought provoking.

There was a general view—even in the local Irish community—that the Irish immigrants were finally making strides to overcome the prejudice they faced in America since the Great Famine. But no one had meaningfully addressed the plight of the single, female immigrants. Their lives, by and large, remained as miserable and unpredictable as ever. For them, establishment of a stable, meaningful life was mostly the by-product of luck.

Nellie Finley's name appeared no fewer than six times in the piece, not to mention three times in a news story in the same paper the same day. Could Charles Bennett III have missed them all? Did he not hear the case discussed in one of his clubs or at a fancy dinner? If he was aware of the case, why remain anonymous? He must have relevant evidence, inculpatory or otherwise. Surely, a former employer would feel some civic or humanitarian obligation to step forward. He never did. There was something afoot here.

Astor Street looked like another planet to Conor Dolan, one with a magnificent view of a raging ocean. The street cobblestones were flawless and new—no ruts, missing bricks, or even the normal discoloration of wear and tear. The street had curbs with a slight grade allowing water to accumulate at the curb where it would run down to underground sewers.

Two, maybe three blocks of Victorian mansions lined the west side, connected by a concrete walkway. Rich red brick, imported stone—each an architectural wonder of engraving, decorative black ironwork, and architecture, and all were less than an hour's carriage ride from the Southside Levee. The Bennett mansion was relatively modest and, like most of its neighboring dwellings, not fenced. The police department was famous for providing premium services in the neighborhoods of Chicago's industrial titans. Brendan once railed about the department's practice of sweeping the homeless and poor from the elite streets. The burglars and petty criminals knew better than to ply their trades on Astor Street or Prairie Avenue.

Maybe, Conor thought, that was why the cops never interviewed Bennett or disclosed his connection to Nellie in reports. It was even possible that Bennett was a monster who paid the cops to cover up his involvement with Nellie Finley. Only a month ago, Conor would have considered such a fundamental breach of trust unimaginable in a civilized society, but he knew better now. Every time he tried to gauge the city's tolerance for depravity, he remembered the sign outside that brothel in the Levee District: "Ten to Thirteen-Year-Olds."

Instructing the driver to wait, Rebecca and Conor approached the rectangular, red-brick structure on a narrow lot. It was a simple three-story, efficient mathematical design, three rows of three windows in front, with a front door in the place of one window. The windows were arched in the Colonial style with grillwork. The arched entrance door was unobtrusive and in alignment with the two first-floor windows. A large brass knocker centered the green-painted oak door.

A middle-aged housekeeper answered the door. The true titans of Astor Street would employ a butler for the task, so the Bennetts were frugal titans.

"May I help ye?" The middle-aged woman asked in a harsh, Dublin accent but with no hint of an unfriendly demeanor.

Introducing herself as a Pinkerton and Conor as a defense attorney, Rebecca stuffed their plan and apparently sensed an opportunity. "We are representing an unfortunate young woman named Nellie Finley, and we understand she once worked for the Bennetts."

"She did, indeed," the woman answered matter-of-factly.

"May I ask your name, miss?" Rebecca prodded.

"Kate," she answered, "Kate Rowland."

The woman showed no inclination to bring them in from the cold, but Rebecca made another try. "If you have a few minutes, we'd be grateful if you would tell us about her. You may have heard she is not well."

Kate hesitated, then stepped back, maybe back from an instinct to cooperate. She seemed annoyed, maybe even frightened, as if she was about to cross a line from which there was no retreat.

The housekeeper is beholden to this Bennett for her livelihood, her survival. It was anything but a level playing field. If Bennett had committed crimes or atrocities, his hold over this woman would protect him

"Oh, I saw it in the newspapers, but I'm afraid ye would have to speak with the gentleman regarding your inquiry, and he's not at home."

Her reluctance was understandable, Conor thought, but not irreversible. "What about his wife?" he asked.

"The gentleman is widowed, sir."

Rebecca tried again. "Mrs. Rowland, how long did you know Nellie Finley? Could you simply tell us about your own relationship with her? Were you friendly?"

Kate looked agitated, now peering north and south along Astor Street to see who might be watching her conversation with the strange visitors. The woman would be wondering whether to tell Bennett about their visit, risking his displeasure, or to simply ignore it, setting herself up for a rebuke in the future. "She was...is a dear lass, but please understand. This is my employment. I live in this house. Ye have no appreciation for my position here. I..."

Kate was terrified, Conor could see, because the visitors had already created problems for her. She would have to report the visit promptly to Bennett and risk his reaction. After all, she had not cooperated in any way with these interlopers. Still, Kate could not mask her obvious affection for Nellie. Conor could see it in the woman's face, so he knew they would talk again.

Kate Rowland was still very much an open door, and this trip was anything but a waste of time. The woman's only possible reason for being afraid or nervous over their visit was Charles Bennett III. Kate Rowland knew things that would incriminate Bennett. There was no other explanation. Conor was certain Rebecca had seen it too.

Rebecca seemed to sense, wisely, that she had pushed Kate to her limit for now. To press further would be pointless and only risk antagonizing the woman. Something was amiss in that house, and Kate could put it into words—if they could convince her to help.

Rebecca handed Kate a card and planted her seed. "Kate, please tell the gentleman that we represent Nellie Finley in the alleged murder of her child and that we would like to interview him regarding the circumstances of her employment. In the meanwhile, is there anything at all you can share with us?" Giving her the card for Bennett was a shrewd move, Conor thought, because it gave Kate access to their contact information. The message from Rebecca might also help shield the woman from Bennett's wrath.

Rebecca's moment had passed. "No, madam. Thank you."

Back at the front gate, Conor asked, "So what do we do?"

Rebecca shrugged. "We wait and see if our seed grows, but what about that charismatic priest friend of yours, the one with the girl-friend in Chinatown?"

It was a great idea. There was nothing more irresistible to an Irish woman than ecclesiastical persuasion, and Father Brendan White had already taken an interest in Nellie's case. Hopefully, the woman was not Protestant. If this housekeeper was harboring dark secrets, surely she would open up to the priest. Whether or not she would testify was another matter.

Tomorrow was Thanksgiving, Conor remembered, and Father Brendan invited Conor to dine at the rectory. He felt bad about leaving Rebecca to deal with Mrs. Kaplan and Mrs. Goldman and the resident barber, but it would give Conor a good opportunity to talk with the priest about the Nellie Finley case.

Chapter 13

The streets were quiet on Thanksgiving afternoon, and the people appeared happier, more relaxed in their holiday mode. Most of the commuters, Conor figured, were off to a relative's home for a family dinner. The area around St. Michael's Parish on Armitage Avenue on the city's North Side was home to a more prosperous brand of immigrant, mostly older Germans and Irish who had emigrated in the 1870s and 1880s and graduated to home ownership. He could see the differences in the clothing, the maintenance of the houses and the more upscale shops. It was a fine sunny day, chilly, but the kind of day Chicagoans would cherish, he thought, as a last gift of fall before an inevitably brutal winter.

St. Michaels's rectory was a traditional two-story directly beside the church, a beautiful, stone masterpiece, complete with spiraled tower and stained-glass windows in the ancient, if garishly inappropriate, tradition of the Catholic Church. Conor knew, even if the parishioners did not, that their pastor would prefer to convert the complex to a shelter for the poor and homeless. His flock would revolt against such a move, for these parishioners, Father Brendan had explained over a beer, had largely kept their roots buried as opposed to nurturing them back to life, with some exceptions among the Irish, of course. "Well on their way to being good American Protestants," was the way Brendan had put it. "Give a man a decent job, his own home, and a good horse, next thing he thinks he's the Duke of Cornwall. Can't find a nickel to save a starving child."

It was not Conor's first visit to the rectory, so he greeted Father Brendan's housekeeper/cook by her name at the door. "Happy Thanksgiving to you, Mrs. Fogarty, and thank you for the invitation."

The woman looked annoyed and appeared frazzled. Conor detected just a hint of perspiration on her forehead. She frowned and, turning away, said, "Come in if ye must and find a seat. I'll not be serving jars of beer. Ye can get up and go to the half barrel when ye like."

The dining room was relatively spacious but, in context, looked more like a closet. There were perhaps twenty sinners at the table including the good Father himself at the head. Conor recognized not a single guest. By the looks of them, Brendan rounded up his dinner party from the Harrison Street Police Station.

He waived to Conor. "Come. I saved ye a place here beside me. Now we'll all say the Grace."

Mrs. Fogarty reluctantly took his hat and coat, and Conor took his place beside the priest. On the other side was an empty chair and, on the chair beside that, a toddler seated on a box. Not just a toddler…it looked like…yes, little Patrick, Maureen Brogan's waif, being tended to by a very old woman in raggedy attire, a *guest*.

At that moment, Maureen Brogan herself emerged from the kitchen balancing two trays of bread and a mug of beer, which she placed in front of Conor. It was a lot to take in all at once.

Father Brendan slapped Conor lightly on the back and laughed. "I didn't want ye to be bored, Conor, so I invited Maureen and Patrick to join us. Sure 'twas good fortune I did, or Mrs. Fogarty might have been overwhelmed. Your Maureen has been working harder than a sheep dog in the field. Ye may not see much of her. Anyway, welcome. Enjoy yourself and make some new friends. Everyone here has a story."

"Your Maureen?" Conor repeated silently. The gathering looked like a convention of homeless policy winners, the lucky few of the unlucky minions. Father Brendan was truly an unpredictable character, one with an enormous capacity for empathy. But, *"Your Maureen?"*

Maureen's presence, while not a shock, surprised him, but then Brendan was full of surprises. He needed Brendan's help with the Nellie Finley matter but doubted he would have the opportunity to state his case with all this holiday mayhem.

This was a new Maureen, fresh and sparkling in a new, frilly white blouse, obviously purchased for the occasion. She wore a simple brooch, a harp fastened to the blouse just under her neck, hair finely brushed back into a single braid tracing the line of her neck elegantly in a perfect line to the small of her back. The girl bubbled with excitement at what must have been her first real dinner invitation.

Within two hours, the once-fat turkey was a mere skeleton, the pumpkin pie was reduced to crumbs, and the cheap brandy scented the room, a slight whiff of the recent past. Smoke enveloped the whole place. By the time Mrs. Fogarty's pie disappeared, Conor had a dozen or so new friends including a former German soldier who had fought in some war or other in 1870 and a middle-aged sign painter from County Cavin forced to accept charity after a fall from a ladder left him partially crippled. The man admitted to being a Protestant named Smith. He was thankful for landing a factory job with Brendan's help. It was the least Brendan could do, he had explained, for a poor soul whose misguided religion would prevent, by accident of birth, his eventual entry into the Kingdom of God.

Brendan bid his "guests" good night around six o'clock—collectively first, then definitively, one by one. Some took a full drink and some bread into the cold night air. One took a bottle. With the last of his guests turned back into the street with full bellies and loaded to the gills, Brendan asked Conor and Maureen to retire to the parlor with him. He seemed to sense that Conor was anxious for a talk.

"I think I should help Mrs. Fogarty with this mess," Maureen protested. Mrs. Fogarty smiled her first smile of the night.

Brendan shook his head. "No. Mrs. Fogarty will watch the child. I hid a bottle of good cognac. We three will have a wee drink and a chat. Then we'll all help Mrs. Fogarty clean up."

When the three were seated around the warm fireplace, Brendan said, "Now then, Conor, ye been busting to get somethin' off your chest all evenin'. Sure what's on your mind then?"

Maureen's presence made things a bit awkward, Conor thought, for such an indelicate conversation. "I don't see that we need to burden Maureen with Nellie Finley business. Maureen's had enough problems of her own."

Brendan waived him off. "Nonsense. Maureen knows as much as I do about the girl, and sure her own experience makes Maureen a kind of expert on the subject in any case. The woman isn't the wallflower you take her for. Sure what is it then?"

So Conor recounted the visit to Astor Street, sharing all the information from the employment agency as well as the substance of the conversation between Rebecca and Kate Rowland, Bennett's housekeeper.

"So," Brendan interrupted, "Ye want me to visit Kate Rowland, get her to betray her employer, possibly incriminate the man, the powerful man he is, and essentially testify against him in court. Is that all?" Brendan was a quick study and a meticulous scholar of human nature.

Conor shrugged. "I suppose it is."

Then Maureen dropped her opinion with no question pending. "I think she'd go fer it meself, providin' certain arrangements could be made to address legitimate concerns about her safety and her prospects for future employment. This gentleman, Bennett, won't be overjoyed to learn his housekeeper is sellin' him down the Shannon."

"We can't bribe her," Conor declared. "Beyond that, what is there?"

"Well, it seems to meself," Maureen began, "that Father Brendan's housekeeper and cook, Mrs. Fogarty, is overworked, to say the least. Sure she's doin' the job of at least two people and for what? How much are ye payin' the poor soul?"

Father Brendan blushed, then pretended to cough while recovering his bearings. "Well, I suppose I could squeeze a few more dollars a month out of the parish for this Kate Rowland, and she could share the second floor with Mrs. Fogarty. If the woman can cook at all, I'll be delighted to reduce Mrs. Fogarty to housekeeping duties. Sure Bennett will fire Kate if she comes clean with us—or worse."

Conor nodded. "That sounds like a perfect solution to me. I get the distinct impression she'd be overjoyed to find a new situation."

"Leave it to me, then. I'll go see the woman within the next day or two." Then Brendan rose from his chair in a formal, almost clerical way—palms up like he was holding a big globe—indicating the evening had ended. "Let's help Mrs. Fogarty clean up, and then I'll say goodnight to ye all. Oh, Conor, I know I don't need to ask ye to escort Maureen and Patrick home for me."

"Of course, I will, Brendan."

ON THE TROLLEY BACK SOUTH, CONOR WONDERED WHETHER Maureen's presence at the dinner, the seating arrangements, even this trolley ride home were coincidence or some sort of sinister plot by his devious friend, Father Brendan. He never thought of his relationship with Maureen Brogan as a courtship, nor had he harbored any desire to court the girl. Still, his initial opinion of Maureen had been unfair, unkind even. There was substance in Maureen Brogan, intelligence to spare, and the kind of independence he so much admired in Rebecca Fletcher. And make no mistake, he thought, Maureen was an attractive woman. There was no denying the fact.

Out of nowhere, Maureen asked from the seat beside him, "So what did ye think of Father Brendan's matchmaking then?"

He laughed. "Yes, I noticed. It was a little embarrassing, I suppose, you and I being more or less business acquaintances—I mean in the matter of my brother's demise and all."

She kept her eyes trained straight ahead. "Of course, in the matter of yeer brother's demise…and all."

Conor found it an uncomfortable conversation, so he tried to inject humor. "Well, I suppose a Catholic priest with a girlfriend would want to see everyone with a girlfriend."

His attempt at humor flopped. "'Tis a myth, if ye ask me. Father Brendan is a complicated pairson. He feels guilty about being a priest, t'inks he has it too easy. He doesn't want people to see him as marally superior, so he makes up sins about himself, sins he never committed. It makes him feel more like the rest of us poor fools. Besides, you already have a garlfriend, and, if you ask me, she's too old far ye, no matter how nice she is. I t'ink the garlfriend is in his fookin' head."

Conor knew better, but Maureen Brogan had effectively shut the lawyer's mouth. Brendan must have told her about Rebecca, but who told Brendan? Outside Maureen's flat, he stopped at the exterior door of the house and tipped his trademark homburg, "Goodnight, Maureen. It was a very pleasant day."

Still holding little Patrick's hand in hers, she took a step toward Conor, raised herself up on dainty tiptoes and kissed him gently on the lips. "Goodnight, Conor Dolan, and t'ank ye for a wonderful day."

On the streetcar ride east, it occurred to him how complicated his life had become in the last two months. He had learned much about women, about sex, even about the basest proclivities of human nature. And that was only his personal life. The more he learned, the more confused he became. He recalled a paraphrased quote from Oscar Wilde to the effect that, *"Experience is the name men give to their biggest mistakes."*

He hopped off the streetcar at LaSalle and caught a southbound transfer with no wait. The car was empty but for a shabbily dressed woman with a young boy playing a harmonica. He sat facing them in the open car, and he was struck by the woman's uncanny resemblance to his own mother. For the first time since his arrival, Conor thought consciously about his mother, about Ireland, the little white cottage, and the road down to the bog. He remembered the music that filled the family's evenings as the turf fire cast its shadows along the stone wall. In that moment, he could almost smell the fire and the song of the kettle on the hearthstone.

Pa was proud of the stone house he and his brother had built; the people in their village, most of whom lived in cottages, lauded him for his craftsmanship.

On rare occasions these days, Conor would still dream about his little dog and the incident at the Cliffs of Moher, but that was more a nightmare than a memory, banished to the whim of his unconsciousness.

He passed Murph's place on the walk home but fought the urge to stop for a nightcap. He would need his rest for the coming days.

Nightfall carried with it a frigid wind off the lake, forcing him to quickstep the last half block to his basement apartment. *Odd that the dog is sitting exposed on the top step in such weather.* It was nearly ten o'clock. He expected the mutt to be snuggled up under the dirty old blanket with his alley cat friend. The dog's muted growl ignited his senses to full alert.

Easing his way down the eight stairs, he stopped a few steps from the bottom in the feeble light from the streetlamp. Nothing but dead silence and his thumping heartbeat. Only a foot from the door, he reached out to check the lock and the dog unleashed a frantic chorus of barking sufficient to roust the neighbors from warm beds.

Retreating to the top of the stairs, Conor heard a window opening above him as lamplight from the second-floor window invaded the darkness. "Conor, is that you?" Rebecca said. "What's wrong with the dog?"

There was only one way into the apartment and one way out, he knew. If someone was still inside, the scene would get ugly in the next few seconds. "Ring up the cops," he said in a pointless attempt to keep his voice low.

Within a matter of seconds, Rebecca was at his side, coat over a nightgown and a pistol in her right hand. "Someone's in there," he whispered, "or *was* in there."

The police responded quickly as Mrs. Kaplan and her sister enjoyed the suspense from the parlor window. The neighbors had a less advantageous view.

The lock was broken and the inside of Conor's apartment thoroughly ransacked, but the evildoers were long gone. The place was a mess, but nothing was obviously missing. Mrs. Kaplan was kind enough to let him sleep on the sofa in the parlor and did her best to make it into a bed for the night. He and Rebecca stayed up and unwound with a cognac in the chairs before the dying fire.

"They appeared to be looking for something very specific," Rebecca suggested.

"It would help to know who 'they' are before speculating about that, but you're right. A search like that would suggest that I have something they're afraid of, maybe something that would hurt them."

"Do you have any ideas at all?" she asked.

"Well, I thought it might be that box of my brother's belongings, but I've been through it carefully several times. There's nothing at all in there that would fit the bill."

Rebecca rose from the chair and reached for his empty snifter. "It's possible they were just curious about how much information you've uncovered. You need some rest now. I'll clean up here, and we'll figure this out tomorrow. There was no real harm done."

"Not tonight anyway," he said softly. "Not tonight."

Chapter 14

Less than a week later, Rebecca appeared at Conor's office just before five o'clock. He knew something was cooking because she warned him that morning to expect a surprise, even suggested he pack an extra shirt in his attaché—a formal one with a winged collar and a cravat. Part of him cringed because he was never comfortable at formal gatherings or society events. They made him feel like an interloper, a fake. Maybe it was a feeling common to immigrants, but he felt like friends should be chosen individually, one by one, not by status or position. It was something about the music, he thought. His ma and pa blessed him with a love of music, and people in America seemed to associate great music with nice clothes. There were several fine orchestras playing in Chicago, and he was thinking—hoping—Rebecca's surprise might involve a visiting orchestra down at the Iroquois Theater.

She wore a long, gray, floor-length coat, simple but elegant with large buttons and an expansive lapel sporting decorative black flowers. The coat was efficient and not tapered to her waist, almost rectangular. He eased the garment from her shoulders.

Her dress was floor length, also simple but royal blue. Unlike the coat, the gown was tightly fitted and perfectly tapered to heavenly hips with see-through lace sleeves to the shoulders and a banded neck. The buttons began at the back of her sculpted neck, descending to just below her waist to that delicious indentation he loved so well. He thought briefly about reaching for the top button, but hung the coat, then held the chair for his guest.

"Happy Birthday, Conor," she said, carefully placing two envelopes on his desk, one letter sized and one larger.

Rebecca was as unpredictable as she was desirable, he thought. Conor was moved. "How did you know? I never said anything."

She smiled coyly and said in a kind of scripted way, "I'm a detective. It's what we do. Open the small envelope, please." Inside he found two tickets to the Auditorium Theater's performance by the Chicago Orchestra for that night. He had been hoping for a musical evening, but this was beyond expectation, not to mention beyond his budget.

"I know how you love Theodore Thomas and his orchestra," she said, "so, unless you have an objection, we'll have dinner at Schlesinger's Grill & Tea Room before the performance. A carriage will pick us up here in half an hour."

He was euphoric. "Not a bad gift for a farm boy from Clare," he said, opening his arms to embrace her.

Rebecca smiled coyly while holding him at bay with her palm. "Makeup," she declared. "You'll have time for that later."

For years, Conor had followed the orchestra's world-renowned director and his campaign for a permanent home. It was said that Auditorium Theater, although considered acoustically acceptable, was far too large to allow optimal enjoyment of a world-class orchestra. The new Orchestra Hall, designed by no less than Daniel Burnham of Columbian Exposition fame, was nearing completion and set to open within a matter of weeks. Conor recently heard rumors that the orchestra would be renamed for the opening. The "Chicago Symphony Orchestra" was the betting favorite. All things considered, he was hardly disappointed.

Conor smiled. "I'm your willing captive for the evening, madam. And may I say that you look stunning?"

They moved to the sitting area where Conor noticed the larger envelope still in her hand. "What's this then?" he asked.

"The rest of your birthday gift."

Inside, he found a file entitled, *Olaf Peterson*. Conor began to scan the documents, amazed at Pinkerton's capabilities. Olaf Peterson, the Hoyne Avenue tunnel employee, was forty-four, divorced, and living with his mother in that house. He was Chicago-born, had no ties to Ireland and no history with Irish Republican organizations. Olaf, however, did own a long history of financial problems, including two evictions related to both legal and illegal gambling debts along with a felony conviction for embezzlement in Indiana.

Whatever else Olaf might be, Conor thought, the man was no ideologue. Within the tunnel operation, Olaf was employed as a rail supervisor in charge of crew scheduling and assignments related to ongoing construction, limited commercial operations, and phone conduit maintenance. He would be privy to details of the royal visit and itinerary. Conor looked up at Rebecca and said, "You got all this without raising eyebrows?"

"Not one," she assured him. "The Agency is fifty years ahead of its time. We don't chase train robbers on horseback anymore. Well, I don't anyway."

"Curious—he's been on that job for five years, so he's probably been a reliable employee up to now. Maybe the money in the pouch from Maureen was enough to drag him back into his old ways."

"There's more. I submitted a formal report to the Agency recommending cancellation of the royal trip, but Scotland Yard, after discussions with the prince, have concluded there is no evidence behind our speculations. They're arrogant and believe the Clan is just a mob of Celtic drunkards."

Conor walked over to the desk where he kept the Jameson. "Plenty of people have been murdered by drunkards, but it's getting interesting. Let's have a drink." He retrieved the bottle from his desk, poured them each two fingers, and returned to the sofa. "So how do we find out the tunnel route of the prince?" he wondered aloud. "Hell, how do we even get inside the tunnels?"

Rebecca sipped slowly from the glass, then announced with just a touch of playful conceit, "We Pinkertons have been very busy, Conor," and explained that Scotland Yard authorized Pinkerton to send two detectives directly to Illinois Telephone and Telegraph senior management to secure their cooperation, just to be certain. The tunnel company was known to be negotiating for the sale of the entire operation, and they would not want a scandal to jeopardize the deal. The company was counting on the good will a royal visit would generate.

Scotland Yard itself recently wired the CEO naming the two individuals who would appear, Rebecca Fletcher and a lawyer named Conor Dolan, but without setting off alarms. "Routine security, they called it. But from now on, we'll both need to take precautions against being followed. The tunnel ceremony will take place in only three weeks, and the royal party will arrive in New York next week to begin its US tour. My office is working to schedule the meeting with the tunnel executives as we speak."

Conor smiled and raised his near-empty glass. They clicked. "Sláinte," he said, "and to the future King. Long may he reign, with his head in a ditch and his ass in a drain."

They saw the cab pull up in front, and Conor was ready with the coats. He nearly forgot to lock the office door in the excitement but managed to remember his escort duties and helped Rebecca into the cab as the horse dropped a remembrance on the cobblestones.

It was clear now that that the Hoyne Avenue man, Olaf Peterson, was paid to do something. But what? They both doubted he was an assassin. It had to be something less bold, most likely information and access. Potential bombers would need to be familiar with the tunnel system and know the route of the royal tour. More than that, they would need to plant explosives. The work would require an inside man.

They both knew the Clan na Gael's history of doing its own killing in the past, even if ineptly. Besides, Peterson's experience was confined to graft and petty crimes. The man was no murderer. So what was the money for? Leave a gate open? Pull a switch? Plant dynamite? They agreed the most likely answer was that Peterson would somehow get the Clan faction access to the timetable and the tunnel itself for the purpose of rigging an explosion. The Clan members could unlock a door (if they had a key) and avoid security (if they knew the plan). They could walk through a door (if it was unlocked), but once inside the tunnel, they would be lost without a guide or a good map.

Rebecca reminded Conor that they did not know whether there were more Olaf Petersons out there. Mr. Hoyne Avenue did not necessarily get the entire $20,000. There could be four or five more out there somewhere, but they had enough information now to mount some counter measures.

AT THE AGENCY FLAT, THEY MADE LOVE LATE INTO THE NIGHT, then talked and talked and talked—about music, about Nellie Finley, about Maureen Brogan, about Rebecca's family, and about Kevin Dolan. Conor even told her about his summer nights in the park with Lori Howard and recounted his boyhood family in Springfield with no particular sense of nostalgia. He tried not to dwell on the Lori Howard thing. It was childish and embarrassing.

Talking with Rebecca was like thinking out loud, like working through his random thoughts and trying to organize them into something with meaning, something that would make sense. As he listened to his own words, it occurred to him that he had no particular affection for Springfield or his Uncle Willie. It was not that Willie Dolan abused him in any way, but the only real affection he could recall from his childhood came from Ireland, from Ma, and from moments like Pa's praise for a little boy's turf-footing skills. His Springfield hosts considered him more a boarder than a relative, more a Christian responsibility than a family member, and his uncle extracted a fair trade in hard work in exchange for board and food. He remembered only the affection and intimacy expressed in Kevin's letters, but he was not able to recognize that reality until now. "I think I was lonely," he had to admit to Rebecca.

"I think in some ways, you still are."

She was right, and he wondered why he had never recognized it before. This was the most intimate conversation of his young life, he thought, one of those brief and rare moments he would carry forever in a secret place as one would a signed Mark Twain first edition. He wanted it to continue, maybe even to grow, but everything was so confusing to Conor. Thoughts of Maureen Brogan plagued him like an annoying fly in a tiny room.

Rebecca was refined and wise, confident in a way foreign to most young men. Yet, despite the calculating, reasoned demeanor and obvious beauty, this woman was slowly dying of her own loneliness and grief. Maybe only someone suffering from the deepest pain and sadness, he thought, could find and touch those hidden venues in another human being. Conor could not label his feelings for her, and that fact troubled him.

He still was not sure what love was—or was not—but what he felt for this woman transcended lust and affection. If it was *not* love, then he could live a happy, loveless life. Maybe a part of what he felt was pity, but there was no denying he was content in her company. To Conor, she was as much teacher as lover, and in her presence, he never failed to learn something new about himself.

"Why are you so quiet?" she whispered. "Sleeping?"

He chuckled. "Just thinking."

"About?"

"Oh, about my brother, about you and me and this damned complicated city, I suppose."

They were both still staring up at the cracked ceiling in a dark room, naked between sweat-soaked sheets under a stack of blankets when she said, "I have a house out west of the city in Oak Park."

"You never mentioned it."

"It's where Jacob and Sarah died. I rarely go there, but I just can't part with it."

"So it's just empty?"

"Hardly empty. Oh, it's not morbid or anything like that. I gave most of their things to the St. Vincent DePaul Society, but there are reminders in every room. The reminders aren't healthy for me; I understand that. It's just that sometimes, not often, I need them because I'm afraid I might forget."

He felt lost in this conversation or more like he was drowning in it. "What kind of work did Jacob do?"

"He was a lawyer."

"What kind of lawyer?"

He could almost feel her sly smile there in the dark. She traced a single finger along his chest through the modest sections of chestnut hair. "What kind of lawyers are there? What are my choices?"

It was her way of letting him off the hook, but he did not want to be off the hook. He wanted to offer her what she needed in that moment. He kind of sighed because he was so bad at this, no matter how much he wanted to be good. His empathy, his passion to relieve her suffering would not translate into words. Is it possible to feel real empathy, he wondered, without the ability to express it?

"I wish I knew what to say, Rebecca. I wish I had the words. I just don't. You're smarter than I am, more experienced. All I can say is that I feel your pain to the point that it's become my pain. I'd like to go to the house with you the next time."

She did not respond to that, so he said exactly what he was thinking. "The only thing I want to do at this moment in my life is help you, maybe ease your grief somehow. Tell me what to say or do."

Silence descended upon the room but for the faint sound of a single horse clapping along in the street below, starting and stopping, the lamplighter on his pre-dawn rounds. Gas lighting was disappearing quickly in the city, like his youth, never to return. He fought the urge to reach over and touch her face because he was afraid to find tears.

Then she said, "I want to have a baby, Conor—your baby."

Chapter 15

Less than three weeks before the tunnel ceremony, Rebecca and Conor suffered a bitterly cold and blustery trip by open trolley; they were then stuck out in the wind awaiting the Jackson Street transfer. The conversation focused on their eleven o'clock meeting with tunnel company executives.

Regarding the royal visit itself, they knew the ceremony with the Prince of Wales would be held in the lobby of the Jackson Street address, Station No. 1, at noon on December 20. They also knew the prince and his entourage would enter the tunnel and ride the mini-train from that location to an undisclosed destination along a secret route. There were over twenty completed miles of tunnel and track of the planned sixty, so they needed specific information and unfettered access.

A white-shirted security guard greeted them by name in the lobby upon arrival. The space was a domed affair occupying parts of three floors with two levels of overlooking balcony on three sides and connected to the ground floor by a single staircase. Conor was no expert, but he immediately decided the location provided a perfect, short-range firing position for a would-be assassin. It never occurred to him that they might just shoot the prince in the lobby and avoid all the trouble of explosives. Still, sufficient staffing and surveillance of the balcony would all but eliminate that threat. He made a mental note to inquire about the balcony and review security procedures for building access on the day of the visit, but Rebecca was well versed on security protocols, and she was already making notes.

The man led them to a second-floor conference room where he formally introduced two Illinois Telephone and Telegraph executives; the vice-president of operations and the chief of security stood to greet them. Pot bellies, bushy mustaches, and receding hairlines were the order of battle, and only a comical difference in height distinguished the two.

Addressing Conor with his eyes, the vice-president—the shorter man—pointed to two chairs across the long table, each with a file in front of it. He said, "Please, Mr. Dolan, sit and be comfortable."

The slight of Rebecca was obvious, and Conor decided to act quickly to reset the rules. He said, "Thank you, sir." Then holding a chair for Rebecca, he added, "But Mrs. Fletcher is the senior member of our little delegation. I'm here only to advise."

"Of course," said the tall security chief. The man was more relaxed than his superior, his voice mellower, the difference maybe a product of their height difference, Conor thought. "We're prepared to assist in any way we can, Mrs. Fletcher."

And they were. The files on the desk each contained a plan for Chicago police protection supplemented by private security, along with the minute-by-minute itinerary for the royal visit. It included a map of the entire tunnel route from start to finish. The tour would begin at Station No. 1 and was relatively straightforward. This was precisely the tactical information they needed.

"How many people have access to this tunnel route?" Rebecca asked immediately.

They whispered between themselves a minute, then the short guy said, "Seven, maybe eight if you count the young woman who made the mimeographs." Then he explained that the prince would exit the train for a demonstration at the newly constructed private elevator entrance below Marshall Field's Department Store where the royal party would enjoy lunch in its Tea Room Restaurant on the fourth floor.

The department store, Conor figured, would offer another stellar opportunity to shoot the prince, but the cops would have Field's covered like a blanket, aided by the store's private security. Detective Flynn would not dare attempt such a brazen suicide mission. Besides, one simple, well-aimed bullet would kill the Prince of Wales, but these Clan men needed more theater for their global audience. The Clan na Gael saw themselves as seasoned bombers, dynamite men. To the rogue Republicans in the Clan, the assassination had to be drama and spectacle. They would opt for dynamite for the symbolism of the explosion, the violent, symbolic exorcism of the British Empire from the Emerald Isle.

Following lunch, the underground mini-train would transport the party under the river at State Street northbound and back south under Clark Street. The security man advised them that he had arranged for Rebecca and Conor to participate in a test run of the route immediately after the meeting. Then he addressed Rebecca with what seemed like his chief concern. "I must ask you, Mrs. Fletcher, do you have any indication of a specific threat?"

Rebecca could lie like a cheap watch. She flashed a look of surprise and said, "Oh, good heavens no, sir. Had we been aware of a threat, we would have taken our information to the police immediately. This is all strictly routine, and it seems you gentlemen have provided a solid security plan. We appreciate the information and the tour."

THE TUNNEL STARTING POINT, LOCATED IN A WAREHOUSE-LIKE industrial space beside the office building, might have been mistaken at a distance for a real train station. Damp and filled with miniature, open freight cars and box-like engines on narrow gauge track, the place was abuzz with the activity and noise of railroading on a miniature scale. Cranes along the roof, machinery and switches everywhere and all aligned above and between the tracks. Massive windows swung open just below the roof high above. To the south end, huge overhead doors lined the wall for loading and unloading of freight. To the north end, the tracks all fed gradually into one another until only a single track disappeared into each of two open archways in a brick wall, presumably descending into the tunnel below.

The rail cars were not built for passengers, but crude, open seating behind the engineer allowed for four moderately sized passengers on the engine. The engine pulled a modified freight car with bench seating for six. The security chief helped Rebecca into the wooden seat, and Conor climbed in behind her. Luckily, she had switched from see-through blue lace to sturdy broadcloth for their day trip. The noise of engines and machinery was deafening. The party did not require the modified freight car.

Conor watched their escort tap the engineer on the shoulder as the tiny engine chugged slowly toward the left archway. The man turned back momentarily to face them. Conor could not hear the words over incessant clamor but nearly fell off the train when he recognized the face of Olaf Peterson, the Hoyne Avenue guy. He should have recognized the man from the hat. By the look on her face, Rebecca had already made the connection.

The descent into the tunnel, forty feet below, was an uncontrolled drop, and Conor thought it must be like riding that roller coaster at Coney Island, the one that the lawyer in Springfield bragged about. He held fast to the side of the car and remembered the instruction not to extend a head or arms out of the car, as the tunnel allowed only six inches clearance on each side. The tunnel system was not built with safety in mind. The train was slow, but it would sever a head as efficiently as a guillotine.

The ceiling, at seven feet, carried huge phone cables along the tunnel.

The cables hovered only a foot above their heads. Electric lighting along the walls was sporadic and dim but seemed sufficient to the purpose. Tracks branched everywhere from intersections—four-way, even six-way intersections—and the bigger intersections clearly allowed a bit of extra clearance, enough for a man to stand and carefully maneuver. Only rats could feel safe walking in the straight sections, Conor thought. The system in general was surprisingly well ventilated.

Conor was careful to mark the main intersections on his tunnel map along with the emergency exits that appeared about every quarter mile, each equipped with a vertical ladder fixed to the wall. He made a mental note to find out how the emergency entrances operated. The ride into the bowels of Marshall Field's Department Store took less than ten minutes. A carved out, concrete loading platform marked the station with a huge freight elevator along the wall. It was truly cutting edge, twentieth century technology.

Conor could see Rebecca recording notes of her own in the near darkness. He thought the Marshall Field's location would draw too much attention during the royal tour to be an attractive target, but they dared not talk with the Hoyne Avenue guy just in front of them.

After another half mile or so, their tour guide, the security chief, announced in a loud voice, "We'll be going under the river in a minute, just beyond this next intersection."

It was a six-way intersection around a circular hub, offering enough room for a man or two to work surreptitiously around the tracks without fear of being run over. The intersection even included an escape ladder leading to the street, the perfect place for an ambush or an explosion. He wondered if a powerful detonation might even be enough to breach the river but dared not ask the question. The question alone might spook them, but such an event would mean certain death to everyone inside the tunnel system and destruction of the entire project. It would be major global news even if the Prince of Wales managed to grow gills and survive.

On the trolley ride back to Mrs. Kaplan's, Rebecca did not hold back. She put his own thoughts into words. "Dynamite is what the Clan knows, and that tunnel is a perfect target. The intersection under the river is too tempting for them to resist. The damage could be catastrophic."

He refrained from telling her he had reached the same conclusion earlier, but hearing her say it raised doubts in his mind. "Right. A big enough explosion could bring the river down and throw the entire city into chaos. It would flood basements and destroy foundations all over the Loop, not to mention erase the tunnel system. But I've been thinking about it. That would go against the Clan's interest, against the interest of any breakaway faction as well."

"Maybe you're smarter than they are," Rebecca replied.

They hopped from the trolley, weaving their way around the commuters, the tracks, and the horse dung until Rebecca stepped into a slush-filled hole in the cobblestones.

Conor grabbed her elbow before she could fall. "You all right?"

"No damage, but you're right. Enraging the people of Chicago and damaging their economy is not in the interest of Irish independence. The IRB raises enormous sums of money here, and an incident like that could kill sympathy with the Irish cause here. Maybe that's the answer. Maybe that's why the Clan proper objects. Doing something like that would be madness." They both went quiet for a minute, thinking, until Rebecca asked, "So what do you think?"

"My money is on madness," Conor replied.

In Mrs. Kaplan's parlor that evening after dinner, Conor was preparing himself for the baby discussion with Rebecca when Mrs. Goldman requested to hear him play a few tunes on the piano before dinner. She and Mrs. Kaplan joined them in a glass of wine. Conor was relieved to postpone the long-overdue conversation about fatherhood.

All the action and drama unfolding daily had effectively buried the subject of Rebecca's bombshell request all week, allowing Conor a few days to consider the existential consequences of fatherhood, especially under such unorthodox circumstances. On the other hand, the subject had largely robbed him of four nights' sleep. He knew they would have to talk about it soon.

Of course, he wanted children one day, but a child needs a full-time father. If he and Rebecca had a baby, he would want to be a part of raising the child. It was cowardly—he knew that—but she was asking Conor for a lifeline, and he was too cowardly to simply say no and let her drown, too selfish to rescue her by putting her needs ahead of his own. That was the simple truth of it.

Mrs. Kaplan and her sister always wanted to hear the most popular song on the planet in 1903, "In the Good Old Summer Time." They sang it together around the piano with Mrs. Kaplan and even the barber joining in. They always sang it together, to the point that Conor was beginning to enjoy it. He especially appreciated the mindless lyrics in these troubled, stressful days:

In the good old summertime
In the good old summertime
Strollin' through the sha-ady lanes
With my baby, mine
I hold her hand and she-ee holds mine
And that's a very good sign
That she's my tootsy-wootsy in
the good old summertime
In the good old summertime
In the good old summertime
(If I could go) Strollin' down a shady lane...

Conor could hear the dog howling from his dog flat at the bottom of the stairs, but Mrs. Kaplan had made it clear she would rather host a pack of coyotes in her parlor than that "insufferable hound." Mrs. Kaplan would never know that the dog had been spending the coldest of nights inside Conor's flat.

The conversation about fatherhood would have to wait, but he knew Rebecca by then. He knew she wanted nothing from him, only that he help give her someone to love—more than that, someone to live for. She would not expect Conor's financial support, not even his participation in raising the child. That in itself was a problem. He could never abandon her with his child—their child. Either he would summon the courage to say "no," or they would marry if she became pregnant.

Knowing Rebecca, she had already considered the issues of stigma and childcare that would make having a baby difficult for a forty-year-old woman with a career in a male-dominated field in the Edwardian Age. She would have thought it all through, carefully, before even broaching the subject. Halfway through the final chorus of the song, he looked at Rebecca across the piano. The glow in her eyes and the sheer joy on her face in that moment obviated the need for any discussion on the subject tonight.

Of course he would have a child with Rebecca. A part of him still knew that marriage was not a good option for them, at least not an honest one. Still, he was not doing this for himself but for Rebecca. For whatever reason, she saw a life for herself in this solution. If not happiness, then at least a meaningful life with the love and commitment a child brings. But if marriage was what she wanted...

Chapter 16

Sixteen days before the royal tunnel tour, Conor was dictating to his new secretary, Mrs. Schmidt, a no-nonsense woman of advanced middle age. They happened to be working on the Nellie Finley case, scheduled for court the day after tomorrow, when Dr. Martinovsky walked in the door.

"That's all for now, Mrs. Schmidt. You can get started on that, and we'll finish later." Then he turned to Martinovsky—"Good day, Doctor"—and pointed to the chair opposite his desk. "Thank you for stopping by. Please, have a seat."

After Mrs. Schmidt took the doctor's coat, he said to Conor, "Thank you. I have zee report."

Conor had been dictating alternative court motions for possible filing in the Nellie Finley murder case. The first was a formal notice of his intent to raise the issue of insanity and would be filed in the event Martinovsky rendered a written opinion confirming Nellie's insanity. The other, which he had been authoring only moments ago, was a request to extend the time for filing of pretrial motions to be filed if Martinovsky needed more time or if his report required further study. The latter was the more likely option as the emergence of Charles Bennett III into this case raised sinister possibilities that would take time to explore. Every detail of Nellie's life prior to the child's death would be gold to the psychiatrist. Curious, Conor thought, that the Russian had given virtually no consideration thus far to all the blank spaces in Nellie's history.

Conor was not expecting to hear from Martinovsky yet, but he decided instantly to hear the alienist out completely and sample his wares before disclosing any new information.

Martinovsky removed a document from his attaché and handed it to Conor. "I feeneesh report. Kheere is oreeginal for judge. Zees patient eez insane ven she jump from breedge veeth child and could not know zees vas wrong."

The announcement caught Conor off guard. He had been expecting the psychiatrist to take more time, at least make additional visits with Nellie. "When did you examine Miss Finley?"

"Monday afternoon."

Conor reviewed the surprisingly brief report. The document was only two pages, all in proper form and perfect English—not surprising as foreign-born doctors were always careful about such things as grammar and were known to use editors. It listed all of the documents and records reviewed and referred to a patient examination at the Hull House facility. Curiously, his "findings" during the examination were minimal. The report said simply that the patient was minimally responsive to questioning. His diagnosis was "acute, trauma-induced melancholia" and it was his expert opinion that Nellie was "insane at the time of the offense and that, due to her insanity, was incapable of distinguishing between right and wrong." Martinovsky's resume was included as an addendum. It was a bold opinion, Conor thought, based on flimsy evidence.

"Tell us about the examination, Doctor," Conor began.

"Een zee seemplest terms, zees young vooman's brain has partially shut down, meanink eet eez in state of lockdown and hass ceased to communicate and react. Zees is common among veemen who suffer great emotional trauma. Zee brain compensates by blocking painful or traumatic memories, sometimes all memories. Zees not diagnosis, but only seemtome of zee brain disease of melancholia, also acute depression. Most important eez zat zees condition exeested at zee moment she stepped off zee bridge."

How can he know that within a reasonable degree of medical certainty? Since last speaking to the Russian, Conor and Rebecca had opened doors into Nellie's miserable life prior to her jump, doors through which they had yet to enter, all pathways into Nellie's mind. This psychiatrist did not know any of those details either. None of it was in his file. Nellie never told him, and he had never even expressed an interest. The man simply made critical assumptions. The fact that he guessed correctly did not boost his credibility in Conor's eyes. Yet, he had reached the conclusion Conor needed   .

"So how long will she be like this?" Conor asked.

"Eempossible to say." Martinovsky explained that thousands of war veterans had endured identical diagnoses, but the science had not yet evolved although study of these veterans helped drive an evolution in psychiatry. Nellie's current condition, he opined, by its very nature, indicated a long history of melancholia before the alleged murder.

Conor thought about asking the doctor the obvious question: *"If she can't communicate her experiences to you, how do you know the death of the child is not what caused her condition?"* He held his tongue because he was now swimming in deep water. If he disclosed even the sketchy information about Nellie's relationship with Charles Bennett III, the doctor would have to rewrite his report or be prepared to admit under cross-examination that he had ignored the information in his report.

The Bennett information might even be explosive very soon and seriously supportive of an insanity opinion. But rewriting the report now was not an option. The man had handed Conor a copy of the report only seconds ago. Conor now was legally and ethically required to show it to the prosecutor if he raised insanity in the case. The doctor could amend or supplement his report, of course, but the damage would be done.

If Conor, on the other hand, said nothing more to Martinovsky, he would have a favorable expert opinion in his hands, certainly sufficient to avoid the death penalty and probably enough to negotiate a manageable sentence of twenty years or so. But this opinion would never result in a not guilty verdict. A good cross-examiner would excoriate this alienist on the witness stand. There was simply no evidence in the man's report that would exclude the child's traumatic death as a sole cause of her insanity. Only the state of her mind and the sum of her experiences *before* the jump could be considered by a jury. This doctor simply rushed out a careless and haphazard opinion. *Why?*

Looking at Martinovsky across the desk, Conor repeated the question to himself. *If she can't give you a history, how do you know the death of the child is not what caused her condition?* After considering all the possible consequences, Conor decided it prudent not to open that can of worms. He would work with what he had.

The lawyer had another important issue to explore with the Russian alienist before ending the session. The altruistic alderman O'Sullivan was on Conor's mind.

"Doctor, I will speak frankly with you. If you should ultimately testify for the defense at trial, the prosecutor will ask you on cross-examination about your fee: how much you were paid and who paid you. They're entitled to explore your motives to testify for Miss Finley. It goes to your credibility, so I need to know what your sworn answer will be. Do you understand what I mean?"

"I receive no fee in zees case, as you know. I veel use my notes and experience to further my research in psychiatry."

"Are you being blackmailed by anyone or threatened or coerced in any way to aid the defense?

"No."

"Did anyone promise you anything in exchange for a favorable opinion in this case?"

"No."

Sometimes, practicing criminal law entailed walking a line, and Conor learned that much in his short career. He had asked all the questions he needed to ask about Martinovsky's fee, so he hesitated before asking the final question. Technically, he did not need to ask it, but *technically*, he wanted the answer, even if it exploded in his face. "What is your relationship with Alderman O'Sullivan?"

Notably, the question did not seem to rattle Martinovsky. He might have been expecting it. He said, "Vee are friends. Vee are both dedicated to helping community." Then the old man huffed. "I am not creeminal, Mr. Dolan. Alderman seemply asked me to help zees young woman as a kindness."

"Of course." Truth or lie, his answer took Conor Dolan off the ethical hook. The Russian was doing this because he loved humanity. Conor had no reason to push it, not now anyway. Besides, it did not take an alienist to see that poor Nellie Finley had lost her mind.

Still, Conor thought, if the psychiatrist knew everything Conor knew, if he had waited for Conor and Rebecca to finish investigating, his opinion might have been stronger and better supported but would not have changed substantively. So Conor decided to leave well enough alone. There was no reason to extend the conversation. What Martinovsky did not know, he could not be cross-examined on. If the facts warranted it, Conor could always have the man prepare a supplemental report before trial.

THE DOG WAS WAITING OUTSIDE FOR CONOR WHEN HE CLOSED UP the office at five o'clock, and the two of them headed into the wind along Custom House Street. They crossed paths with the lamplighter, fighting off the descending darkness lamp by lamp with his horse and cart. It would not be long until the flip of a single switch would illuminate the entire city with electricity.

They passed Andy Murphy's Bar only a block from his flat, and he decided to pay the proprietor a quick visit before dinner. The dog would have stopped in front of the place anyway. It was becoming a habit, even on Saturday. The day drinkers were sleeping it off, and the night drinkers were just vacating the stockyards, mills, and factories, leaving a comfortable section of bar for Conor and the dog. Murph always enjoyed the opportunity for conversation.

The proprietor was already drawing a beer as Conor dropped a few coins on the bar. "Good afternoon, Counselor, Dog," said Murphy, placing a full beer glass onto the bar and a small bowl beside it. First one for Dog is on the house," Murph announced. "After that it's a penny a bowl and so on and so forth."

"Thanks, Murph," Conor replied. "You know, I didn't want to give him a name for fear of abusing his independence, but I think Dog is a good compromise. I like it, and he's been hearing it anyway."

"Just promise me you won't go all Jack Johnson on me this afternoon, Counselor," Murph joked. "Oh, I almost forgot. Your priest buddy left a note for you last night. Being the nocturnal creature he is, he didn't want to bother your landlady on the Sabbath." Murph reached behind the cash register and retrieved a folded note, which he placed on the bar. "Brendan figured you'd be stopping after work today, you being a practicing member of God's one true Church and so on and so forth."

Conor downed a healthy sip from the glass, then unfolded the note:

Conor, come by the rectory in the evening when possible to discuss my visit with Bennett's housekeeper, Kate Rowland. That poor child, Nellie, lived through more misery than you will ever know.

—Brendan

Conor stuffed the note into his coat pocket and headed for the door. Dog was not happy; he had beer left. "When he finishes this beer, send him home, Murph."

Conor figured he would grab something to eat on the way back from seeing Brendan. Mrs. Kaplan would not be pleased, but it could not be helped. The Clark Streetcar would be the best way up to Father Brendan's parish.

On the streetcar, he considered the note's implications. It could only mean Kate Rowland revealed some incriminating details of Bennett's conduct toward Nellie Finley. They had been expecting that. But was Bennett the father? Did he force himself on the girl? Worse yet, did Bennett have any active role in what happened on the bridge? But the more helpful the information, the more horrifying the experience for poor Nellie. That reality quickly tempered Conor's natural, lawyerly excitement.

AFTER CLIMBING THE RECTORY'S STEEP STAIRS, CONOR NEARLY keeled over and back down into the street when Kate Rowland, Charles Bennett's housekeeper, answered the door. "Good evenin', Mr. Dolan," she said pleasantly. "The good Father has been expecting you. He was just sitting down to dinner. May I fix ye a plate?"

All he could think of to say was, "You…work here now?"

She smiled broadly, as one does when proudly announcing a promotion. "Indeed I do, sir, and sure I live here now as well with a beautiful suite of two rooms I share with Mrs. Fogarty. We even have our own toilet closet."

Conor smiled. "Lovely. I'd be delighted to dine with the good Father."

OVER A DELICIOUS LAMB STEW, FATHER BRENDAN RECOUNTED his conversation with Kate Rowland. The woman had been living in a state of terror and only opened up to Brendan because he offered her a job and a place to live. She felt the priest would protect her. She knew

Bennett had repeatedly assaulted Nellie sexually over the course of her employment. Nellie was planning to go home to Ireland, distraught and completely unraveled by the situation. But before she could save the money, she got pregnant. It was not long until the world could see her dilemma, and Bennett threw her into the street, even accused her of being a whore.

The housekeeper was fond of Nellie but not in a position to help. Nellie came back about two months later with a baby, but Bennett would not see her. He had the housekeeper give the girl twenty dollars and deliver a message that he would have Nellie arrested if she came back. When he had gotten it all out, Father Brendan added, "I think she knows more—and she can cook."

"But will she put all that on paper for me?" Conor asked.

"I'd say she would now. She loves her new job."

ON THE COMMUTE HOME, HE TRIED TO PUT HIMSELF IN NELLIE's place during those many months of her nightmare. Nellie knew that, for an immigrant girl in Chicago, unemployment meant homelessness, and homelessness was a death sentence—or worse. No immigrant woman could find alternative employment without a current reference. This was the reality that bonded her to Charles Bennett III in a savage state of slavery. The poor child must have curled up in her bed night after night in terror, knowing that the lock on her door offered no protection from the satanic creature prowling the hallways.

Whatever hardships and pain Conor endured in Ireland paled in comparison to this child's nightmare, and try as he might, he could not put his mind into her sacrificial bed in the dark room in that evil house. Nothing in his life prepared him for that task.

Such was Kevin's protective umbrella over little Conor Dolan that the boy's awareness of the cruelty, hardship, and poverty in Ireland—not to mention on the oceanic voyage—came largely from secondhand accounts of Springfield relatives and books and newspapers. His memories of the family's burning cottage and the drunken constables remained his only firsthand experience with colonial barbarity.

There was no Kevin Dolan in Nellie's life. She had no brother to turn to, no mother, no priest—only the long torturous ordeal to relive every day and every night, over and over. In the Bennett house, she lived completely alone with her misery, and her only crime was being an Irish immigrant, a girl forced from her own land by foreign plunderers into a hell of someone else's making.

Conor thought briefly about killing Charles Bennett himself. He could do it. He could get Rebecca to help; she would know how. They could surveil Bennett for a week or two, find his favorite restaurants, his barber, maybe his mistress's flat. They would do it at night. Bennett would appear from a doorway and head for his new Ford. Two hooded figures would emerge from an alley, one holding a shotgun, the other a pistol and…it's done, and the world's a better place.

But killing the man would be an act of desperation, and Conor was still far from desperate. Bennett was a dangerous and vile predator, a criminal, and Conor a trained and skilled officer of the court. His primary mission in the Finley case was still to save Nellie from an unjust verdict. But, in the process, he swore to himself that Charles Bennet III would be made to pay for his transgressions—one way or another.

Chapter 17

Even with less than two weeks until the tunnel ceremony, Nellie Finley's case required attention. "Ah, good morning, Mr. Dolan," said the Honorable James Buck, peering down from his throne. Conor was not surprised the judge remembered his name; the newspaper assault on the Finley prosecution had already begun. Nellie stood beside Conor passively, a burly bailiff nearby. "Seems we're here for the filing of pretrial motions this morning, gentlemen." He looked at the young prosecutor, Mr. Groth. "Anything from the State?"

"No, Your Honor."

"All right, then," said Buck, turning to Conor. "Looks like Mr. Dolan has something interesting in his hand."

"Yes, Your Honor." Conor handed up the original with a copy to the prosecution. "The defense seeks leave to file its Notice of Intent to raise the issue of insanity. A report of the expert psychiatrist is attached, finding my client was legally insane at the time of the offense."

"Mr. Dolan, does the opinion address the defendant's fitness to stand trial?"

"It does not, Your Honor."

"Very well," said Buck. "And there is no petition before this court alleging mental unfitness to stand trial. Is that correct?"

Conor answered like the lawyer he was. "Not at this time, Your Honor."

Both Buck and the prosecutor seemed almost giddy—at the very least, relieved—because all the lawyers knew that an insanity opinion would likely generate an easy negotiation for manslaughter. For Nellie, Conor figured, there was no downside. He could always withdraw the insanity plea, try the case without the issue being raised, or file a supplemental report later.

Buck announced, "Leave is granted to file the notice and report. The prosecution will have sixty days to reply. See my clerk for a motion date. Oh, gentlemen, how is discovery proceeding? Any potential issues you are aware of?"

Both counsels agreed that discovery was proceeding without issue although Conor made a record of the fact that his investigation was ongoing and he expected to name additional witnesses going forward.

Outside the courtroom, Groth caught up with Conor at the top of the staircase. "Mr. Dolan," he said politely, "do you have a minute?" It was a good sign. Conor had made inquiries about Groth. The man was known to be overzealous generally in his prosecutions but was considered to be a person of integrity and good character, itself a rarity here.

Prosecutors in murder cases did not chase down defense lawyers in the hallway for an audience unless they were holding a bad hand. *I have an hour if this is what I think it is,* but he said simply, "Of course," and the two men settled onto a wooden bench along the wall. "I'm at your disposal, Mr. Groth."

"Well, sir," Groth began, "the insanity opinion certainly casts this case in a different light, and my boss wants only justice for both the poor victim and for the defendant."

Is he going to do it now without even reviewing the opinion in detail and consulting with the State's Attorney? Apparently, their consultation had already taken place in a cart-before-the-horse kind of way. For the State's Attorney, this was the way out of a prickly case. "I'm happy to hear that, Mr. Groth, but my idea of justice for Nellie Finley is a dismissal of all charges." Conor had no reason to kiss the man's arse. If the prosecutor was in a begging mood, make him sit up on his hind legs and bark, he thought. No lawyer ever got a concession by exhibiting weakness.

Mr. Groth came straight to the issue, no doubt as instructed. "I'm going to make a hard offer on a reduced charge of manslaughter: ten years in the penitentiary. Please don't answer now. Take some time to discuss it with your client and consider the implications. Contact me whenever you want to talk."

Lawyer negotiation was a foreign language to most English speakers, an exercise in nuance and insincerity, implied ultimatum, and surrender. Such a conversation usually required careful consideration and analysis after the fact to unravel the subtle messages and innuendo. It was perpetual gamesmanship. Had they been playing chess, Conor concluded, Mr. Groth would have just checkmated himself with a bad move.

Because of the prosecutor's loose tongue, Conor now knew that the state's real bottom line sentence was likely between five and eight years, not the ten Groth had articulated. Had it been a serious offer, Groth would have ended with, "Contact me *with your answer.*" Instead, he had said, "Contact me *to talk.*" Groth was negotiating against himself and was most likely aware of it. "I'll do just that, sir, thank you."

Only a fool would discuss the plea offer without time for further study and analysis. As Conor got up to leave, Groth added, "We will have to pursue our own psychiatric opinion very shortly." Then the man shrugged his shoulders. "So I'm afraid the offer will be automatically withdrawn in three days."

I doubt that very much, Conor said to himself. He tipped his homburg. "Good day, Mr. Groth, and thank you."

On the walk back to his office, Conor thought about the hastily conceived plea offer. It occurred to him that maybe it was not truly hasty. After all, everyone was acting like the case was already over. It was as if all the players were hoping—even expecting—that Conor would raise insanity. They wanted this case to go away and concluded that Conor was on board with the script.

Of course, ten years was out of the question now, but a plea made sense. The current Cook County State's Attorney was a hardcore reformer and not a fan of the corrupt city administration, but the man was a Protestant Anglo-Saxon who could likely trace his ancestors back to Plymouth Rock and cared nothing for one lowly Irish maid. He would simply welcome a quiet resolution to this troublesome case.

The sympathetic newspaper barrage was raging in favor of Nellie Finley with no winning hand in sight for the prosecutor's office. Reform organizations across the city engaged in a coordinated campaign to generate sympathy, prodded by a certain activist priest with a pipeline into the political cesspool. If he played his cards right, Conor thought, he might get Nellie three or four years. *But don't get greedy, Boy-o.*

The likelihood of a favorable plea offer raised a new issue. In order for the Court to enter Nellie's guilty plea, she would have to convince Judge Buck that she understood the nature of the pleadings, the roles of the judge and lawyers, and that her plea was voluntary. It would necessarily involve in-depth questioning, and poor Nellie Finley was simply not there yet.

Just before lunch, Conor noticed a crowd gathering on the street in front of Dr. Camp's office. He recognized some of the people as local business owners and neighborhood residents. Some were carrying crude signs. One said, "White Women White Doctors." The barber across the street, an Irishman from Mayo, no less, held up one side of a white bed sheet with his wife at the other end: "No Nigger Infiltrators Here." *An Irishman and his Irish wife*, Conor thought.

Apparently spotting Conor on the sidewalk, the doctor walked out of his office with a surprisingly stoic look. Ignoring the rumblings from the crowd, he said, "Mr. Dolan, can you spare a minute for a talk?"

"Of course. Come in." Turning to the crowd, he looked directly at the barber who had cut his hair only last week. "You won't be seeing me in your shop again, Flanagan. You have a short memory. Shame on all of you."

They shouted obscenities at Conor, and one threw a rock that shattered the doctor's front window, drawing the landlord to the door beside Conor and the doctor. Raising his arms, the man pleaded with the crowd. "Please, don't destroy *my* property over this. I had no idea the man is a Negro. I assure you the doctor is leaving today."

Conor sneered at the greedy little man. "See if you can keep your friends away for a few more minutes."

Inside Conor's office, the doctor explained that the landlord had just paid him a visit and demanded he vacate the office immediately. The man expressed sympathy, even offered to pay for the move, and give the doctor fifty dollars, but he was emphatic that the move was not optional.

According to the doctor, the two colored men in that delivery wagon the other day were not just deliverymen. The doctor introduced them yesterday to a mortified patient as his father and brother. The patient fled the building, and by this morning, the street was abuzz with vicious gossip.

The landlord appeared inside forthwith, frantically declaring to the doctor that he would be ruined and driven to the poor house were he to knowingly allow a Negro doctor to occupy his premises, let alone treat white women with his hands. When the doctor reminded him that the two had signed a contract, the landlord's response was chilling. He would not, he insisted, be responsible for the doctor's safety and would hold Dr. Camp responsible for any uncovered damage to the property in the event of mob action.

Dr. Camp was surprisingly realistic about the whole affair and simply sought Conor's help in moving some of his more valuable equipment to a place of safety.

Conor's first reaction was disbelief that quickly morphed into defiance. "I'm a lawyer," he reminded Dr. Camp. "I'll bring suit on your behalf. Surely, you'd win and accrue damages in addition to the right to stay."

Dr. Camp flashed a look of...*what? Amusement?* "Your heart is in the right place, Mr. Dolan, but have you ever considered what it might feel like to be lynched...or tied onto a horse blindfolded? My father was right. He warned me this would happen. *'Stay here in the colored neighborhood and help your own people,'* he said. The thing is, I never thought about it. I didn't lie or hide my racial identity. As a doctor, a light-skinned Negro doctor, I just haven't had the same experiences as my family."

The doctor's perspective made sense, Conor thought. The man would gain nothing through confrontation. If life was difficult for female Irish immigrants in this city, it was downright dangerous to any Negro who defied the de facto rules of segregation. Even if the man fought the eviction and won, he had examined his last patient in that office. He would never see another white patient here, and Negroes had no reason to travel to this neighborhood for medical care. They had their own hospital. Monroe Camp was being sensible and practical, no more and no less. *Had there not been a war over this? Was this to be the permanent state of freedom for freed slaves and their descendants? And what of the thousands of Negroes who risked their lives in service to the Union cause?*

WITH A RENTED WAGON, THE TWO MEN LOADED UP AS MUCH AS they could into the bed and headed out into the cold for the South Side, Dr. Camp at the reins. It was not the way Conor had expected to spend his afternoon.

One could never take this city for granted, he thought. It was always there, ready to jump up and knock you down. Sometimes you could see the trouble with your eyes, other times it ambushed you. The former situation was more manageable. If one disdained debauchery and depraved human conditions such as extreme poverty, one could largely avoid the sight of them by avoiding places where they were known to fester. *If you don't see it, then it doesn't exist.* He suspected the practice was routine for folks on Astor Street and Prairie Avenue.

The depravity in men's hearts, however, was another matter entirely. It was as formless as a cloud and as pervasive as the air we breathe. It might confront you in your own home or in the street. It might draw you in without consent and force you to face demons in your own soul. As a child, Conor himself rooted for his brother, Kevin, to wipe out the wild Indians when the latter served out West in the cavalry. There was no sanctimony or self-righteousness in Conor's feelings, only disappointment.

Conor never experienced open hatred in Springfield. Pettiness?—yes. Cruelty?—of course, but not these things, things specifically designed to debase and destroy human beings face-to-face. The ugliness one could see with one's eyes was bad, but the ugliness one could not see was infinitely worse. Nellie Finley knew, somewhere in the void of her broken mind; she knew all too well of such things.

Crime, corruption, vice, and hate permeated the city like the damp soot of industry, enveloping the entire population, punctuated here and there by technological advancement, art, wealth, and the breathtaking beauty of the lakefront. If there were a natural scale of evil for the four iniquities, hate was the worst because the only way to fix it was to alter human nature.

Nobody was immune to the iniquities. Conor Dolan was a corrupt lawyer, he admitted to himself. Was he not on the payroll of at least one alderman, one beat cop, and two court clerks? There was no such thing as "a little bit" corrupt. Someday, someone would try to leverage his corruption. What then? But at least corruption was not hate.

Had Springfield really been different? Or had Conor Dolan simply not been paying attention? Maybe it was only a matter of cramming too many people with too many differences into too small a space. *Ten people confined in a small room—one with smallpox—versus the same ten people scattered across the Great Plains.*

They drove the wagon south on State Street through a corridor of Negro housing, long and narrow, only a couple of blocks wide, but stretching from Roosevelt clear down past Forty-Seventh Street where they unloaded at the house of Camp's father. A post-fire dwelling constructed of brick, it was well maintained, painted, and had a nice lawn—clearly the home of a prosperous man. But the area of Negro housing was different; prosperous, middle-class people lived side by side with their poverty-stricken neighbors.

The doctor introduced his mother, who invited Conor to dinner, but Conor sensed the family would have other fish to fry that evening and politely declined. The doctor's parents had no notice of the sudden move, yet asked no questions of their son as if they fully understood the situation. The restraint was conspicuous, and Conor wondered whether it was simply a product of experience. Dr. Camp was severely wronged that day, but he had a place to go—people to turn to, confide in, and draw support from. *Maybe it's the lack of those things that makes people go mad.*

On the ride back in the empty wagon, the doctor explained that his father owned a successful restaurant on the South Side and had accumulated enough money to send his son, Monroe Camp Jr., to the University of Chicago with the aid of a scholarship and then on to medical school.

"What will you do now?"

"I'll get back to work," Camp declared. "I worked five years at Provident Hospital. I imagine they'll welcome me back for another five."

"What about having your own practice?"

The doctor turned to him and smiled. "I come from very determined people, Mr. Dolan. I consider myself privileged. My grandfather was a slave in Mississippi, and my mother's two brothers fought for the Union. I will start saving, start preparing, and try again one day. But I'll think more carefully about my address."

Conor offered his hand. "Well, wherever you go, you're my doctor as long as I'm here."

"Fair enough," Dr. Camp replied, smiling, "but best not mention it to your neighbors."

Chapter 18

Conor was not surprised to find O'Sullivan waiting comfortably on the office sofa early Wednesday morning with eleven days left before Conor's date with the Prince of Wales. Mrs. Schmidt, Conor's secretary, was still wearing her coat. She seemed relieved that Conor was on time and delighted to be rid of the stuffy alderman. She took Conor's coat and hat. "Coffee, Mr. Dolan?" she asked.

He nodded. The men shook hands politely and settled down for a chat, Conor into the comfortable armchair Dr. Camp had given him. "You're fortunate to have caught me, Mr. O'Sullivan. I nearly headed directly to court."

"I see you've acquired a telephone since my last visit," the alderman observed, looking at Conor's desk. "I shall phone ahead next time."

"Marvelous invention. Now then, how may I assist you, sir?"

"It's about our mutual cause célèbre: poor Nellie Finley. I was delighted to hear that Dr. Martinovsky has been of service to you. I'm told he has rendered a favorable opinion and you've given notice to the court of your intent to raise her insanity in the case."

"Yes." Conor wondered whether the alderman's knowledge extended beyond the public record of a court proceeding. "I was very pleased to get his expert opinion." He would not volunteer any more information. If the alderman had another purpose for this visit, Conor would not help him disguise it.

"May I ask whether the report has generated any change of attitude from that damned prosecutor's office?" *Does he know about the ten-year offer or not? More importantly, why would this self-important jackass consider Nellie Finley's plight worthy of his personal attention over something as mundane as plea negotiations?* The alderman's standard practice was to dispatch heelers and precinct captains to conduct his off-the-record shenanigans. There appeared to be an invisible engine driving this train.

For whatever reason, O'Sullivan maintained a direct pipeline to the helpful Russian psychiatrist but held no influence in the State's Attorney's Office. Frustration and anxiety drove his visit to Conor's office today, the lawyer thought. The real reason for the alderman's involvement in the Finley matter was not altruism but something sinister; that much was clear now. O'Sullivan needed inside information on the case. *He has nowhere else to go for what he needs, so he goes to the horse's mouth. It must be humiliating for him.* But what was driving the alderman's obsession with Nellie Finley's welfare? Could there be a connection between Alderman O'Sullivan and Charles Bennett III? The possibility was growing more likely all the time.

Conor decided to be coy rather than lie. "It certainly will help. Now the prosecutor will need to engage his own experts."

"Have they made you an offer?" O'Sullivan asked directly. If the man knew about the pending plea offer, he was doing a good job of concealing it.

The door opened, and the mailman walked in carrying his bag and a handful of mail. For Conor, it was an opportunity to terminate the awkward conversation.

He rose to greet the postman. "Good morning, John. I'll take the mail. Thanks. I was just on my way out."

There was only one option for Conor, and it would not serve either man's objective. Returning to the chair, he said, "Alderman, I'd better head for court or I'll be late." Extending his hand, he added, "I'm certain you can appreciate the sanctity of the attorney-client relationship and confidential information. I wouldn't feel right discussing the substance of plea negotiations, if in fact there were such talks in progress, especially before those negotiations were finalized. I'd consider them confidential. Thank you for coming by personally." *That should get rid of him.*

O'Sullivan made no move to leave, seemingly considering his options, and possibly feeling boxed in. Finally, he stood up from the sofa. "I've taken enough of your time, sir." As they moved toward the door, he added, "You see, I'm worried about the poor girl. Could you simply tell me whether she would be inclined to accept a shorter prison sentence if the prosecutor were to reduce the charge? It would be a terrible risk to go forward on the murder charge."

He's trying to push me toward a plea. Why?

As Conor reached for the front door, Father Brendan appeared with Kate Rowland in tow. They were early. The woman was scheduled to give her sworn statement at half past nine. Conor's lie about being late for court was exposed to the underhanded alderman. *Just as well. Let him squirm.*

If O'Sullivan was shocked, he concealed it well. If he knew the woman's identity and her relationship to the Finley case, his expression did not betray him. Surprisingly, he held out his hand to Brendan, smiling. "Father White, what a pleasant surprise. In need of a criminal lawyer, are you?"

On second thought, it should be no surprise that two prominent politicians were well acquainted. The men exchanged pleasantries, and O'Sullivan left without an introduction to Kate Rowland. Conor's multi-talented priest friend could even assume the ethos of a rodent when his altruistic obsessions demanded it.

In contrast to Conor's first meeting with the housekeeper, Kate seemed remarkably relaxed and confident that morning, and he credited the improvement to his friend Father Brendan White. Conor conducted the interview with only himself, Rebecca, and Mrs. Schmidt, the secretary, in the room. Mrs. Schmidt would formally witness the interview and statement signature. She would make a perfect witness—a *prover* lawyers called it—in the unlikely event Kate Rowland would disavow the statement later. He had Brendan take a long walk while he conducted the business. Conor knew the whole story already from Father Brendan, but now it had to come formally in Kate's own words with no unnecessary third party present to avoid the appearance of impropriety.

Kate began to paint a portrait of young Nellie Finley as a woman living in terror of her employer, Charles Bennett III, and under constant assault from Bennett, who was basically a compulsive sexual abuser.

According to Kate, Nellie was initially delighted with her new position in the Bennett household, and her employer treated the young girl politely and with deference. Nellie and Kate formed an instant bond, and within a few months, Kate confided in her young co-worker that Bennett was not who he seemed and had severely abused another Irish girl the prior year.

"Is the girl still in town?" Conor asked. "Do you know how we might contact her?" Finding another victim would put another arrow in Conor's quiver.

"I'm sorry, but I haven't a clue. If the poor thing is alive in the city, it's likely she's fallen prey to *immoral* practices, Lord have mercy on the poor soul."

Despite Kate's warnings, Nellie stayed on with Bennett, and all was good for a number of months until Bennett's mood changed and he began drinking heavily. Kate had seen the pattern before and warned Nellie again, but to no avail. One night, he burst into Nellie's room after a bout of drinking and forced himself violently upon the young maiden. Kate described her anguish as she listened to every vile moment of the attack from the next room, powerless to halt the assault.

"Why didn't Nellie leave after the first attack?" Conor asked.

"Ah, sure it's an easy t'ing t' say but the child had nowhere t' go."

Bennett would be well behaved for a period of time, sometimes lasting weeks, before engaging in a late-night bout of drinking at home or out with friends before descending into a state of unrestrained savagery. During such episodes, young Nellie Finley simply could find no refuge in the house, Kate explained. During the six-month nightmare, Nellie endured no fewer than half a dozen such assaults. According to Kate, whose room was down the hall, Nellie would scream at first, perhaps through the third such incident. Thereafter, the poor girl would try to prepare herself and lie as stoically as possible while Bennett had his way.

All the time, Kate recounted, Nellie frantically sought other employment, but no reputable employer would accept an Irish girl without a letter from Bennett. During the duration of this nightmare, Bennett constantly threatened both Nellie and Kate against going to the police. If either of them spoke of the abuse, he would ensure that both women would starve to death on the street. The details were even worse than Conor had imagined.

As Conor carefully approached the topic of Nellie's pregnancy, Mrs. Schmidt seemed to sense his awkwardness and came to his rescue. She simply picked up the questioning in a natural, low-key way. "Now, Mrs. Rowland, did there come a time when you became aware that Nellie was with child?"

Kate nodded. "Yes, ma'am."

"And how did you come to learn that?" He thought he might have to give his secretary a raise in pay.

"She told me privately one night although I had figured for several days the poor child was in that state. She asked what to do, how to handle the situation. I told her we should both go to the Mister and confront him together." Kate began to cry, but Mrs. Schmidt consoled her as only a woman could. "I was terrified, but I couldn't watch the child be destroyed, her with a little one inside and all. So we went to the Mister one evening and told him."

With the secretary's gentle support, Kate seemed to become more comfortable in her storytelling. She explained that Bennett seemed truly terrified at the news at first. Then he told the women he would make an appointment with an abortionist forthwith and that Kate would accompany young Nellie to the procedure, after which all would remain as before and Bennett would adjust his behavior.

The women kept Bennett's appointment with the abortionist, whose filthy office they found located in the seediest part of the Levee District. Nellie refused to undergo the procedure. Later that day, Kate Rowland gave Nellie forty dollars from her own savings, and Nellie did not return to the Bennett house. Kate reported that Nellie "fled from the office in a panic and disappeared."

Nellie stayed in touch with Kate and used the money for hotel and food until giving birth at Cook County Hospital. When the money ran out, she came back to the house with the baby to see Bennett—alone, desperate, and begging for help. Bennett threatened her again, gave her twenty dollars, and turned her out onto the street. She used the money for food and a hotel until it ran out and she was evicted. The next Kate heard about Nellie was in the newspapers.

While Mrs. Schmidt prepared the formal statement, they had coffee and chatted. Kate was troubled by her own role in Nellie's nightmare. "I didn't do enough for that child," she declared somberly. "I should have gone to the police straightaway."

"Nonsense, Mrs. Rowland," Conor said. "Drive those thoughts from your head. You did everything you could under the circumstances, and you're very brave to be helping Nellie now."

"She never wanted to leave Ireland, you know," Kate said. "Most of them don't. Sure Ireland is a curs-ed place, Mr. Dolan, and shall remain so until she casts the boot of the invader from her neck."

Kate Rowland was a woman with her own story to tell and her own memories, oppression, and hardship. It had not occurred to Conor before, but Brendan, Rebecca, and he had freed this woman from a form of captivity, slavery even. She was a completely different person from the timid housekeeper who answered their knock on Bennett's door.

The statement transcribed and signed, Conor escorted Kate to the door. He was left almost speechless over the sadistic details of Kate's revelations. He now had the evidence to save Nellie Finley, not only from the death penalty but probably from a five-year prison sentence, and he owed her the duty not to stop there. There just might be more out there, something that might set her free, even if freedom in her state held no real meaning.

He said to Brendan, "I had no idea..."

"Sure we're on the right track now, but when this is all over, there has to be a reckoning for Charles Bennett III."

"I look forward to it. If Nellie jumped off that bridge, we know why, so now let's see if we can find out exactly what happened that night."

Considering Bennett's business—telephone equipment manufacturing—it was not hard to speculate. O'Sullivan, Brendan explained, as Chairman of the City Council Contracts Committee, would be in a perfect position to aid the wealthy industrialist as his committee was responsible for selection of recommended bids and city contracts approval. Even a criminal lawyer could see that contracts for city telephone equipment, including for its many agencies and departments, had to be worth millions. Bennett was likely adding obscene amounts of money to O'Sullivan's coffers in exchange for contracts. And what would they gain with Nellie adjudicated insane and confined to an asylum or sent to prison for ten years? The answer slapped Conor square in the face like a board—*her silence.* It was as if they had already killed her and were looking for a way to get rid of the body.

And if O'Sullivan was helping Bennett—what then? Did the alderman help Bennett, knowing the torture that man inflicted upon Nellie Finley? This would never be over until Conor knew the answer to that question and justice had been dispensed.

Chapter 19

Even with nine days left to foil the Clan plot, Nellie Finley's case could not wait. The Pinkerton Agency provided a carriage for their late-night excursion to the remote bridge from which Nellie supposedly jumped with her newborn. Conor and Rebecca wanted to view the scene at about the same time of night she jumped. He was more suspicious than ever that O'Sullivan was trying to cover up for Charles Bennett III, but what was the linchpin?

On the short trip to the Twenty-Second Street Bridge along the South Branch of the river, he told Rebecca about Kate Rowland's statement and the link between O'Sullivan and Bennett. Conor could almost overlook the run-of-the-mill graft and corruption that permeated Chicago politics, but the thought that O'Sullivan might have knowingly helped cover up Bennett's crimes dogged him like a blister on his heel. It was possible, even plausible, that Bennett kept O'Sullivan in the dark as to why he needed help. In fact, it made perfect sense by Chicago Rules: *da less you know, da better*. Plausible deniability. If that were the case, Conor could live with it. Justice for Nellie did not depend on the answer, but peace of mind for Conor

183

Dolan did. This would never be over until Conor knew the answer and justice was dispensed. He got no argument from Rebecca Fletcher.

The bridge stretched over a dimly lit industrial area about a half mile east of the Levee District. The area was dark and deserted. Conor and Rebecca descended the stairs to water level and viewed the bridge from the dock on the west side of the river. Looking up, they could see the bridge clearly against a slightly moonlit sky. A jumper's silhouette would have stood out because the night she jumped was clear with a half moon. It all confirmed the witnesses' statements.

Two crewmen on a river barge at this dock had spotted her falling then flailing in the current beneath the bridge and managed to save her with a small skiff. The two found no sign of a baby. The bargemen reported the incident to police. Cook County Hospital had records of her childbirth several months earlier, so no one questioned the assumption that her baby was dead. They dredged but never found the baby's body. The report contained personal contact information on the two bargemen, and Rebecca and Conor agreed they should speak with them.

Conor spotted an old skiff tied to the dock not far from where the barge would have been that night. The low-riding craft lay three feet below the dock walkway. "I think I should check out the skiff. I'm certain the police ignored it, and you never know—might find something interesting."

They stood near the dock's edge, looking down toward water level, and Rebecca said, "I can barely see it from here. It's just too dark, Conor. We could come during the day. If you fall…"

Conor was already sitting on the edge of the dock, calculating the easiest way down. "It will be fine, Rebecca. It's only a few feet."

He could make out her face because he was looking up. He could see she was worried. "I can't swim, Conor. Be careful."

Conor eased carefully down the structure and into the little boat. His eyes were completely useless, and he began to feel around the inside of the hull for…anything, hopefully not a fishhook or a sharp knife.

"Are you all right, Conor?"

He felt a life jacket, a small anchor, a cloth of some kind, maybe a wet shirt. "I'm fine. Just another minute."

No sooner had he answered, than Conor heard a muffled scream from the walk above, followed by a scrum of heavy footsteps and stomping on the oak planks. As he moved across the boat toward the structure, he felt the bow come loose and start to drift. Turning to the stern, he saw a man's head and shoulders in silhouette. The man was kneeling, masked he thought though it would hardly have mattered. Before Conor could react, the stern came free and Conor was drifting aimlessly in the South Branch of the Chicago River as Rebecca struggled on the dock with at least two assailants.

He had never felt more helpless. Drifting downriver on a fast current, he dared not hesitate. He would do Rebecca no good from the bottom of the river, and the procedure left him yards further away from a possible rescue. Diving into the oily mess, his body struggled to survive the icy shock of the plunge. Conor willed himself toward the dock where he found the commotion had settled into eerie silence, only the clatter of crickets along the bank to greet him.

Back on the dock—panting, shivering, and streaked with filth— Conor was too late. Not a sign of Rebecca or her attackers, not even the sound of a fleeing horse. *They might still be here, but the carriage? The waiting driver?* He had to make it back up to the carriage before freezing to death, shed the wet shirt, and get a coat. *I must send the driver for the police.*

STILL FREEZING BUT NOW WEARING THE DRIVER'S HEAVY OVER-coat, Conor returned to the scene of Rebecca's abduction. Factories, warehouses, and vacant lots surrounded him in the dark. He was a man groping hopelessly in vain. Why had he left her there alone in such a vulnerable position? He had been so careless. They knew they were being followed. Conor himself was attacked a few weeks ago. Questions dogged him, frozen and exhausted as he was. *Were they the same people who attacked me? If not, then it might have no link to my brother or to the assassination plot. But if it was about the Nellie Finley case, why would Charles Bennett go so far as kidnapping?*

More importantly, why would anyone kidnap Rebecca? The answer could only be to extract information from her. Anyone who wanted her out of the way could have killed her easily and quietly on the dock. Whoever did this did not want Rebecca dead, he figured, not yet anyway.

Try as he might in his diminished state, Conor could think of no reason why the kidnapping would be related to the Nellie Finley case. Charles Bennett wanted Rebecca and Conor gone—not kidnapped. He did not need any information from them. His story was self-contained. Exposure was Bennett's problem. Bennett would have killed her straightaway.

The logical suspect was the Clan na Gael rogue faction preparing to assassinate the Prince of Wales. They would want to know how close Rebecca and Conor were getting to them and whether it was still safe to proceed with their plan. If it was the Clan faction who had taken Rebecca, it meant they knew nothing of Rebecca's interactions with the tunnel company. He hoped Rebecca would have the sense to tell them everything. Knowing their plot was exposed, surely they would abort the operation. Then they would have no need to kill Rebecca and risk a murder charge.

What about Maureen? They knew Conor was in contact with Maureen Brogan, but that would not raise alarm bells because they were foolishly confident that Maureen was oblivious to their plot. Still, Maureen's contacts with Conor had increased lately, raising the possibility that she picked up valuable information from him. At this point, he knew Maureen was in danger, and her safety was his responsibility.

At last, Conor saw the light from lamps approaching in the distance from the direction of the bridge. Barely conscious, he stumbled toward the light. The police had arrived…but Rebecca Fletcher was gone.

Conor woke up in a bed at Provident Hospital. Someone had checked him into a private room the night before, but all he could remember was that feeling of numbness and peace that descends right before you freeze to death. Then he recalled Rebecca's kidnapping and tried to swing his feet onto the floor. Dizziness overtook him sitting on the bed. He was facing a window that sometimes appeared to be two or three windows, but it was early because the sun was still low in the sky, unless that was an electric light.

"Easy, Mr. Dolan," came a familiar voice from the door. He eased back down onto the bed until the face of his friend Dr. Camp came into view above him. Maybe they were twins, he thought. "You'll be all right in a little while. We'll get some more fluids into you and get you something to eat."

"So I guess I didn't freeze to death," he managed to say.

"Not far from it, but no permanent damage. Your friend got you here just in time. He's in the waiting room now. I'll order you some food, then we'll get you into a wheelchair. We'll have you walking before lunch. Then you can resume your *interesting* lifestyle."

As the doctor turned to leave, Conor asked, "What day is it?"

"Sunday," said Camp.

"What happened to Saturday?" Conor asked with no humor intended.

Beyond a doubt, the Clan na Gael was killing and kidnapping people. He did not know which group was behind the deeds: the official Clan hierarchy or the rogue faction. Worse than that, he was not sure which players played for which team: the police chief and Detective Flynn, the Hoyne Avenue man, even his own brother, Kevin. Not that a dead man figured into the equation at this point.

He was in the wheelchair when Victor Harris, the Pinkerton, entered the room. It was nearly eleven in the morning, and his only thought at that moment was to get out of the hospital. "Victor, glad to see you. Help me get out of this damn chair. I need to leave this place."

As they wheeled out of the room, Victor said, "Dr. Camp told me to get you walking down the hallway. As soon as you get steady on your feet, we can get out of here. Oh, the police have nothing on Rebecca's kidnapping."

Conor turned his head and flashed Victor an angry stare. "You reported it to the police?"

"Easy, Counselor," Victor cautioned. "I think you need to slow down and think." The big man opened his jacket to expose the "Pinkerton Detective" badge pinned on the inside. "Rebecca was one of us. She was a Pinkerton. We guarded presidents. We investigate political assassinations all over the world."

"You did once," Conor snapped. "But you don't anymore. No offense, but now Pinkerton is more of a giant labor-busting, goon force. People haven't forgotten the Pullman and Homestead strikes. Paid thugs for industrialist millionaires. So don't pull that 'leave it in our hands' malarkey with me, Victor. It's just a company churning money."

Victor was not a particularly imposing figure, lean and muscular for a man in his fifties. Victor's big smile had likely played a role in his success at Pinkerton. But now Conor was facing the other side of that big smile. It was fierce and equally emotive. He had touched a nerve.

"Well, the decision to report her abduction wasn't yours to make," Victor admonished. "Besides, there was no other choice, and you know it. The report won't make her situation with Flynn or the police chief any worse, and we need there to be an official investigation. Our agents will be supplementing the cops anyway."

Conor's legs were already feeling stronger as they slowly walked the hallway and he had stopped seeing everything in bouncing pairs. "Of course, the cops have nothing," he said. "They're probably holding her somewhere right now or…"

He was walking on his own now with Victor rolling the chair beside him. Victor said, "It had to be the rogue faction that took her. You know, to protect their assassination plan."

"Possible," Conor replied, "but they could have just killed her straightaway. We know they have no issue with murder. Dead, she solves their problem. Alive, she's still a pain in their asses. But they might have sweated her for information. If she knew too much about their plan, they could still cancel the whole thing. It could have been the Clan proper. They might be trying to stop the assassination attempt and would have a reason for kidnapping Rebecca, to find out all she knew about the assassination. But I don't see them killing her."

"Hell," Victor said, "the police chief himself might even have ordered her kidnapping as a personal matter just to bury her knowledge that he's a Clan na Gael leader. If that were the case, why would he let her go?"

There was no denying Victor's logic, but the most immediate thing now was the threat to Maureen Brogan and her child. "We need to get to Maureen's now. She's in danger. When she's safe, we can think about Rebecca. Can you arrange for someone to stay with Maureen if we put her in a hotel with the child?"

"Of course."

Conor heard Dr. Camp's voice from behind them in the hallway. "Mr. Dolan, there's a Detective Flynn down at the information desk. He wants to see you. Should I have the nurse let him up?"

So the case is already assigned to Flynn. The last thing Conor needed now was to deal with the murderous detective. "Do me a favor, Doc. Hold him there until I can get dressed and get out of here. Victor and I will find a side door."

ON THE CAB RIDE TO MAUREEN'S FLAT, CONOR TRIED TO GET INTO Flynn's head. The detective landed this case either because of its relationship to Kevin Dolan's supposed suicide or because the police chief specifically wanted him on the investigation. In either case, his objective would be to go through the motions of an investigation while protecting himself, the chief of police, and his Clan associates. He would, of course, make certain the kidnapping was never solved. At the same time, he would use the investigation to figure out how much Rebecca and Conor knew about the Clan's internal problems. Whichever Clan group Flynn was with, more violence was on the horizon.

Conor's options were limited. He could confront Flynn directly and threaten to take what he knew to the papers, but that would not help Rebecca. They would surely kill both him and Rebecca for that. It was clear now that his brother did not commit suicide. High-ranking cops kidnapped Rebecca and killed Kevin because he was behind the assassination plot or Flynn and the chief were part of the faction planning to execute the prince. Rebecca might be beyond help by this time, but if it was still possible to save her, he would need help. Victor was right.

Chapter 20

A sleepless Sunday night did nothing to sharpen Conor's instincts and even less to help Rebecca Fletcher. He was bathed, shaved, and sitting on Mrs. Kaplan's front steps with Dog when Victor arrived in a hansom cab. He and Conor had decided to check on Maureen and Patrick at the hotel before heading to the dock where Rebecca disappeared.

"We'll have to stop downtown at the home office first if you don't mind," Victor announced. The invitation did not sound optional. "The big guys would like to speak with you."

"Why?" Conor asked abruptly. After all, Rebecca's kidnapping was now in the hands of the police.

The big Black man looked even more sleep deprived than Conor, but he was ready for the question. "Because this is the most important contract Pinkerton has had in years."

"Well, who are the 'big guys?'" Conor asked. "Are they real detectives or just money counters?" He wanted to know why it was so important to talk with the Pinkertons first.

"Probably the latter," Victor admitted. "I can tell you that this contract was to play a central role in the Pinkerton resurrection. If they can stop the prince's assassination, Pinkerton will garner headlines all over the world. That means big money, contracts, and a huge boost to Pinkerton's prestige. Why do you think they assigned the Agency's top investigator to the case?"

"Rebecca Fletcher?" She had not hinted at any special status among the hundreds of Pinkerton Detectives, but that was Rebecca.

"Of course."

The dynamics were becoming clear, and it all made sense. A series of Pinkerton missteps over the last ten years generated horrendous publicity and a loss of respect for an agency that once guarded presidents and kings and operated a spy network for the US Government. They were known more now for providing hired thugs to anyone with enough money to pay. The Agency had blundered away its reputation for excellence and trail blazing in criminal investigations, coupled with the growing responsibilities of the US Secret Service. The days of the dime novels were over for Pinkerton, and apparently, the Agency had tapped Rebecca Fletcher to fuel the franchise toward a return to the glory days of the legendary Kate Warne, arguably the Civil War's most effective and famous Union spy.

But the decline had been inevitable since the creation of the US Secret Service in 1865. As a branch of the Treasury Department, the Secret Service's responsibilities had been steadily expanding since its creation. If that was not enough, police departments were becoming more sophisticated each year, transitioning from their traditional social services model into a crime-fighting/sleuthing model. As a result, Pinkerton could not compete with the massive availability of public funding and had turned its focus toward simply making money using the once-honored name.

The current contract with Scotland Yard to investigate and stop the assassination plot was a notable exception to the downward trend and an opportunity for Pinkerton to regain a measure of respect.

The Pinkerton executives obviously wanted to interview Conor to protect the company from more bad publicity. Conor doubted that Victor Harris shared his conclusions and, for that reason, avoided any conversation on the subject.

Had Rebecca made mistakes? Had she foiled the investigation? Had she stepped on the wrong toes? Most importantly, they would want to know every detail relating to the current state of the plot. Conor Dolan was not ready to go there today. "Turn this contraption around," he commanded the driver, "and please do it without killing us."

"The man turned his head back and said, "Sorry, sir. There are rules here. Just give me the new address."

"Fuck your rules," Victor snapped, "and do as the man told you." Turning to Conor, he added, "There's a black Ford following us, two men. We'll have to lose them or we'll broadcast Maureen's location to anyone who wants her."

Victor simply instructed the driver to pull the vehicle over in the northbound lane on State Street, in front of the Central Music Hall. The two passengers disappeared into the mass of Christmas shoppers and office workers, heading north toward the crowd surrounding Field's festive holiday window displays. "Follow me," said Victor, ducking into Marshall Field's revolving doors.

He led them into the massive department store and directly toward the rear of the building, adjacent to an alley that served as a shipping and receiving location for Field's. "They'll be expecting us to leave through the Washington Street entrance, but they'll be disappointed."

Through the service doors and onto the loading platform, they scurried into the alley southbound, emerging on Madison Street, free and clear of any pursuers. Victor looked over at his friend Conor, smiling. "We're still a detective agency. Come on. We'll catch a streetcar on Clark Street and head for the hotel."

They found Maureen and the child safely tucked into a comfortable room with a no-nonsense-looking female detective. Young Patrick was asleep in the bed only feet from the detective's double-barreled shotgun, lying along the mantle beyond his reach. Conor quietly asked the three Pinkertons to wait in the hallway while he spoke with Maureen. When they were alone, he pointed to the small table and two chairs across from the bed. "Please, I have something to tell you."

She did not protest or even speak. He took the chair across from her, laying his homburg on the wooden table. This was the real reason he had been determined to see her today. "You know about Rebecca's kidnapping," he began. "I mean, of course you do. It's the reason you're here."

"Oh, Conor," she sighed, "sure this isn't a confessional, and I'm not a priest. So say it straightaway, please."

She was making this difficult, but that's who she was. "Well, it's gonna get very dangerous for all of us now that they've taken Rebecca. I want you to know that, if anything happens to me...I mean..."

She silenced him with a wave of her hand. "Ah, sure I'll hear no more of that rubbish, Conor. There's nothin' will happen t' ye a'tall now."

Conor reached a hand across the table, placed it gently on top of Maureen's, and whispered, "You and Patrick will be cared for if anything happens to me. I need you to know that." This woman, he knew, had been ravaged by life and remained a rock through the testing. She did not surrender easily to tears. Yet there they were, crawling sensuously down rounded, red cheeks and marking a trail to soft, salient lips.

They both stood, as if answering a secret clarion call, and embraced with the passion of a thousand scorching embers, the moisture of her tears an erotic baptism for the smitten, young lawyer, a reincarnation into a new world where his own petty concerns, ambitions, and even his stubborn-headed fixation on his brother's murder faded from consciousness. There was only Maureen and little Patrick.

Gently, he raised her chin with his hand until their eyes met. "There's something else you need to know, Maureen, something about Rebecca—I mean about Rebecca and me—that I never told you."

And she smiled through the tears—almost laughed, he thought. "Oh, Conor," she said, "ye are such an irresistible twit. Will ye kiss me now?"

And he did.

On the ride to the Twenty-Second Street Bridge, Conor wondered why Rebecca had really been assigned this case. If the assignment was a reward for service to Pinkerton, did she know it? Or were the motives behind it more sinister? Was she perhaps a clueless, sacrificial lamb? Hers was a dangerous mission by any definition, one that exposed her to mortal danger from multiple sources, including corrupt cops. She would have realized that, questioned it. Why did she never let on?

Victor turned to him in the back seat. "How badly do you want Rebecca back?"

Conor knew what was coming. In a way, he had been considering it himself. "What do you think?" he replied rhetorically.

"Then we take Flynn and make him tell us," Victor said matter-of-factly.

It would be a suicidal choice for both men, Conor knew. "All right," Conor said. "We take Flynn, but it has to be tonight. We've only got a few days until the ceremony. After that, she's dead either way. But what if it isn't Flynn?"

Victor shrugged, clearly intending to do this thing with or without Conor's help. "In the war," he said, "I was young and scared and angry. I saw and did terrible things, things I would never speak of. Well, I'm not young anymore, but I'm just as angry—angry and scared as hell. This is our best chance to help her."

But this would be a qualified conspiracy, Conor thought. "I won't be a party to hurting him."

"No more than we need to," Victor replied. "I promise you."

"Then let's do it—unless we find something down around that dock that tells us Flynn's not involved." Neither man spoke again on the last minutes of the drive.

Maybe Conor's unexpected intrusion into Rebecca's investigation had increased the danger to her. He should have realized that. But Rebecca was always so poised, so controlled...except when sharing her personal pain. She had trusted him like no one else ever had. *I encouraged her, exposed her to more danger by getting her involved with Maureen.* Did she know about his feelings toward Maureen? Had she guessed? Did he betray himself somehow?

Had she seen it coming? Was she afraid? More than anything, was she still alive? Rebecca had revealed herself to Conor in a way that no one else ever had. That kind of trust brings responsibility, he thought. *A bit late for that, you eejit. You should have considered her vulnerability, exposure to danger a long time ago instead of pandering to your own selfish desires and planting barriers.*

The river around the Twenty-Second Street Bridge was teeming with barge traffic this mid-morning and the dock below a hotbed of activity, in stark contrast to the night Rebecca was kidnapped. They hopped from the cab in an empty lot adjacent to the cluster of warehouses and were immediately surrounded by a dozen armed cops led by none other than Detective Flynn.

"Checkmate," Conor whispered.

"Good morning, Gentlemen," Flynn began smugly. "I assume ye're looking into the Rebecca Fletcher case. Sure we stopped by your office, but nobody home. Mr. Dolan, we'd like ye t' come with us to Kedzie Avenue. We've a few questions far ye."

"Like...?" Conor said coldly.

Flynn stepped forward and smiled maliciously. He was barely arm's length from Conor's face. "Like where is Mo-reen Brogan? She's a known Clan operative, and if ye're hiding her, it will be trouble far ye, Mr. Dolan."

"Oh, you're a piece of work, Flynn. A known Clan operative, is she? I have nothin' t' say to you, Flynn, and I'm not going anywhere with you unless it's in shackles."

Flynn nodded to a pair of burly cops on his left. "That's the way, then. Ye're under arrest, Conor Dolan, for obstructing an investigation."

Something inside Conor snapped. There were limits to how much hypocrisy and deception he could endure. "You've got a lot of gall, Flynn," and he launched a vicious left hook that connected squarely with Flynn's prominent chin. "There, you murdering trash. Now you have something to charge me with."

Chapter 21

His suit was destroyed, torn so badly from his ride in the police wagon that it was headed straight for the trash. He stunk so badly, he could smell his own odor. He was cut, scratched, bruised, and humiliated after standing before a circuit judge for an early morning bail hearing. Aside from that, Conor was feeling pretty well.

"Thanks for bailing me out, Brendan," he said after breathing deeply of the fresh fall air on Hubbard Street.

Father Brendan White was in his element here, Conor thought. Careful not to add to Conor's self-loathing, Brendan said simply, "Come now, me boy. We'll get ye home and cleaned up. You still have work to do." Conor had not forgotten. Nellie Finley was still in dire straits. They had to confront Kate Rowland's employer, Bennett. As for the assassination, Conor's stupidity had blown up their plan to snatch Detective Flynn, leaving Rebecca in a hopeless situation with only four days left until the tunnel ceremony.

WITHIN TWO HOURS, CONOR AND BRENDAN WERE RIDING A northbound trolley to confront Charles Bennett III, Kate Rowland's former employer. Kate had painted a picture of a monster, a sexual predator and abuser as guilty of murder as if he had strangled the baby with his own filthy hands. The statement, signed and witnessed only two days ago, was locked in Conor's desk.

He had decided to hold off for the moment on tendering Kate Rowland's statement to the young prosecutor on Nellie's case. The man seemed trustworthy enough, but informing the prosecutor inevitably meant informing the police, and that meant informing the corrupt supervisors, ward politicians, and Lord only knew who else. It hardly mattered now that Detective Flynn knew. Or did he? He might only know that Brendan went to visit her at Bennett's house.

The result could be disastrous if he timed it poorly. Tipped off in advance, political allies and pay-rollers of Bennett could fabricate all manner of specious defense to the allegations or even take action against the Good Samaritan, Kate Rowland, who exposed the evil deeds. Witnesses against corrupt politicians had been known to stumble in front of moving trains in the past. They would paint poor Nellie as a prostitute and God knows what else to cover up their evil deeds.

The wind off the lake assaulted the open trolley with Chicago's bone-chilling December wind. It felt cleansing to Conor after his experiences of the last twenty-four hours. Brendan sat across from him, but neither man spoke. He knew Brendan was giving him space and time to put recent events behind him.

Conor and Brendan had concocted a plan at Andy Murphy's to either expose and humiliate Bennett for the foul creature he was or force a confession to his crimes against Nellie Finley. Father Brendan himself agreed to play a key role in the production. Both men were ready to have a go at the millionaire pervert.

The State Street trolley carried them up the lake to within walking distance of Bennett's telephone equipment plant. They arrived at the massive facility just after ten o'clock, the time most wealthy industrialists favored as a starting time. The front of the heavily windowed, brick structure housed the executive offices. They had no appointment, naturally, but they did have a plan.

The entranceway was small and nondescript, but a wide, decorative staircase led them to a palatial reception area with velvet chairs and sofas on marble flooring. No fewer than a dozen fine oil paintings, all in the American Western style, decorated the walls. A single reception desk of hand-carved oak commanded the room, complete with an impeccably dressed and coifed young receptionist. The woman was alone in the spacious room until Conor and Brendan entered.

"May I help you gentlemen?" she asked politely.

"Yes," Conor replied. "We're here to see Mr. Charles Bennett III."

"And your names?"

"Conor Dolan, attorney for Miss Nellie Finley, and this is Father Brendan White."

The smile disappeared as she woman looked over the appointment book on the desk. "I'm sorry, gentlemen, but I have no appointment for you this morning. In fact, I don't see one here looking to the end of the month. Perhaps if you would care to ring Mr. Bennett's secretary, something might be arranged after the first of the year. Is it a solicitation for charity? We do have someone who will handle that."

Brendan apparently could not resist. He said, "No charity in our bag today, miss."

Conor flashed his most sincere smile. "Pity," he began. "Perhaps we could impose on you to check personally with his secretary. I believe she may confirm. Just tell her that this good priest, will announce from his pulpit on Sunday that Mr. Bennett committed unspeakable sexual crimes against an innocent young nanny, causing her to drown her own baby in the river."

The young woman was aghast and leapt from her chair. "Wait here, please."

Within ten minutes an older woman appeared, accompanied by a muscular, bald-headed brute looking most uncomfortable and restricted in a high-collared shirt. "Come with me, gentlemen," she said.

The older woman opened double doors inward and led them into the private chamber. Conor figured the doors were designed to create the effect of entering a king's lair. The office itself was predictably opulent, precisely what one might expect of a wealthy, narcissistic rapist.

When the woman had closed the doors behind her, Bennett, seated behind a massive desk that made him look tiny, said, "You realize I could have you both arrested for extortion." It was not a question. Looking at Brendan, he added, "I've heard of you. What kind of priest are you, harassing an immigrant housekeeper or nanny or whatever this person is?"

Brendan spoke softly. "I can see the headline in my mind," he said. "'Priest arrested in sexual extortion case.' I think my reputation could survive that with all the facts on the table. How about you, Mr. Charles Bennett III?"

Bennett fumed but did not stand, Conor figured, because he was short and preferred to use his palatial office to maximum effect. He would try to intimidate them with bluster and threats. He and Brendan expected as much. Conor could almost see Bennett squirming in his oversized chair. He was in his forties, thin with a severely receding hairline and grayish mutton chops creeping well below his ears.

Bennett would know by now that Kate Rowland had spilled the beans and was working for the priest, and he would be worried, looking for a way out. If there was an escape for Bennett now, Conor could not see it. Once Kate's statement made it into the prosecutor's hands, the game was up for the telephone man. Even murder could not prevent a scandal that might land him in prison and certainly land him in the poorhouse.

"Be my guest," said Conor. "Telephone the police."

Father Brendan chimed in again, not to be left out. "Oh, we'll go to jail peaceably, Mr. Bennett."

Bennett glared at the priest. "What makes you think you can walk into my place of business and threaten me without consequence? If either of you makes a single slanderous allegation against me, I will bury you and break you with lawyers and police. What is it you're after? Money? State your business and your intentions before I have you thrown into the street."

Telephone Man did not invite the two interlopers to sit, and Bennett was still glued to his chair, so Conor decided to deliver his message looking down on the lecherous tycoon. "Well, Mr. Bennett, I apologize for not delivering our entire message to the receptionist, but we wanted to save some just for you. Not only will the good father announce your murderous sins from the pulpit, but I will personally take this entire story, including Kate Rowland's sworn statement, to every daily newspaper in town. Kate Rowland's notarized statement is already in the hands of prosecutors."

It was not, but it *was* in the mail, and he wanted Bennett to know that killing Kate would not help him. "I know how many good friends you have in the blue uniform. But you'd be surprised how friends run and hide under newspaper pressure, Mr. Bennett. By the way, you'll be interested to know that young Nellie has begun to remember details of her long nightmare and will make a valuable witness."

Conor had, of course, lied about Nellie's recall of events, but the moment just seemed to carry him away. Besides, a partial recovery for Nellie had never been ruled out. She had yet to see a treating psychiatrist, only the Russian, and the human mind was only recently beginning to reveal its secrets and its undiscovered paths to healing. He hoped with his entire soul that Nellie might feel and think and live again one day. But today's task was a more immediate and strategic.

"What do you want?" Bennett said it like a man begging to make a deal.

"We want your confession, a civil confession to start with," Brendan answered. "Nothing more and nothing less. Oh, and I am prepared to offer ye full absolution for your sins, should you wish to make a farmal confession to God afterward. On second thought, it might be better if you see another priest. I have a conflict of interest in this matter."

The tycoon was apparently not as smart as he professed to be, so Conor gave him a nudge. "It's possible that you never raped the girl as Mrs. Rowland alleges. Maybe the two of you had an affair and she became with child. You panicked and turned her out. No crime in that, not if you come clean now. On the other hand…"

For just a moment, Bennett looked like he might fold his cards, but he regained his equilibrium and pressed a button under his desk. The burly bald man suddenly appeared. He used only one door. Bennett, still looking down at his desk, said simply, "Get them out of here."

Conor thought briefly about mentioning the link to Alderman O'Sullivan as added pressure but decided against it. They did not need more pressure. Besides, there was a slight chance now that Bennett would not call O'Sullivan about their visit, so why alert the alderman at this point? Conor had separate plans for O'Sullivan—special ones—that he did not want spoiled, but he was ready to deal with the alderman either way.

So how would Bennett react? His options seemed limited. If he followed through on the threat of arrest for extortion, Bennett would be digging his own grave. The evidence would all come out now. If the man were charged—a distinct likelihood—he may not be convicted, but the damage will have been done.

He could have Conor and Brendan killed, but then he would have to kill Kate Rowland as well. It was too late for that, and even O'Sullivan would not ride the horse that far. Conor figured there was a chance that Bennett might come clean, clean enough to clear Nellie Finley anyway. He could deny the rape charges and claim the two had an affair. He could avoid prison, but his reputation and standing would be savaged, likely his business as well. It was not nearly justice for poor Nellie, but the best way to hurt someone like Bennett was to take away his money.

Any lingering doubt of a connection between Charles Bennett III and Alderman O'Sullivan evaporated after lunch when Conor found the alderman waiting at his office. It had been barely two hours since Conor and Brendan left Bennett's telephone factory. He had not considered that the alderman would show up so quickly but would hear him out.

Sending Mrs. Schmidt to lunch, Conor and O'Sullivan took coffee on the sofa in front of the heater. "I was in the neighborhood," the alderman began, "and decided to stop in and see how poor Nellie Finley is doing."

"Actually, she's improving," Conor confided with as much sincerity as he could falsely muster. "It looks like there's more to this case, much more." Conor decided to play with the alderman a bit.

"For instance?"

Without time to think, Conor called on his trial skills. Adjusting on the fly was a difficult art to perfect, but all good trial lawyers develop the skill. O'Sullivan was here at Bennett's request, certainly to confirm the facts as presented to Bennett that morning and maybe for other reasons as well. Conor would want to give the alderman enough information to convince him that Bennett was a cooked goose but not enough to reveal Conor's knowledge that the alderman was working in Bennett's interest. Conor would have his own fish to fry with O'Sullivan later, depending on whether or not the alderman was acting with knowledge of Bennett's unspeakable crimes. "Turns out that Nellie was the nanny for a local industrialist who raped her repeatedly and then impregnated her. When she showed up with a baby, he threw her out in the street."

"Horrible," O'Sullivan declared. "Do you know the man's name?"

"We do," Conor replied. "We even have a witness statement from his former housekeeper inculpating him in horrific crimes, but of course, I'm not at liberty to reveal his name."

Conor could see O'Sullivan beginning to sweat. "Of course. I understand. But my goodness. It's just unthinkable."

O'Sullivan would now be thinking only of himself. If he were implicated in something so sinister and depraved through his dealings with Bennett and even Dr. Martinovsky, his career would end—or worse. Conor actually felt a pang of guilt at having so much fun with O'Sullivan.

"So where do the plea negotiations stand?" O'Sullivan asked. "I'm sure this new information will push the prosecution to a better deal, maybe even a year or two—even probation."

That was why the man was really here, one last shot at forcing Nellie to plead guilty. *You'd like that, but chew on this instead.* "Oh, there won't be a plea. We're taking this information to trial. I will be withdrawing the insanity defense. We'll get to the bottom of this and put the blame where it belongs."

From O'Sullivan's expression, you would have thought his own mother just disowned him. The man was no altruist. He was working hard to protect Bennett, now even harder to protect himself.

The Russian psychiatrist was indebted to O'Sullivan somehow, and O'Sullivan leveraged his claim to help Bennett. Somewhere in the mud pile, an aggressive, honest prosecutor like Mr. Groth would find the golden nectar of graft and plenty of it. O'Sullivan now wanted desperately for Nellie Finley to plead guilty and go away in order to get Bennett and himself off the hook. Nellie could do them no harm from inside an institution. Even if she recovered her memory of all the horrors, she would be recounting it only to four white walls. The only question was whether the alderman knew Bennett for the monster he was.

In the space of three short hours, Conor had put the fear of destruction and hellfire into two of Chicago's most prominent and powerful citizens. It was satisfying in a lawyerly kind of way, but it was not nearly enough to solve his problems. They were still dangerous, Rebecca was still missing, and somebody was getting very close to blowing the Prince of Wales to kingdom come.

Chapter 22

The next day Conor was leaving the Harrison Street Police Court on a damp and foggy morning, only three days before the tunnel ceremony, when a young man in a suit approached him on the sidewalk.

"You Mr. Dolan?" he asked.

"I am."

"I'm Detective Johnson. I work with Detective Flynn. Would you be willing to come to the morgue with me to identify a body?"

Conor had been expecting this moment, dreading it, and wondering about the details: the where, the when, the who. The chances of Rebecca's survival diminished each day she remained missing. It also occurred to him that the body might not be Rebecca's. "Sure. Let's go."

He had not heard anything from Maureen since visiting her at the hotel, but she was well protected and surely safe. But what could a single bodyguard do against a planned execution attempt? They might all three be dead, he thought: Rebecca, Maureen, and the child.

"Tell me what you know, please," Conor said.

"It's a woman, about forty, pulled from the river early this morning.

Hasn't even been in there a day. Appears she was beaten and strangled."

Conor felt the air rushing from his lungs. Then, for a second, he could see it, a whitish cloud slowly rising in the frigid air and, little by little, absorbed into that grayish filth that blankets the city on mornings such as this. *What a dehumanizing place.*

SHE HAD NOT SAID A WORD, HE KNEW, ABOUT THEIR STUPID, meaningless investigation of a man who was already dead, a mean, murderous man he wished had never been his brother. And fook the Prince of fooking Wales! Conor hoped in that moment that the Clan would blow his ass back to England where it belonged. With all the misery and pain England had inflicted across the globe, how could the safety of their overfed, overindulged prince justify the death of such a beautiful human being as Rebecca Fletcher?

The detective was equipped with a two-seat Model A Ford, complete with a soft top, which he drove himself. It was a short ride to the county morgue on Polk Street, housed in the Cook County Hospital and known as the "Deadhouse." Conor toured the facility less than a month ago on an orientation trip sponsored by the bar association. The morgue, occupying the entire basement of the three-story, three hundred-bed facility, doubled as a teaching facility for the hospital.

Despite the short distance, the journey was arduous. The streets were mobbed, all of them, stuffed to the edges like Polish sausages with pedestrians and freight wagons of all sorts, nothing moving save the ant-like humans, dancing and weaving among the stuck traffic. Long lumber wagons blocked intersections, trolleys and streetcars backed up behind one another as if in a parade, and more people, more chaotic dancing through the black-sooted air. The Ford did not help. The automobile was a novelty. It was said, Ford had produced fewer than two thousand of its Model A automobiles to date. Everywhere people called out or pointed, even stepped directly in front of the machine to get a better look.

Conor just wished for the ride to end, for his thoughts took him ever deeper into dark places. How long had he stalled over Rebecca's honest and straightforward plea to have a child? She had to sense his hesitation but never hinted of it. He had lacked the courage to simply decline or the compassion to lift her unbearable loneliness and grief.

Rebecca would not have loved him less as the price of an honest answer. She knew the complexity and the lifelong, existential consequences of such a request to responsible people. It was a plea for help, he knew, not a request at all. She never would have emboldened herself to that extent, never exposed her vulnerability in such absolute terms had she not loved him and trusted him. His silent answer to her plea had been, *"I'll get back to you on that."* A coward's exit from a sinking ship. *"Well, I just happened to be near the only lifeboat. I didn't know those women wanted to leave."*

In truth, the morgue was really a huge warehouse with a little ancillary hospital on top because the dead bodies, at any given time, outnumbered the capacity for live ones by at least three to one. Corpses lay everywhere in the frozen chamber, stacked on racks along the walls— tagged, numbered, and bagged—most patiently waiting their turns to be diced and sliced on the dozens of rolling, metal carts by an army of white-coated, blood-soaked, would-be physicians. The stink of the place made Conor long for the sweet aroma of the Harrison Street jail.

Gunshots, starvation, disease, exposure, alcoholism, and syphilis. The hundreds of bodies stacked and catalogued along these racks told the real story of life in Chicago for the poor immigrant—whose real story was death. Death visited his world daily, never invited but always expected like the natural offspring of illness or injury or greed. It was more affordable than long illness and less painful than shattered bones, but most of all, you could not catch it from your friends—like cholera. A funeral, a mass, a little crying and storytelling, then everyone gets on with the business of survival. Still, he thought, they keep coming, and many of the strongest survive to give their children better lives.

The detective escorted him to a section labeled, "Forensics" in block-lettered wall paint where Conor spotted Victor Harris, hat in hand, head down, over the table supporting the remains of what appeared to be a woman under a white sheet.

Conor put his hand on Victor's shoulder and said softly, "Rebecca?" Victor only nodded in the affirmative.

Detective Johnson respectfully pulled back the sheet from the face and said, "I'm sorry for the necessity of this, Mr. Dolan, but we would appreciate a second identification. Do you know this woman?"

There was nothing peaceful or contented or resigned about Rebecca's expression or the map of her once beautiful face. She looked cold and ugly and something less than human, a state that might have mortified Rebecca quicker than death itself.

Her lovely hair was mashed, the nose too big, lips too wide. Thank God, her eyes were closed, for those inescapable eyes had been his window into a beautiful soul. Maybe it was someone else, he tried to convince himself, but he knew the truth, and the truth was on this cold, harsh table in this damp basement.

"It's Rebecca Fletcher," he declared. "Now let's get her out of here and put some clothes and makeup on her."

He and Rebecca were not in love, he knew, just two lonely people, each filling a void in the other. Conor was more determined than ever to complete her mission, to avenge her, to find the answers about his brother's death, but they were getting too close. Today it was Rebecca's turn. Tomorrow it could be Conor or even Maureen. There was no more time for nibbling around the edges. Conor needed to act if he was to stop the assassination and prevent more deaths. Still, he could not shake the feeling that he was missing something, something within his grasp if he could only open his eyes and see it.

Conor and Victor, the big man with the stoic demeanor, did not discuss Rebecca on the ride over to the Pinkerton office on

State Street. They sat side by side on a trolley, then a streetcar, both in silent mourning. Conor could recognize Victor's grief. The big man knew Rebecca years ago, before Pinkerton—known her as Conor had known her. Conor could see it in the way Victor mourned. It was deep and personal with a solid foundation built through a relationship without boundary or propriety, without witnesses or guilt, a relationship that was honest.

He turned to his companion, whose eyes were fixed on some meaningless distraction out the window, and said, simply. "Was it in Urbana, all those years ago?"

Victor, the proud Pinkerton, did not turn back from the window, but he could not conceal the moisture in his right eye. He said stoically, "Yes, Urbana, a long time ago, before she met Jacob."

Conor looked at Victor on that streetcar, maybe for the first time. In the big man's face, he saw his friend Dr. Camp; he saw a little of Father Brendan and a trace of his favorite newsboy clients, the Hawk brothers. As they stepped off the streetcar near the Pinkerton office, Conor said, "There's no pressing need to go there now. Is there?"

"I suppose not. Why?"

"Then let's go have a drink to Rebecca. There's a bartender and a dog I want you to meet."

So they did the whole trip again, but in lighter traffic, until Conor recognized his own neighborhood and stepped off across the street from Andy Murphy's.

Dog had somehow picked up Conor's scent before the two men entered the bar and had joined them by the time Murph slapped down the first round of beer.

"Murph, meet my friend, Victor Harris, the Pinkerton detective." As the two shook hands, Conor pointed toward the floor. "And this is Dog."

Victor patted Dog on the head and, bending down, offered him a lick of beer, but Dog passed. Conor took the bowl from Murph and placed it in front of the animal who promptly lapped it up. "It's not personal, Victor. Dog has decided he only likes Schlitz."

Victor raised his glass. "To Rebecca." They clinked and drank, then lowered the mugs to the bar. That's when Conor began to hear the low grumbling from down the bar. By the time Murph brought the next round, the volume had increased along with the bravado. Conor did not recognize the group of four men, but some were clearly Irish. From the grumbling, Conor began to recognize words; "coon, spook, and nigger" were among them.

Murph had obviously heard it too and quietly approached the group to issue a warning, but they were too well greased, and the ugliness prevailed. When it became obvious that Murph could not bypass trouble, Victor straightened up from his hunched position on the bar. Elbows on the bar and bent like a chicken, he had seemed a normal-sized Negro man, which he was not.

Victor removed his Brooks Brothers coat, handing it to Conor. He did not say a word, but walked straight to the little mob of weasels and stopped. "I'm going to have one more drink with my friend and then leave," he announced. "We would like to drink in peace for a little while. If you have a problem with that, let's the five of us step outside now and finish the argument. I wouldn't want to damage this fine establishment." Victor's face said the rest. He looked unconcerned about the outcome. He was prepared to deal with the situation either way.

Predictably, the bravado dissolved quicker than a sugar cube in hot coffee, and the two men and one dog quietly finished their last drink. They did not speak of Rebecca again, but Conor knew they had forged a bond, a bond among a son of Irish peasants, a steadfast Negro detective, and an alcoholic dog.

As they prepared to leave the bar, Murph looked uncomfortable, unlike the usual gregarious publican, as if he had bad news to deliver. "Something wrong, Murph?" Conor asked.

"I suppose you could say that. It's about Brendan," whereupon

Murph placed a copy of the *Daily News* morning edition on the bar. The paper was neatly folded to a story on page two, "Local Catholic Priest Removed for Embezzling Funds."

A prominent local priest has been ordered to leave his post as Pastor of St. Michael's Church on the city's North Side. Father Brendan White, an Irish immigrant and cleric of fifteen years has been accused of embezzling funds from the Archdiocese of Chicago, according to a press release from the Administrative Office of the Archbishop of Chicago. The release goes on to say that, following a routine audit, an unspecified sum of money was found missing from church coffers. ... Father White will be reassigned to a diocesan retreat house in rural Wisconsin effective January 1. ... The Archbishop has personally requested a criminal investigation.

"I can't believe it," Conor said quietly.

"Look," said Victor, pointing at another story down the page. Conor had to read it twice to be certain:

Telephone Tycoon Dead in Violent Suicide.

It was a busy news day. The article reported that, instead of going to work that morning, Charles Bennett III had locked the door of his home office, decorated with the heads of his own victims from the wilds of Africa and the American West, and blown the top of his head off with the barrel of a shotgun in his mouth. A poetic ending for a vile example of Homo sapiens, Conor thought. The day had not been a total loss. For every curse, there was a blessing.

He knew Brendan was no embezzler. The man did not even own a suit of decent clothes. Whatever it was about, it was either a frame, or Brendan spent money to help someone the archbishop did not like. It was surely a dark time for his friend.

But Conor, God forbid, was becoming comfortable in this city, and getting involved would not help his chances at sainthood down the road. Despite his complete ignorance of details and evidence, Conor smelled Chicago politics at the root of Brendan's problem. Beyond the City Council, the Roman Catholic Church was the most powerful political institution in Chicago—and maybe the most vicious.

With Rebecca still lying on a cold morgue slab and Nellie Finley still on the hook, Brendan's defrocking—or whatever they called it— would have to wait. Conor would find a way to help his friend, but right now, the priest just needed to know he was not alone.

Conor thought about writing a letter to Nellie's sister in Connemara. It was the only postal address Nellie used. There was an aunt in Westport, County Mayo, but no name or address in the file. He dismissed the idea as quickly as he hatched it. What would he tell them anyway? Their lives were most likely miserable enough already. *"Dear Finleys, Nellie had a child as a result of rape. It was a girl. Then your beloved Nellie jumped off a bridge with the baby. The baby is dead and Nellie is a lunatic about to go on trial for murder. The good news is that the man who assaulted her blew his own brains out. I will keep you posted on future developments..."*

No. *If* and *when* he had something constructive to say, he would revisit the question of a letter. For now, he had some serious strategizing to do. As for Charles Bennett III, a quick, painless death was an insufficient measure of justice for the violent pervert, not to mention for a young woman named Nellie Finley.

Chapter 23

With only two days until the ceremony, Victor went to the Chicago Tunnel offices to work on security arrangements for the rail tour, leaving Conor free to check on Father Brendan and work the Nellie Finley case. The tunnel company agreed to conduct a thorough search of the tunnel route and rail track secretly tomorrow night in the wee hours with the Pinkertons. Conor would be there. The ceremony and royal tour would commence at noon.

Olaf Peterson remained Conor and Victor's secret for the moment. If the Hoyne Avenue man became suspicious, all bets were off. According to the plan, Peterson would be detained on the way to Tunnel Station No. 1 on the morning of the twentieth by a team of Pinkertons who would "mistake" him for a wanted criminal. The tunnel company would simply assume Peterson was ill or had overslept and assign another engineer.

Conor found Father Brendan in the church basement cleaning up after one of his resident "disciples" who had moved into a hotel earlier. The basement housed three other homeless residents at the moment, all women, all in scraggly condition but clean and fed. Conor thought it would not be a bad place to flop in a pinch—clean mattresses on a dry floor and warm.

"How are you holding up?" Conor asked. "It's crazy."

With the broom in his hand, Brendan pointed to the corner of the spacious room. "Would ye bring me a clean mattress from the pile over there?"

He spread the mattress on the floor. Brendan was sweating, but he stopped sweeping to answer the question Conor had not yet asked. "Did ye know the archbishop himself sent two auditors over? They spent a day and a half with the books and another half day in this very basement, conducting an 'inventory,' they said, of the unauthorized supplies and furniture, even the food we have for these poor divils. But sure 'twas the three hundred I used for poor Nellie's bail that did me in. It was like they knew I posted church money for her bail."

"It all makes sense. How much money are we talkin' about in total?"

"Oh, just over three hundred, I t'ink. Maybe another hundred for the poor souls in the basement."

"So no diamond rings or holidays for your girlfriend over in Chinatown?"

Brendan made a feeble attempt at laughter. It failed miserably. "They say 'twas archdiocesan funds I used. The thing is…'tis true, all right, now that I think about it. It never occurred to me that helping the poor with church money was stealing." This time he laughed for real, even slapped Conor on the back. "Isn't that irony for you now, Conor? Come now. Let's go up and have a bit of lunch while my two housekeepers still have employment."

On the way up the stairs, Conor said, "Murph told me they want to send you to some snowbound monastery in the North Woods. What's that about? Will you go? "

Brendan shrugged his shoulders. "Sure what choice have I? Listen now, Conor. The ladies still haven't seen the papers, and the news will devastate them both, so not a word about this at lunch. Promise me now."

"Of course."

"I have a couple of good employment opportunities for them both and should be able to finalize the details soon. The news of my demise will go easier on the poor dears knowing they won't be turned into the street."

Even now, his reputation savaged, his career destroyed, this man's only thoughts were for the welfare of others. Conor stopped at the top of the stairs and turned to face Brendan. He did not want to make small talk for an hour with the overriding question hanging over the room like a cloud of industrial soot.

"Why, Brendan? Whose toes did you step on? The archdiocese has more money than God himself. It makes no sense that they'd do this over $300 spent on the poor. And why *now*? You've been doing this for over ten years. Have they ever objected before?"

Brendan shook his head. Conor could see he had touched a nerve. "Sure that's the t'ing now. A few years ago, I even took the bishop himself into the basement to show him the work, and he was delighted with my mission. 'A fine example of Christianity' he called it."

"Something triggered it then—or someone—and I have a good idea who. But what about this retreat house? Will you really go? That's not the kind of priest you are. It's not what God called you to do."

Brendan threw up his hands in a gesture of frustration. "I have no choice in the matter. Maybe I can teach the visiting priests to play poker or shoot dice." It was a melancholy attempt at humor. "I might even unionize them. Now wouldn't the archbishop love that?"

"You could leave the priesthood." It's what Conor had been hinting at all along. What was the big deal? He thought. But he knew better. Conor Dolan, like other Irishmen, understood the extent to which the Church invades the inner sanctums of young, naïve minds and plants its flags of loyalty, fear, and submission. The only reason Conor could articulate the process was because he had managed to climb that great wall of confinement to embrace the liberation that comes only with freedom of thought and expression, with questioning. It was Kevin who had motivated the long climb out of that prison. Poor Brendan—however intelligent, noble, and generous—had simply never taken that first difficult step.

They found the two women in the rectory kitchen, and Brendan said, "Sure we'll have a guest for lunch now, ladies. We'll just have a glass of wine in the dining room." It was as if the priest had not a care in the world.

Conor did not linger after lunch. Despite the mad pace and high stakes of the Clan na Gael investigation, Nellie Finley still needed his attention. He would follow up with the Finley case this afternoon by tracking down the two bargemen. They had been the subject of his last conversation with Rebecca on the bridge. He carried the addresses for both men and figured Saturday afternoon would offer the best chance to find them at home.

One of them lived way out west near Garfield Park, so he opted to visit that one first. It was a forty-five-minute journey for nothing. The flat was vacant and undergoing renovations and repair. The landlord explained that the tenants, William Sanders and his wife, had only weeks ago broken their lease, leaving abruptly. None of the other tenants saw them leave, so the man figured it must have been at night.

The landlord could not be certain precisely which night they fled, but the small window of possible dates all fell within the three nights after Nellie Finley's jump from the bridge. In addition to all the family's furniture, Sanders left a note on the table announcing that he had obtained better employment in another city. In it, Sanders pledged to settle the issue of rent when the landlord had secured a new lease. The landlord had no clue where they went and would be grateful if Conor would follow up with him.

The story was suspicious enough to require a follow up investigation, but without more information, there was simply no trail to follow. Victor could check the train stations and interview ticket clerks, but without an address or a photograph, they would be pissing up a rope. Conor asked the landlord, "Did they leave personal belongings in addition to furniture?"

"Yes," the man replied. "I filled several boxes with the things. I have them in the basement. You can see them, if you like."

Most of the items were old clothing, male and female in adult sizes, confirming it was only a husband and wife. He was looking for an address, a letter from a relative, a note, anything that might give Pinkerton a place to start. In the last box, while going through a stack of books, he spotted a framed wedding portrait of Sanders and his wife. It was not as good as a destination, but it was a start.

THE OTHER BARGEMAN WAS A YOUNG IMMIGRANT NAMED STANislav Naganska. He lived in a boardinghouse down on Bunker Street, west of Jefferson, in the Maxwell Street area.

The landlord did not seem overly concerned or fastidious, unlike the landladies he knew, and simply motioned to the staircase. "You go," the man said. "Room numba tree." He held up the corresponding number of fingers.

At first Naganska did not answer the door, then Conor heard signs of life from inside the room. He knocked again. "Mr. Naganska, I'd like to speak with you. I'm a lawyer." Conor figured it was always good to let people know you were not the police.

Naganska finally answered the door. A cigarette hung precariously from thin lips, threatening to drop ashes on his hairless chest. The man's long johns sported more holes and stains that an old wash rag. He had obviously rolled out of bed to answer the door. A night worker, Conor figured. "Whadda ya want?" Naganska asked. "Who are ya'?"

The man did not sound like an immigrant, but then neither did Conor. He must have arrived with his parents. The door opened inward, and the smell of alcohol exploded into the hallway into Conor's face.

Naganska looked even worse than he smelled: emaciated, around twenty, a chaotic mop of yellow hair, and unshaven. Behind the man's bloodshot eyes, Conor could see a woman's legs moving on the bed, partially between two sheets. A second glance revealed black leg hair. Conor decided to let well enough alone and have the conversation there in the doorway.

"You deserve credit for saving that woman's life. She would have died if you and your friend hadn't plucked her out of the water."

Naganska's face showed no response.

"I'm a lawyer for the girl you rescued from the river."

Naganska was coming around. He looked nervous, although in his condition it was difficult to be certain. "I don't know nuttin'. It's good the girl didn't drown."

"Look, I just have a couple of questions. Did you see the baby? I mean actually in the water or hit the water?"

"Yeah, I seen the baby," he mumbled, "but it went under before I could get it. I don't know nuttin' else."

Naganska tried to shut the door, but Conor jammed it with his foot. "Just one more question, please." At that moment, a naked body strolled nonchalantly through Conor's view in the background. It was not a woman...not by any *stretch*. "Sanders's landlord told me your friend and his wife moved out of their flat over near Ashland and didn't leave a forwarding address. Do you know where they went?"

"He ain't my friend. Not no more. They all moved down to Kankakee, and that's all I know. Now go away," he said, closing the door. "I don't know nuttin' else and I don't want no trouble."

Trouble? Had the two bargemen once been friends? Conor wondered. Did they have a falling out? Over what? More importantly, why was the Polish kid so nervous? Why was he so reluctant to talk about that night on the bridge? And *trouble?* The bargemen were both heroes. Conor would have to find this Sanders fellow to get his answer, but something was afoot. Kankakee was at least a good start. If they did flee to Kankakee, the photograph would be even more helpful, but it would take time and resources.

It was dinnertime when Conor arrived back at his flat. He would get something to eat, then have an hour nap before heading over to Station No. 1 to meet Victor. As he put the key in his lock, Mrs. Kaplan called out from the stairway above. "Mr. Dolan, I have a message."

He looked up. "Yes, Mrs. Kaplan?"

"Alderman O'Sullivan called on the telephone. He asks that you meet him at your office right away."

There was no telling what was on O'Sullivan's mind this time, but at least Conor was about to get some answers, the easy way or the hard way.

Chapter 24

On the short walk, he thought about how to handle the alderman. He would know about Bennett's suicide, of course. For one reason or another, Bennett's death would be connected to the visit. Knowing these politicians, Conor knew the visit was motivated by O'Sullivan's instinct for self-preservation. His arse was on fire, and he intended to extinguish the flames. Conor needed to know what started the fire and whether O'Sullivan had knowingly covered up for a depraved rapist. Without Father Brendan's help, the whole…

Then Conor had an epiphany.

Charles Bennett had every reason to hate and fear Father Brendan—even once openly expressed his rage at Brendan in the corporate office. Beyond that, Bennett had to know it was Brendan who wooed a timid Kate Rowland from the shadow of fear into the bright light of an accuser. Could Bennett have somehow pulled the strings to arrange Father Brendan White's demise out of a sense of hatred and revenge? It made sense. Then Conor remembered Brendan's chance meeting with Alderman O'Sullivan at the law office. They knew each other. It was not a stretch to suspect that O'Sullivan used his well-known connection to the current archbishop of Chicago in aid of his felonious friend, Charles Bennett III. Everything pointed to the conclusion that O'Sullivan made a deal with *God's one true Church* to ruin Brendan's life. If true, the gall was staggering.

He must be seriously worried, Conor thought when he spotted the alderman standing outside the office on this freezing cold evening. Conor waved to O'Sullivan while digging for his key. "Sorry, Alderman. I just got your message and came right over."

O'Sullivan smiled. He did a lot of that. They all did, so Conor knew by now it was meaningless. "Nooooooo need to apologize. Sure I was coming your way this evenin' and t'ought I'd stop by."

Sure, Conor thought. *I believe that.* "Come on in. Leave your coat on while I heat the place up." He thought about a casual sofa chat but opted to use the lawyer/client format at his desk. *This might get touchy.*

Surprisingly, O'Sullivan kept the small talk to a minimum before digging in. He said, "I was just wondering how the Nellie Finley case is progressing now that you have an insanity opinion. Sure I can't get that poor girl off my mind, herself coming from the old sod and all."

Immigrant women were being held in sexual slavery less than a mile from there, hundreds of them, and this parasitic politician had the chutzpah to feign empathy for Nellie Finley. Conor recalled meeting the alderman for the first time in this very office and being taken in by the man's pseudo-humanitarian facade. He had learned a lot about human nature since that day and almost none of it good. It was difficult now to believe he had once been so naïve. "Well, of course, I need to be careful what I say. Privilege and all. You understand, but it's a dynamic situation, changing every day. We've been very successful at filling in the blanks in her history."

O'Sullivan kind of shifted his weight in the chair as if his long johns were on the move. It was a really nice chair, a gift from Dr. Camp, soft and velvet, so no need for fidgeting. "Really?" said the alderman. "Good or bad, if I might be so bold?"

Conor kind of shrugged. "Could be either one, I suppose. Just depends which side you're on—or for whom you are working."

O'Sullivan flashed the look of a fish that had just tasted the bait. "How so?" he asked. "Are ye able to share?"

The shrug had worked pretty well, so Conor used it again. "Of course. It doesn't matter now because Charles Bennett is dead."

O'Sullivan began playing with the brim of his bowler. "Bennett, the telephone equipment guy? Is he, now?"

"Same one," Conor confirmed. "Blew his brains out. The thing is, we're pretty sure the suicide was related to the Finley case. You see, his former nanny gave us a sworn statement the other day. That's when you encountered your old friend, Father White at my office with her. Only yesterday, I sent a mimeograph duplicate of her statement to the prosecutor. It changes everything."

The politician did his best to look pleased, but the result was comical. "Does it, now! And how so? What had he to do with the Finley girl?"

It was time to throw his best pitch. "It turns out Bennett was essentially a white slaver and a rapist. He recruited poor Nellie all the way from Ireland on the pretense of legitimate employment. It wasn't long until the swine unleashed his depraved proclivities. He began a pattern of rape and physical abuse, each followed by threats to ruin her and see her starve if she complained to authorities. The poor child had no one, but for the terrified, old housekeeper. Nellie made a plan to escape back to Ireland but, before she could make good on it, found she was with child. That's when it got even worse, until…well…"

By that time, O'Sullivan was white as a sheet, perspiration pouring from his forehead. "All he could produce from the silvery tongue was, "Holy mother of God."

Conor sat back in his chair, folding his arms across his chest. "It's unspeakable, all right, but at least it will serve Nellie's interest. By tomorrow, every newspaper in the city will have it on the front page. No right-thinking jury would ever convict her of murder knowing what she's been through. I'll withdraw the insanity pleas, of course. So I want to thank you for your kind assistance in her cause."

O'Sullivan appeared to be in a coma, but snapped back quickly. "Oh, you mean Martinovsky. Don't mention it. Happy to help."

"Still, there is one thing that might concern you, Alderman. I feel I should warn you."

The man was leaning forward on the chair now. "Warn me?"

"It's a matter of record that Dr. Martinovsky assisted us free of charge. The police will want to know why, and I'm afraid I am obligated to disclose that the doctor offered his services as a favor to you."

A long silence followed. Alderman O'Sullivan appeared to relax in the chair, realizing he had been outplayed at his own game. Once O'Sullivan's name was linked to this affair, he would be finished in Chicago—and maybe worse. When the State's Attorney started investigating, who knew what other filth might surface? He could end up in prison. Finally, O'Sullivan smiled and said, "Sure you're a very shrewd man, Mr. Dolan, shrewd, indeed."

The two men now had an unspoken understanding. They were playing a game that O'Sullivan had mastered years ago. Still, had it been chess, the grand master would have just been checkmated.

With all the cards on the table, Conor said, "I don't want to know what you had going with Bennett, maybe because it's all too obvious and it would help my conscience not to hear it spelled out. I want to know just a couple of things. Did you know what he was doing to Nellie Finley?"

This was a new Alderman O'Sullivan, a person only his own mother would recognize. Eyes down, he was completely defeated. "I swear to you on my dear mother's grave, Mr. Dolan, I knew nothing of all this. Bennett and I had an arrangement, and friends like that help each other from time to time. It was about contracts and telephones. If I had known… If this comes out, I'm finished, but you know that already. I underestimated you, Mr. Dolan. So what do you want?"

Conor was convinced this politician had no knowledge of Bennett's deviant behavior, but this time he was not fooled by partial truth. O'Sullivan did not know because he never wanted to know, because he and Bennett both knew the *Chicago rules of play.* The most important rule was to maintain deniability. *"I never saw it. He never told me about it. Had I known, I never would have..."*

So, this is a pivotal moment in your life, Conor boy. Until this moment, Conor Dolan had never committed extortion or bribery in his entire life. Oh, he had lied a few times, but he was Irish, after all. He had already agreed to participate as a victim in bribery and extortion but tried to convince himself that morality was a relative virtue and that a qualitative difference existed between paying extortion and the act of extorting. By that loose definition, he still considered himself an *honest* lawyer and an *honest* man, but the answer to O'Sullivan's last question could redefine Conor's character for the foreseeable future.

Although he still considered himself a recovering Catholic, Conor wondered how a priest might handle the situation, not just any priest but a particular priest from St. Michael's. Conor had an opportunity at this moment to right a handful of wrongs, to help some people who deserved a break by committing a thoroughly dishonest and corrupt act.

For whatever reason, it occurred to him that he had been thinking like a lawyer up to now, parsing elements and dissecting definitions, a decidedly dangerous endeavor. Father Brendan's real message finally broke through to him.

Conor sat back in his chair and smiled, tapping his pencil on the desk. "I believe you, Mr. O'Sullivan, and that brings me to my second question. How is it that Bennett was able to influence the archbishop in the little matter of Father White's dismissal from his parish?"

O'Sullivan seemed ready for the question and answered with a sense of resignation. "I think you have a good idea about how this all works now, but Bennett had his own relationship with the archbishop, and I don't know exactly what fueled it. Money, I'd say. The point is

I can't help you with that. The archbishop was looking to get Father White for years. Why not simply tell me what you want?"

And with that, Conor knew he had hit rock. "To answer your question, I have three wishes. First, I have two clients named Hawk. I think you've heard of Lefty Hawk, the labor-organizing newsboy. He and his brother are charged with minor crimes: theft, pickpocketing. Lefty lifted your friend Alderman Tully's wallet. I want all charges dropped."

O'Sullivan was already nodding his head. "Done."

"We're still on the first wish. I want good city jobs for both boys. Lefty would make a wonderful police officer."

"Done. What else?"

"Next, I'm finished paying monthly graft to your organization. I operate my business here hassle free as long as I please."

"Done."

Details were important when applying the Chicago Rules. "That goes for the local cop too."

"Of course."

"Lastly, I have a friend owns a bar in the Nineteenth Precinct. Andy Murphy. Other than Schlitz, he's only allowed to carry one brand of beer. I think you know why. As of today, he sells any fucking beer or whiskey he likes."

O'Sullivan offered his hand. "We have an agreement, Mr. Dolan."

Conor let the hand dangle. "I won't shake your hand. We're both thieves now, and there is no honor among thieves. But I'm curious about one thing. What did you have on that Russian psychiatrist that would make him do all that work for nothing?"

O'Sullivan laughed. "That's easy. He has a lucrative contract with the insane asylum in Elgin. My brother is the State Rep who controls those contracts. There's always an angle, Mr. Dolan. You only need to find it."

"I'll tell Father Brendan you said that," Conor quipped.

Conor was officially off the fence. He would no longer pontificate over self-serving distinctions between good and bad, or major and minor corruption. He had officially extorted his first victim, quid pro quo, but he felt only euphoria. No guilt whatsoever. From now on, he would evaluate the morality of municipal corruption on a case-by-case basis as Father Brendan would. If his conscience started to bother him, there was always confession—or a bartending job.

BACK IN HIS FLAT THAT NIGHT, HE POURED A JAMESON AND thought about the approaching climax to this chaotic swirl of events. He and Victor would spend the night searching tunnels before the noon ceremony and tour. They would be looking for dynamite. But where? Maybe the assassins would not use explosives at all. They might simply shoot the damn prince getting out of his carriage or poison him at lunch, although Conor was betting against it. The Clan's penchant for drama was legendary, and nothing said drama like an explosion and a flooded city.

Even if they knew what to look for, they still did not know who the would-be assassins were. Had it been Kevin? If so, who were his helpers? Or had Kevin been trying to foil the plot when they killed him? And who killed Rebecca?

He was sitting on the bed, throwing a ball across the bedroom for Dog to fetch. On the third toss, the ball disappeared under the bed, and Dog could not free it. Conor knelt and reached under the bed where he found the ball stuck behind the box of Kevin's belongings, the one Kevin's landlady gave him. He had moved it to the apartment after the break in. The safest place was the place his adversaries already searched

He looked down at the box, then thought about his conversations with Maureen Brogan…and suddenly realized he had the answers all along, right under his nose. At last—at long last—everything made sense. He opened the box. The answer had been there all this time, and it chilled him to the bone. He reached for his coat…

Chapter 25

Conor and Victor lay crouched in the bone-numbing dampness forty feet below the south bank of the Chicago River. The rail intersection included the last possible northbound escape route to the surface south of the river. The intersection itself was diagonal, with the tunnels converging into what resembled the hub of a wheel, offering some measure of clearance from a passing train. The position offered the best possible observation in all directions—such as the poor lighting would allow.

It would be just over an hour before the little train carrying the Prince of Wales and his entourage came chugging up from the south, Conor noted. He and Victor were exhausted from lack of sleep, but many of their questions were answered in the last twelve hours; many others were not.

Whatever was happening inside Station No. 1 at that moment was beyond their control. He and Victor were tactical actors now, responsible only for what was about to happen there in the tunnel in the coming minutes.

Despite all the frantic maneuvering during the night and the nervous tension building in his gut, Conor kept thinking of Rebecca Fletcher.

He felt a personal responsibility for her death. He had failed her miserably, gone missing in action, and taken refuge in his cowardice when confronted with her plea for help.

It did not matter whether the damned English prince lived or died or converted to Catholicism. This entire venture was doomed to failure from the moment he boarded the train in Springfield, like a train speeding along in the dark toward a collapsed bridge. Part of him wished he never left Springfield. Rebecca would still be alive.

Victor had been silent for the better part of the last hour but seemed to sense Conor's thoughts. "You didn't set this course. You followed it. There's a difference."

"Is there?"

"I'm fifty-four years old. I was one of a handful of colored men at the University of Illinois back in 1880, old for a white student, bold for a colored one. That's when I met her."

He had figured this Pinkerton for a younger man, and despite his curiosity, Conor had determined to respect Victor's privacy on the subject of Rebecca. The big man was telling Conor this because he wanted to for some reason.

He could see Victor smile in the hazy light. "She was young, even more beautiful than she was when you knew her." Victor adjusted his position on the damp, concrete floor, stretching out long legs toward the track. A crack in the wall oozed a slow drip that puddled water in the low spots. Ice formed between the rails. "I was once a slave, escaped and came north from Virginia with a kind man after the Emancipation. Joined the Union Army at sixteen. That's where I learned to read and write properly between the fighting. After I was wounded, I worked as an orderly for a white doctor."

Conor heard footsteps coming from the south and saw the figures of two men standing along the tracks, part of their team changing positions.

Conor said, "I'm listening."

"Years later, I applied for a university scholarship through a private Reconstruction foundation and found myself in Urbana. They even gave me a job in the kitchen to cover my expenses."

"That's when you met her?"

"Yup, or you might say she met me. Central and southern Illinois had strong pro-slavery leanings back then. Urbana is kind of in the middle of the state, so there was conflict on the subject, a lot of conflict sometimes if you catch my meaning."

"I do."

"Let's just say Rebecca took a stand, made her feelings known to all comers, and we became friends. As a rule, Jews don't think much of slavery. Later we became good friends, but we both knew that part wouldn't last. Pinkerton hired me ten years ago, and we met again. Just a coincidence. Rebecca was happily married then, but our friendship was still there. I knew what she was like inside…I think you did too. I don't know much about Jews, but they know what it's like to be on the wrong end of a whip."

Conor looked at his watch. *The train will be entering the tunnel about now.* At the moment, he heard what he had been hoping never to hear: someone opening the hatch forty feet above them from street level. The maneuver required two separate keys. Neither man spoke but dispersed to preordained positions. Conor tapped three times on the track with a wrench to signal the team. His heart felt ready to burst from his chest.

Conor could see a man's silhouette emerging from the ceiling and moving slowly down the ladder. Inch by painful inch, he saw what he had hoped to see so badly and then what he had hoped never to see again.

The man moved quickly and quietly to that point of the track where Conor expected. Finding that the explosive charges had all been removed during the night, the silhouette straightened up and appeared to deflate before Conor's eyes.

Conor stepped out into the shadowy light. "Hello, Brother," he said.

Kevin sighed. "Oh, Conor, Conor…'tis a fine job I did with you now, a fine job, indeed, that ye would be after spoiling the crowning moment of me tired life."

"What in the name of God are you doing, Kevin?" Conor pleaded. "Are you mad?"

"Just looking after you, Brother," Kevin replied. "You had no idea what you were stirring up."

"I got that message, Kevin, when your goons jumped me in an alley."

Kevin shrugged. "I'm sorry, Conor. I never meant for all this to happen. I tried so hard to keep you from coming to this godforsaken place."

"And Rebecca, Kevin? Why did you have to kill her?"

"It's a war, Brother, and people have to die sometimes. Your friend was working for the British. I'm sorry."

"And the poor soul they pulled from the river dressed in your uniform, Kevin? That was your friend from the bar. Wasn't it? The one who looked like you? They told me at the bar that he disappeared around the time you went missing. Did you murder someone only for the misfortune of having the same build and hair color?"

"That I did, Brother, but it was for the cause of a free and united Ireland that he died."

Conor walked slowly towards his brother until he could see Kevin's face clearly. It was much older than he had imagined, and weary—so very weary. "There are two children on that train—children, Kevin. I couldn't let you do it." The distant sound of a train rumbled faintly.

Two figures emerged from the murky light behind Kevin, and he turned to face them. Conor could see Detective Flynn and the chief of police clearly. "So you've turned informer on your old brother, have you now, Conor?"

As the train's rumble grew louder, Conor reflected on the long road to this moment. He had indeed betrayed his brother, informed on him, but he could not allow innocent people to die. He had suspected for some time that Kevin was still alive and behind the plot.

After re-examining the box last night—the box of Kevin's personal items—everything became clear. Conor went to see the police chief and the detective. As it turned out, they were the ones trying to stop the assassination all along, but they did not know any details of the plot. Kevin was always behind it. Faking his suicide gave him some breathing space. Conor knew his brother was resourceful and bright. He just had to put himself into Kevin's head, painful as it was.

"So how did ye know, Conor? How did ye know it was me?"

"It was the packet of postcards. You left them in your room. The landlady gave me a box with all your belongings. I missed the significance of the postcards at first, but last night, thanks to a dog, I went back and looked again. They were all the Chicago World's Fair, all of them, the same postcards the Clan would use to signal Maureen Brogan. It was you who sent her to Hoyne Avenue with that pouch of money for your saboteur, not the Clan.

"As for the fake suicide, I just tried to think like you. Even as a youngster in Ireland, you would always find a solution. You were never afraid to do the hard thing, like boarding a ship to some foreign shore without a nickel to your name."

"Ahhh...and so ye informed on me, Brother. Sure Maureen is a fine looking girl. Well, no matter. Ye ended up exactly who I wanted ye to be and I'm proud to death of you, Conor, as would be our dear mother, the Lord rest her soul."

The train was close now, the single headlamp visible. Kevin pulled two dynamite pipes from his pocket and said, "I only have the one detonator left and a couple bombs. It might not be enough, but we shall see."

As Kevin produced a detonator from his pocket, Detective Flynn took a step forward and fired a single shot into Kevin's chest. Conor himself could almost feel the impact.

The chief of police pulled Kevin's lifeless body from the tracks just before the little train rolled slowly past with a loud rumble. The four men waived to the prince, who returned the gesture without a clue that his entire family barely escaped assassination. He would be free to return to England and resume his role in the subjugation and murder of the Irish people—Conor's people, Kevin's people.

Conor looked up. "Is he dead?"

Standing over the body, the chief said simply, "Your brother was already dead, Son."

ON THE WAY HOME, CONOR RELIVED THE PREVIOUS TWELVE hours in his head. He had learned that the chief and Detective Flynn had been assigned by the Clan to eliminate Kevin Dolan, but Kevin faked his own suicide to fool them. The cops had their suspicions about the suicide. They were never certain he was dead. The bullet destroyed half the corpse's face, and the fishes finished the job. Kevin was smart.

The cops had been tailing Conor to find Kevin. Even if Kevin had been dead, he was never acting alone. He was head of a radical faction and had plenty of help. The assassination might have gone ahead without him. Conor was thankful he and Victor were not able to act on their plan for Flynn. He might still be a villain, but he did not kill Rebecca.

Disaster was avoided. The world had not changed in the last twenty-four hours, but Conor Dolan himself and the way he viewed the world had both changed forever.

He stopped at the newsstand for the latest evening paper. Not so much as a hint that anything went wrong with the royal visit. The prince even gave a speech citing the "industrious nobility" of the city's people. A woman named Rebecca Fletcher had saved the bloody Prince of Wales, and the world would never know of her bravery and sacrifice.

And yet, he could almost sympathize with the Clan na Gael. This Prince of Wales was a notorious admirer of Oliver Cromwell, the great persecutor of Catholics in Ireland and the most hated figure in Irish history. Now this fucking prince would live to become King of England, and only time could judge the cruelties yet to be inflicted on the Irish people. If only Kevin had not killed Rebecca.

As he reached the stairs down to his flat, his thoughts turned to his most important client. In retrospect, Conor figured, he would rather save Nellie Finley than have saved the Prince of fucking Wales, but saving her from prison would mean condemning her to a life of pain and misery in Elgin. There had to be another way.

He put out a bowl of water for Dog along with some scraps of beef he had saved from last night's dinner. He had been feeding Dog at home lately out of concern for the animal's health. As a result, Dog gained weight. He was getting lazy, and Conor determined that the two would start walking regularly and watch their diets. He was doing what he had sworn never to do: he had started treating Dog like his property. He told himself it was out of love for the animal, but he knew better. Maybe it was just human nature, a triggered response to fear of loss like Brendan's passion for the poor immigrants. Father Brendan would never remove his finger from the pulse of this city and be happy just saying mass and hearing confessions. It was against his nature.

But humanity had changed Dog's life forever, and not for the better. There was no going back, only forward, and Conor knew that too. He had not seen Dog's alley cat friend in over a week, and they did not need a funeral invitation to know what that meant. The streets of Chicago claimed Dog's friend as they had Rebecca Fletcher. It was another common experience in the ties that bound the two. Dog seemed ready to start a quieter life, deciding to hook up permanently with this lost Irishman. They were stuck with one another now. Still, Dog smelled better these days.

Inside, he put the kettle on and turned up the heat. It was still an hour until dinner. Just time to read the paper. It occurred to him that he had been up to his ears in everyone's problems lately, ignoring his own. So the prince was spared and Kevin was really dead this time, but the Clan na Gael was still out there and knew that Conor Dolan was walking around with the goods on the chief of police. People at the tunnel company saw the explosives, saw the chief himself at the scene. The fact that they bought into the "secret mission" *bullshite* Victor had given them meant nothing because they were tickled pink that the Chicago River did not wipe out their operation.

For now their lips were sealed, but what if one person—just one person—opened his mouth? Faced with an accusation that the company aided the Clan na Gael in the person of the Chicago police chief, they would sing like Irish linnets. The chief and Detective Flynn would be skinned alive in the papers. The British government would want them extradited for the murders in the Dynamite Campaign. If Brendan was right about Chicago, then the chief, the Clan, and maybe even the mayor himself would not leave Conor alive with the leverage he now held. But that was tomorrow's problem.

The kettle whistled, and he poured his tea and turned to the sports page where he read of high hopes for his favorite baseball team. The deal for Ducky Holmes last June had worked out for the Chicago White Stockings. Following another losing season, the Stockings might be ready for a run at the new World Series competition with the National League. The Red Sox had certainly made the National League take notice last year. At six thirty, he headed upstairs for dinner.

Christmas Eve was coming up, and Mrs. Kaplan had replaced her menorah with a beautiful little porcelain Christmas tree on the dining room table, a respectful concession to the gentiles in residence. Conor had not given Christmas a thought until seeing the tree at dinner. He had come to dinner tonight only at Mrs. Kaplan's insistence as she had expressed concern over his late hours. Conor assured her he would get more rest. Her kindness and empathy had blossomed since Rebecca's death. With Mrs. Kaplan's help, he had managed to avoid the parlor and the piano the last couple of days despite Mrs. Goldman's passion for his music. The entire place haunted him with memories of Rebecca. The ladies understood that. There would be a move in his near future.

Chapter 26

Conor managed to avoid Mrs. Kaplan's parlor and left out the front door at half past eight, down the stairs, and then to the basement entrance. As a rule, Dog would be in his little stairwell flat by that time. He was running late. Conor unlocked the door and felt for the oil lamp hanging on the right. As he adjusted the flame, the soft light highlighted a man's silhouette sitting quietly at his small kitchen table. It was not entirely unexpected.

"Well, Detective Flynn," he said calmly, "I can't say I was looking forward to seeing you again. The door was locked. Can I ask how you got in?"

"I'm a detective," Flynn said. "I have magical powers."

Dog was lying beside the cop, looking unconcerned. "Your dog likes me."

"He picks his own friends," Conor snapped. "I don't own him, and I'm beginning to question his taste."

"Your brother wasn't a dog person," Flynn observed.

"He wasn't a people person either, seems like, but you're right; Kevin saw the world in its worst light from an early age. He couldn't afford an emotional connection to a dog. To Kevin, they were working animals. At home, everything and everyone had responsibilities. You wanted to eat, you worked—except me, of course. So you knew my brother well? No reason we can't be truthful."

"I knew him but not well. I liked it that way."

Conor was still standing. "You want a whiskey, coffee, before we get down to business?"

"Whiskey is fine. Thanks."

Before turning to the cabinet, Conor said, "You won't put a knife in my back while I pour?"

Flynn was holding his cards close. "Nothing of the sort."

Conor took out two glasses and the bottle of Jameson. He poured the two whiskeys and sat opposite Flynn at the table. He patted Dog on the head. "You're a horse's arse of a watchdog. I should start charging you rent." Then he looked across the table at the steely-eyed old detective. "I still don't understand why he killed Rebecca."

Flynn was in a mood to talk and had an answer but kept his right arm under the table as they spoke. No mystery about what the hidden hand was holding. "Somehow, you and Mrs. Fletcher managed to keep him in the dark about how much you knew, how close you were getting. I think he just killed her out of spite when she wouldn't talk."

"Madness." Conor still had not come to terms with it. Rather than struggle endlessly over motives and causes, Conor preferred to believe his brother had simply lost his mind. It was the only thing that made sense, the only thing he could live with. "Was he on the take?"

"Does it really matter now?"

The detective had a point. "I suppose I never thought about it that way," Conor admitted. "So tell me, Flynn, who was my brother—really?"

Flynn smiled. He picked up the glass with his left hand and held it. "Sláinte." They clicked glasses and downed the whiskey. "Sure after everything that's happened, don't ye know the answer to that question, Conor Dolan? Sure it's only yourself can answer that question because not a soul on this earth knew him better than did his baby brother, whether you believe that or not."

It was a strange thing to hear after everything he had been through. Maybe it was even true, Conor thought, but being patronized by the man who was about to kill him was too much to bear. He knew that's why Eammon Flynn broke into his flat quietly in the night. The whole trip to Chicago was a terrible waste of life for nothing. Now it would be his own life, but he did not want to die and would fight with his last breath to live. *What a fool you were to turn down the pistol. She tried to hand it to you.*

He knew Flynn could not afford to shoot him there in the flat. It would attract too much attention. He tried to gather his thoughts through the gripping fear. Flynn would suggest either they go for a ride or try to overpower Conor right there. But had he come alone? Was someone hiding in the next room? Flynn was too old—too experienced—to have come here alone expecting Conor to go quietly. If there was a fight, Flynn would lose.

Conor decided to put his cards on the table. "So did you come here to kill me?" he asked softly.

"Hadn't thought about it," Flynn said sarcastically, "but sure it's a good idea. Easiest way to look after meself and the chief." Then Flynn glanced down at the useless dog, begging for a bowl of Schlitz. Surely, this detective would not kill the dog. "But if we threw ye in the river, this homeless man killer of a hound would come after us for certain. Besides, it would raise a *fuss*."

"I think that sounds reasonable."

They talked more about Kevin and about the Clan na Gael. Conor refilled the glasses, and they talked about Springfield. Flynn was a Wexford man. The more they talked, the more Conor's hopes rose that he would see tomorrow.

Flynn laughed. "Relax. Sure you know I'm in the Clan na Gael and so is the chief. Our mutual problem is that you know too much."

"In the event it will help, I have a terrible memory."

"That's good to hear, and nobody's going to kill you, Son, not today anyway. I only came to have a chat. Officially, you might say."

"Officially for the police?" Conor asked.

Flynn shook his head *no*. "If ye expose the chief and me, it would ruin his career and his reputation. As for me…well, I'm fifty-nine years of age…ready for my pension anyway. They can't bring charges against us for some fifteen-year-old murders in London. We'll not do a damn thing to ye. We haven't reached the point where we'd start killing honest men doing their duty."

Conor started to breathe easier. "*Honest* isn't exactly how I'd describe myself," he confessed. "But I misjudged you, Flynn."

"You're not the first, Boy-o."

"So why do you do it? How do you do it? They say no one can serve two masters."

Flynn seemed to relax and become reflective. "I wish I could wear a Clan na Gael badge on my coat, Conor, but I can't. Being an Irishman is different from being a German or Italian or a Pole. You carry it right here." The cop struck his heart with a fist as though doing a mea culpa. "If you're an Irishman, you've known the famine and the cruelty of Cromwell through the memories and stories of your people. You've watched your neighbors and families waste away and die with your own eyes, seen your land stolen, your people starved, ravaged by greed and cruelty while the crops are shipped to England."

It was more complicated than that, Conor knew, but he was starting to see beyond his own mortality, even feeling a bit emboldened. "None of that justifies killing innocent people."

Flynn was up to the challenge. "You're forgetting that we worked hard to stop the assassination. I've never murdered anyone, and I don't think the chief has either. The Clan na Gael is not what it was fifteen or even ten years ago. We raise money to help the IRB in the struggle for Irish freedom. And if the struggles turn violent again, I'm certain we'll send them weapons. But if the day ever comes when we bite the hand that feeds us—I mean, inflict violence on American soil or even while living here under its protection—I'll quit."

The chief of police, Liam O'Casey, chose that moment to step purposefully into the dim lamplight from the bedroom. Looking directly at Conor, he said in an even tone, "Sure I'll quit as well before that happens again, Mr. Dolan. What I'll never do is sit in saloons and listen to fake Irishmen sing drunken songs about great men like Wolfe Tone or James Stephens. So go to the newspapers if you've a mind. Go. Tell them we're bombers and killers and whatever strikes your fancy. We'll deal with the consequences. Only remember one thing: you're a born Irishman, Conor Dolan."

In truth, Conor had never thought of himself as a "born Irishman," but this had been a long and instructive three months. "So I am."

O'Casey said, "I can't believe Kevin fooled us about the suicide. We never expected him to start killing innocent people. Sure a part of me hoped he would blow that fookin' prince to kingdom come. But I'm not just Irish now. I'm American as well, and I'm no traitor, and neither is Flynn here."

"I won't go to the newspapers," Conor declared, "or anywhere else. It's over as far as I'm concerned. I have other problems." With that, Conor rose from the chair and offered his hand to both men. There was work to do.

Flynn was not quite finished. "Sure there's still one or two more items on our little agenda. All along, we knew more than you thought we knew. We know about Nellie Finley. We know you're looking for a fellow, a barge operator, in Kankakee. The chief and I figure we owe you." Then he handed Conor a piece of paper from his pocket. "This is your man Sanders's address in Kankakee, Illinois. He's the bargeman who left town. He got a job with a local riverboat company."

"And what will I find down there?" Conor asked.

Flynn smiled. "You never know, Laddy, but I suggest you get down there right away. Might be something interesting. There's a train leaving at 7:10 in the morning from Central Station. Sure you'll have to spend the night somewhere, but there's a noon train back on Christmas Eve. A little bird told me you're on the right track. Consider it a gift from the chief and meself. I hope it all works out for you, Conor Dolan."

"Thanks, Flynn. Oh, you said there were a couple of items."

I did, indeed," Flynn said. "I did, indeed."

With that, the chief stepped forward and handed Conor an envelope. "Open it. There's a police report inside."

Conor unfolded the papers and held them under the dim light. It took less than a minute for him to understand what he was holding. Within two minutes, he had read every word. Within five minutes, he had read it three times. Each time he read it, the paper became heavier, more powerful, far beyond anything Conor had imagined. The paper had the power to save lives, to destroy lives, even to topple institutions.

He sat there quietly for a minute, holding it until he had reconciled his spinning thoughts and then said to the chief, "Why? Who?"

"It's your copy to do with as you please. Ye might even call it your brother's legacy. I got a call from Alderman O'Sullivan. He instructed me to retrieve the report from my desk and to provide you with a copy. Nothing more, nothing less. So, whether this is a gift or a curse, it's from him, not me."

Until that moment, Conor had not even considered his own predicament, but this was as good a time as any. "Oh, there's still the small matter of the pending felony charge against me for assaulting an officer."

Flynn laughed. "Well, much as I'd like to hold that over yer head for a year or two more, I t'ink the judge might be permitted t' drop the charges."

Chapter 27

Victor Harris had his own wife and kids in Chicago but agreed to accompany Conor on the overnight trip. In Kankakee, they checked into an inn near the train station and took lunch at a little diner on the picturesque town square, a community of businesses a few blocks south of the train station and surrounding the mid-nineteenth century Kankakee County Courthouse.

Private residences followed the hub-and-wheel pattern out from the town square in all directions except to the east where the river valley revealed a surprisingly bustling commerce and industry area that included stone quarries, modern port facilities, warehouses, barges, even a fancy riverboat. A line of fine houses wound north with the river along the far bank. The houses seemed to shrink in size the farther one walked from the square. Construction materials varied as well. Two blocks out, brick disappeared, replaced mainly by wood frame. They headed out to find Sanders an hour or so before the supper hour.

William Sanders and his wife lived in a modest frame house nearly a half mile west of the town square, but it was nicely maintained and in good order. A light snow fell as Conor knocked on the front door.

Sanders, only thirty-five, looked older and carried a slight paunch but a welcoming face framed by salt and pepper-colored hair.

"Good afternoon, sir. I'm Conor Dolan, an attorney. This is my associate, Victor Harris, a Pinkerton detective."

"Hi, I'm Bill," the man said in a melodic Dixie dialect that reminded Conor of Mark Twain, despite the fact that he had never met the great humorist and author. "How can I help you folks today? It 'peers to this ol' boy that you fellers came down here from the big city. Couldn't be just to see ol' Bill."

They both removed their hats. Victor said, "Actually, sir, that is precisely the case. Would you mind if we took a few minutes of your time?"

Bill opened the door all the way. "Come on in. Have a seat. Can I offer you a whiskey?"

"Whiskey will be fine," Conor said, whereupon Bill produced a bottle of Sour Mash and three glasses. The visitors were seated on a settee in front of the window.

The whiskey burned, then settled, a perfect warmer-upper for the task at hand. "You might have guessed," said Conor, "but we're here about the Nellie Finley case. She's the woman you and your friend saved from the river."

Bill shook his head back and forth. "Figured as much. I ain't likely to fergit that night. All happened so fast, we nearly missed it. How do y'all figure a woman would do that to her own child?"

"That's one of things we're looking into," said Victor. "Mr. Dolan is her lawyer."

Conor saw his opening. "That's right, sir. The report is sketchy, to say the least, so we'd like to go over a few things with you. Is that all right?"

"Don't see why not," Sanders replied.

"It's not clear that you actually saw the child in the water, or falling from the bridge for that matter. They never recovered the infant's body, so we'd just like as clear a picture as possible."

Sanders leaned forward in his chair and scratched his chin. "Well, sir, It all happened so quick like. We was just sittin' there on the barge after unloading. The Polish kid had a bottle and, you know...it was a long day. Well, somethin' caught my eye from the bridge, and I seen this female body fallin' from the bridge. Looked like she was holdin' an infant in her arms."

"So you didn't actually see the baby?"

"Can't say as I did," Sanders confessed.

In that moment, the unmistakable sound of a crying baby punctuated the silence, not loudly but definitely, and only for a split second. *It came from behind that door*, Conor thought. The sound had turned the atmosphere in the room on a dime. Nervous tension engulfed the space, and no one moved.

They had all heard the baby cry, but Bill showed no reaction. Conor said nothing, and Victor seemed to read his mind. Maybe there was nothing wrong, but they wanted Bill to talk first, and he did not disappoint. "Oh, sorry, that's my wife. She's feeding the baby. Had a baby a couple months ago, right after we moved down here."

"Congratulations," Conor said. "Boy or girl?" He remembered Nellie's baby was named Elizabeth.

Sanders ignored the question. *Possible he didn't hear the question, but not likely.* "So how can I help you gentlemen?"

"We're just turning over rocks," Conor said, "trying find out why the woman did this. Anything to help her. I know it's a terrible thing, but no mother would do that unless something drove her to it. Maybe she said something to you, a name, an incident. Maybe you found something. We're looking for anything that might help."

Bill Sanders stood up, held up his hands, and said politely, "I'm sorry. We used the skiff to fish her out of the water. I stayed with her and sent Naganska for help. She didn't say nothin' to me. She was out of it. I don't know nothin' else."

Sanders tried to escort them to the door, but Conor kept thinking about Eammon Flynn. The crotchety old detective had a hunch there was something here that might help Nellie. He was too close and was not about to leave the house without an answer. He and Victor made no effort to rise from their seat.

Then it came to him, the conversation with the other bargeman, Naganska. According to the young Pole, the Sanderses had "*all* moved away the next day." *All* moved away the next day, he repeated to himself. Realizing he was stuck, Sanders walked back from the front door.

"Do you have other children?" asked Conor.

"No."

"Does anyone else live here with you?"

"No."

Detective Flynn had been suspicious about this guy leaving town so quickly. He was telling Conor how he would have investigated the case himself. Naganska implied that three or more people left town, not simply Sanders and his wife.

"It's a strange thing," Conor said, "but when I spoke with your old landlord, he didn't say a word about your wife being in the child-bearing way. Is it a boy or a girl?

"It's a girl," Sanders replied.

Was it possible Nellie's baby was alive? Conor was not going anywhere until he knew the answer. "You understand we'll need to check it out. Can you tell us her birth date?" He needed Sanders to know this was not going away without answers, without proof. "Think about this clearly for a minute, Mr. Sanders. If you don't answer our questions, the police will be back until this is resolved. If that's the baby from the bridge, you could be in a lot of trouble. But you haven't done anything wrong yet. If that is the same child, she's only alive because you saved her. If you come clean and give her back now, there's every chance you won't even be charged. I'll represent you in the matter in the event they charge you with anything at all."

Conor's answer came from across the room, in a female voice. "We don't know her birth date." The woman was holding a baby and sobbing. "A part of me knew it was too good to last, Bill. You should know, Mr. Dolan, we would have turned the child over to authorities if the girl was convicted of her murder. We'd not have let her go to prison or..."

She tried to hand the baby over to Conor. The move startled him. What if he dropped the infant or her neck snapped? He had no clue how to hold a baby.

Victor came to his rescue. "Ma'am, why don't you hold the child for now? Looks like you're doing a fine job anyway."

Bill Sanders more or less collapsed into a chair near the door, head down, his hands cradling it like a watermelon. "She came out of the river, from God's hands into mine," he muttered. "I saved her. How could I give the child back to a woman who threw her from a bridge?"

The revelation started a frank conversation during which Sanders revealed that he and his wife had tried unsuccessfully to have children for years. That night, he managed to snatch the baby alive from the murky water in the blackness. In her delirium, poor Nellie Finley never had a clue. The Sanders saw the child as a gift from God. These people were not criminals, Conor knew.

The Sanders agreed to cooperate and return the child. But return her to whom and where? Conor had no clue. The man and his wife agreed to accompany Conor and Victor back to Chicago the next day and make a statement to the police. They would need Mrs. Sanders to care for the infant in any case.

"You both best be clear about one thing," Conor warned. "You never intended to keep the child. Never. You only wanted to keep her safe until you figured out how to return her and to whom. Do you understand how important that is?" He made them both say it out loud.

"Yes," said Sanders.

"Yes, I understand," said Mrs. Sanders.

Conor would tell the police that the Sanders contacted him after seeing his name in the newspapers. He and Victor would take them both directly to Detective Eammon Flynn. He was convinced the couple would not be charged. After all, Bill Sanders saved two lives in the river that night. Conor knew he was about to *fix* his first criminal case, but somehow, he felt no need to rush to a confessional.

At the inn that night, with the baby safely in the Sanderses' custody, Conor and Victor discussed where to take the infant and decided to deliver her directly and immediately into the hands of Nellie's social worker at Hull House. Then they would track down Flynn.

Since the infant had been declared dead, the Sanderses faced no current legal problems, but that could change if they told the wrong story. Thankfully, Conor figured, they were not Irish immigrants or colored. Justice seemed to be a little less blind with immigrants and employed perfect vision in dealing with Negroes. Besides, the factors mitigating their actions so far outweighed their illegality so as to demand complete exoneration. Together, the two saved the infant's life and lovingly nurtured her.

They speculated about Nellie and the baby. Hull House would know what to do. There would be no tearful reunion between mother and child on Christmas Day. Nellie's condition had not changed, and she would likely not be cured instantly by the baby's appearance. A reunion would come, hopefully soon, but only in consultation with psychiatrists and the professionals, and only under supervision for a time, maybe a long time.

Nellie might never be well enough to take custody of the child. If not a happy ending, it would at least be favorable because the charges against Nellie Finley would be dismissed and a flicker of hope for her eventual recovery was sparked. Conor's more immediate concern was who would care for the child during the long months or years of Nellie's recovery.

As for the Sanderses, Conor was determined to guide them past the legal pitfalls. He could never lift their pain—but he might arrange something to lessen it considerably.

Chapter 28

On Monday, morning, January 4, 1904, the entire city of Chicago was still in a state of shock. The New Year's holiday weekend had gone literally unacknowledged across the city, and the disaster story still dominated every edition of every paper after five days. Conor had picked up an early edition on his way to the office and unfolded it on his desk as Mrs. Schmidt delivered his black coffee.

"Theater blaze death toll may reach 600" was the double-sized headline emblazoned on page one of the *American*. Through page six at least, the Iroquois Theater fire was the only item of news in this grieving city. The venue had only been open for five weeks and was touted as the "the most fire-resistant building in America." The saddest part was that most of the victims were women and children attending a performance of a popular children's musical. It would be years, he thought, before the whole story was revealed. Even then, there would likely be another story, a sinister tale of greed and politics that might never surface. City inspectors, permits, favors, bribes, contracts—all of it was likely in play, and little, if any of it, would ever be known to the survivors, even to the newspapers. For every step forward in this city, there were two steps back.

He saw Mr. and Mrs. Sanders outside the office door and slipped the paper into his drawer.

"IT'S AN INFORMAL AGREEMENT," CONOR REITERATED TO MR. AND Mrs. Sanders. "As of yesterday, all charges against Nellie Finley have been dropped, but that also means no court has ruled on the issue of her insanity. It took two weeks to get the poor baby back onto the rolls of the living, so I wouldn't look for any rulings on her sanity until near the end of 1904. It really is a Happy New Year for little Elizabeth.

"Technically, Nellie is still Elizabeth's custodial parent. It may take several months for the court to rule on our petition for guardianship of her person, but in the interim, you will be acting as foster parents. When the judge issues a guardianship order, we will formalize the agreement, but you're free to return to Kankakee with the child for now."

Mrs. Sanders could barely speak through the joyful tears. "Thank you, Mr. Dolan. I just don't know what to say."

For perhaps the first time in his brief career, Conor felt proud to be a lawyer. That something good could emerge from this long nightmare filled him with a sense of possibility. He wondered what Ma and Pa would say if they could see him now. They could never have foreseen he would become a lawyer and help change people's lives for the better. Conor was thoroughly cured of religion and a belief in afterlife, but a part of him wished he could share this feeling with his parents again some time.

The Sanderses had spent the last few weeks in a hotel, visiting Conor's office nearly every day, and he was delighted to send them *all* home. "I'll notify you as soon as Hull House okays a reunion between Nellie and Elizabeth. After that, you should be prepared to come for monthly visits."

Bill Sanders said, "Does Miss Finley know Elizabeth is alive?"

"They've told her," Conor answered. "I only know the response was encouraging. Nellie is getting good care, and the staff is hopeful. You can head over there now and pick up Elizabeth if you like."

Conor helped with their coats and escorted the emotional couple to the office door. As they left, he added, "Detective Flynn asked me to convey his best regards. He's very happy for you."

Flynn was sympathetic to the Sanderses from the moment they all walked into the station on Christmas Eve. He simply noted that the infant had been found alive and returned by Good Samaritans. The law required no further action. Bill Sanders and his wife saved two lives, and neither was the worse for encountering them. The Nellie Finley file was closed. Conor regretted that Rebecca never got to rejoice in the outcome. It would not have happened without her.

On the cold walk back to Mrs. Kaplan's, he reflected on the irony of the situation. The corrupt police chief, whose loyalty was at least partially to a foreign nation, was the one who ultimately saved him. Men like the chief had managed to overcome half a century of anti-Irish bigotry and wrest a measure of political power from the Anglo-Saxon establishment. Of course, the real power in the city had always resided, and remained, with the titans of industry, the upstanding men of Astor Street like Charles Bennett III. Some said that men like Pullman and Marshall Field just let the Irish run the city subject to their veto power—to save them the nuisance. Maybe it was true, maybe not.

Conor looked down to see that Dog was tracking him home as usual, hoping to stop for a beer at Murph's. He had lost some of the extra weight. Dog would be disappointed this evening because Conor was feeling tired and very confused about his future.

The sting of Kevin's death—his real death—was raw and deep. Despite his murders and cruelty, Kevin believed in his dream of a united Ireland even if driven by deep-seated hate and revenge. He had good reason to join the Clan na Gael, Conor thought, but hate and bitterness hijacked his judgment and dissolved his capacity for discipline and reasoned actions, even love.

Maybe there was no getting away from his Irish heritage, Conor admitted to himself. By putting it out of his mind, losing his brogue, and assimilating into the world of the Anglo-Saxon Protestants, had Conor wrongfully denied his Irishness? His entire family, going back generations, suffered or died under the Crown's yoke, all except Conor. Assimilation was compromise, and Conor had become adept recently in the art of compromise. It was what Kevin wanted for him, but it felt dirty somehow.

Chicago opened Conor's eyes to reality. Nothing was as it seemed. Nothing worked quite as designed, and no one was quite who he claimed to be. Yet it managed to work, to grow incessantly. Chicago was a long way from Clare. He could never go back, not even to Springfield, his adopted home, and especially not to his Ireland. Chicago was in his blood now. It had welcomed him, bloodied him, and overwhelmed him with a sense of awe and possibility. He had seen it naked and raw, even abhorrent and corrupted, but the trials and hardships, debilitating to many, helped to forge a brave and resourceful people. Those people desperately needed his skills to help level the tide of injustice and bigotry.

Despite all the obstacles, the Irish immigrants and others continued to endure, survive, adjust, and eventually thrive here, he thought. The harsh environment, the bigotry, the institutional corruption, and labor abuses combined to make a place for them to plant roots and see their children prosper. Conor wanted to be a part of it, to grow with it, and to grow old with it. As for Kevin, Conor knew he might never fully understand the nature of the demons that fueled him.

MRS. GOLDMAN HAD SPOTTED HIM AT THE STAIRS TO HIS FLAT and called down from the first floor window. "You have two visitors in the parlor, Mr. Dolan."

Maureen and Patrick were there waiting for him in the main house. Mrs. Goldman was delighted to occupy little Patrick in the kitchen while the two adults spoke. Conor sat at the piano as he did when Rebecca was alive. It felt good again now, right. His fingers played some gentle tune he had been humming earlier. Maureen sat beside him on the bench and said, "Mrs. Kaplan invited us for a kosher dinner. What is it?"

He smiled. "You won't even know the difference. It will be delicious."

"I haven't heard from you all week. We've been worried. So much has happened since you got here."

He shrugged. "I've been trying to figure things out. It's hard to believe my brother was a murderer. I grew up believing in a man, in a world that never existed. In a way, Kevin never left Ireland. His grievances were justified; I know that, but he let hate drive them and turn them into something evil."

"You're an eejit, Conor Dolan," she scolded, "a bloody eejit. Anyone can hate; I hate."

He had been thinking only of himself, and shame enveloped him. "What do you mean, Maureen? Who do you hate?"

Her eyes turned away toward the floor. In a barely audible voice she said, "Do ye remember the story Father Brendan told ye about my young fella leaving me alone on the keel?"

"Very well," he answered. "It was terrible."

She looked up and directly into eyes, gently running a sleeve across her cheek as if to wipe away tears. But there were no tears. "There was no young fella," she confessed, "only three animals, Black and Tans, they were."

Conor was stunned. "You mean…"

"I mean exactly that. 'Twas late one night on the road home from me grandmother's. They were drunk in a cart, the lot of them. The royal bloody British constabulary they were, foreigners, German or Belgian mercenaries. Well—"

Conor held up his palm. "No, stop, Maureen. You don't need to say more." Still no tears, he thought, save his own. He reached across the piano, and they embraced as she began to sob, her tears bleeding in waves across his chest.

Conor felt completely helpless, dunce that he was, and dared not move or speak. When she righted herself, the tears were gone, beaten back by resolve and…hate. "Yes, Conor, I hate. I hate the English as I do Lucifer himself. Why do ye t'ink I'd get mixed up with yeer brother in the Clan na Gael but for hate? Did ye t'ink I was naïve? Daft?"

His smile was not forced. It just happened. "I'm an eejit," he declared and they both laughed.

But she had something else to say. It was there in her eyes. She placed her hand over his heart and whispered, "But there's none of my hatred on yeer own head, Conor, nor your poor brother Kevin, the Lord rest his soul. Jaysus, now could ya t'ink dat to be an accident? Sure it's Kevin who made you the good man you are. Don't you understand what that hateful son of a sow did for you, Conor? His letters and his moony helped build you into someone he could be proud of, someone I'm proud of, someone Kevin himself could never be."

Mrs. Kaplan walked into the parlor. "Dinner will be ready in ten minutes," she announced. "But do keep playing, Conor. I love to hear the music."

They were quiet for a minute as Conor improvised along the keyboard, then Maureen said, "Play something Irish, Conor, something really Irish."

He knew what to play for her and fumbled through his music until he found the paper, the one he found with Kevin's personal belongings with the lyrics to an old Irish ballad, "(My Own Dear) Galway Bay." He remembered the tune and had worked out the chords over the last weeks. It was well suited to Conor's limited voice range, but he never sang the whole thing before.[3]

It's far away I am today
from scenes I roamed a boy.
And long ago the hour I know
I first saw Illinois.

---

3 https://www.youtube.com/watch?v=Ha9jB_kecDg

But time nor tide nor waters wide
can wean my heart away.
Forever true it flies to you,
my own dear Galway Bay.

Had I youth's blood and hopeful mood
and heart of fire once more,
for all the gold the earth might hold,
I'd never quit your shore;
I'd live content what'er God sent,
With neighbors old and grey,
and lay my bones 'neath churchyard stones
beside you, Galway Bay.

The blessing of a poor old man
be with you night and day.
The blessings of a lonely man
whose heart will soon be clay.
'Tis all the heaven I'd ask of God
upon my dying day—
my soul to soar for evermore
above you, Galway Bay.

They sat in silence for a moment. The January evening sun was low in the west, shining directly on Maureen at the piano. He knew she was crying. From the corner of his eye, he could see the glistening tears reflected in the glow of sunset. Then she whispered, "Kevin never deceived you, Conor. He just raised you to be better than himself. His great love for you kept all the hate and meanness from his letters, and I don't mind sayin' he did a fair job of it as well. Hate consumed your brother, and I hated him in return. I still bear the scars, but he made it his life's work to be certain it would not consume you. What greater gift can a brother bestow? God bless him for the difference he made in your life, Conor Dolan."

He kept doodling some soft melody on the piano. "I swear, Maureen, I could have understood if it had only been about the Prince of Wales. Sometimes lately I think I would shoot the bloody prince myself, given another chance. But the innocent people Kevin killed...I can't forgive him that. I prefer to think he simply went mad. He wasn't the person whose letters I read and cherished over the years."

Maureen moved one hand onto her hips and scowled. He stopped playing. "Was he not, now? Well, let me tell you a story, Conor Dolan. Your mother did not die of old age in a quaint turf cottage in County Clare overlooking Galway Bay."

"What are you talking about?" he asked, annoyed.

Mrs. Kaplan reappeared and announced, "Dinner will be ready in a minute, folks. Mr. Dolan, I never heard you sing before. What a beautiful song."

With Mrs. Kaplan gone, Maureen said, "Your brother didn't talk a lot, but he told me one story ye need to hear. Sure Kevin was determined that you never know. When yeer father died, the family lost its tenancy. Ye were reduced to begging. Kevin took it upon himself to build a turf hut with a grass roof for yeer mother in the bog. 'Twas only mud bricks, Conor, with not a window a'tall and boogs everywhere. A kind neighbor provided the plot. One night, Kevin stole a cow and a donkey from the English landlord and set out for Galway City with yourself atop the donkey. It was that or sit on the mud floor of a wet shed and watch his baby brother take his last breath."

"Yes, I remember the donkey."

"In Galway, he sold the animals and bought two steerage-class tickets to New York from a shipping agent. Ye were in Galway a week waiting for the notice of sailing and slept in a church. When they announced the sailing, ye boarded a train for the port at Queenstown.

"Kevin knew full well he'd sentenced your poor mother to death, the Lord have mercy on her soul, and left her to die alone as Kevin himself set off to make you a new life. Sure the memory of the deed tormented him until that bullet pierced his troubled heart. He often told you she was well and living with neighbors until only a few years ago, all the while suffering the guilt of her inevitable, cruel fate. He never wanted you to know, Conor, but you needed to know."

"Kevin told you all that?"

"Sure even the divil himself has his unguarded, drunken moments. And where would Patrick and I be today, sure but for Kevin's intervention, twisted as it was? We'd have ended up like that poor soul, Nellie Finley. Ye were his one and only living dream, Conor. Sure Kevin knew his own life was a mook. More than anything, he wanted to help make yourself into the man he might have been."

She was right, and maybe he knew it all along. With all his baggage and damaged humanity, Kevin was determined to save his younger brother, not only from the consequences of hunger and deprivation but also from the crippling grip of hate, guilt, and revenge. Not unlike Christ on the cross, he thought, Kevin shielded him altogether from the scars of misery, hardship, and pain. He imagined how miserable Kevin must have felt, forced to choose between saving his mother or his little brother. The story, heartbreaking as it was, revealed to Conor his brother's complicated nature and the madness that drove him to kill innocent people like Rebecca. It was as if Conor understood his brother for the first time.

Had Kevin not done the same thing for Maureen in his own twisted way? She might have been driven to desperation like poor Nellie Finley.

She was right, and Conor knew he was seeing this woman in a new light these past few weeks. Maybe the light was always there but could not penetrate his thick skull. Her red hair was a burning bush there in the deep orange sun over the piano keys, loose and wild, raging like a prairie fire. Her eyes, far from lacking color, radiated a kaleidoscope of colorful emotions. They spoke in the Gaelic: pale gray for deep thought, emerald green for the scalding fury Conor had glimpsed only a second ago.

He turned to face her at the piano, the last rays of sunlight beating onto her fair skin and dancing through her hair. For the first time, he could see the natural color of her eyes. His mother had called it "County Leitrim green," the rare, hypnotic color God himself created only for crimson-haired Irish colleens. Maureen's Leitrim eyes had won young Conor Dolan's heart and his soul. *This is a remarkable and desirable woman, a woman with enough radiance and strength to fill my life.*

She touched his cheek gently and whispered, "Sure we were all damaged, Conor: ye, me, Kevin, Rebecca, even the bloody dog. Lovely Father Brendan, deviant soul he is, told me all about yeer little collie back in Ireland. All of that aside, the next time I see that three-legged mutt of yours, sure he had better be washed and groomed. I'll not tolerate that smell in my house, Conor Dolan. Am I clear?"

He reflected finally upon his brother, the meaning of brotherhood, and the irreconcilable duality of human nature. It all made him appreciate the three-legged dog more than ever. Dog was immune to all the duplicity and did not understand the concepts of lies or hate or concealed motives. He liked a good steak or rib bone now and again, shared his home with a needy stranger sometimes, and did not give a damn where another dog came from or what color he was. If only Dog could talk. What a conversation they would have over a Schlitz.

Like Father Brendan White, the animal had adapted and evolved to a point of perfect coexistence with a city that loved and laughed and killed without apology or excuse. Conor thought he might do the same if he was not alone. He was coming to love this city as he had this woman, but Maureen needed to know everything…everything.

"There's one more thing you need to know, Maureen—now before we speak another word."

"Ah, sure what could be so impartant now after all the shenanigans we've only just put to bed?"

"I'm thinking of joining the Clan na Gael, and I've spoken to Eammon Flynn about it. I'll do my part from this day forward in support of the Irish cause. As bad as Kevin was, it was the one thing he saw clearly since we left Ireland. I had to come to Chicago to see it for myself. How many lives were ruined or lost here only since the Great Famine? How many Nellies and Maureens boarded the iron coffins at Queenstown and the other ports, only to die in the filthy hole of a ship, in a frozen street or a brothel—or worse—five thousand miles from home? Until the British are out of Ireland, Maureen, no Irishman is free. Kevin knew that. His mistake was in forgetting that the end never justifies the means. I think my brother went mad of loneliness and guilt—of hate."

Maureen smiled and kissed his lips as if he had been complimenting her looks. "Is that all?" she asked playfully. "Sure you're an Irishman, Conor Dolan, even if you only just figured it out. And didn't your brother know it all along?"

Epilogue

"**S**ure this is pintless, Conor. How did I let ye talk me into this? Sure priests don't hire lawyers in matters of Church discipline."

"You know, for someone who rubs noses and makes deals with the most powerful men in Chicago, Brendan, you're remarkably naïve. You violate every rule of clerical conduct routinely; you don't believe half the gibberish you spew from the pulpit, and you spend half your time worrying whether your Chinese girlfriend is pregnant. Let the lawyer decide when you need a lawyer."

The velvet, hand-carved, antique chairs in the archbishop's private waiting room were elegant to the point of discomfort. The private mansion on Michigan Avenue might have gone unnoticed among the trophy estates along Astor Street or Prairie Avenue. But here, in the heart of the city, it commanded submission to the authority within its walls.

"You're going to embarrass yourself, Conor," Brendan protested. "Sure this is not how the Catholic Church operates. Ye have no influence here. Reason and logic, even truth, have no standing within these walls. It's an autocracy, pure and simple. There are times ye can't act like a stubborn eejit."

"Fine. The only thing I ask is that you keep quiet and let me do the talking—all the talking."

Brendan nodded. "That's the way then."

No less than a monsignor escorted them into the inner chamber where they stood in a medieval throne room amidst a blizzard of red and green fabric around an army of Jesus paintings, each in a gold frame and depicting increasingly painful levels of suffering. The great, oversized archbishop sat stone-faced in his work clothes, a black cassock with red trim and tassels, behind a desk that surely consumed the entire lifetime of a master craftsman.

"Father White, Mr. Dolan, His Most Reverend Excellency, the Archbishop of Chicago."

Conor would not have known whether to genuflect or curtsy or salute, but Brendan had carefully explained the protocol. Brendan even made him practice the procedure by dropping to his right knee, head down and kissing the ring.

Sure enough, the fat old cleric rose from his throne, walked carefully to the front of the desk, and extended his wrinkled hand, palm down, ring up for a smooch. But with the moment at hand, Conor recoiled from the certain trauma and, in so doing, failed his friend miserably. Standing tall, he took the archbishop's hand in his own as he would the hand of any man. He was left to imagine Brendan's reaction. The archbishop displayed no reaction whatsoever but asked, "Are you Protestant, Mr. Dolan?"

"No, Your Excellency." There was no need to be rude.

"You may be seated," the monsignor announced.

"Gentlemen," said the bishop, "this is most unusual." Staring directly at Brendan, he added, "I must say I'm extremely disappointed that one of my priests would find it necessary to involve a lawyer in Church matters."

Conor expected as much. The bishop agreed to his request for a meeting simply to eliminate the possibility of blowback. He wanted

Brendan gone quietly with no fuss and no questions. The man's intent, no doubt, was to make that clear.

The monsignor had obviously been choreographed to stand behind Conor and just off his left shoulder, not completely out of sight. They appeared to be confident, well-prepared, if condescending soldiers of Christ. Conor decided to state his business straightforwardly. "Your Excellency, we came here today hoping we might get you to reconsider your actions against Father White."

The three-chinned cleric slowly formed a condescending, pastoral smile. "Did you, indeed, Mr. Dolan? May I ask what qualifies you to conclude that my edict was intended to act *against* Father White?"

"I'm not certain I understand your question. Father White, as you know, has done laudable work in his community and has never asked anything for himself. The allegations involve a small sum of money, and I ask you to consider that all of it was used in service of the poor. Isn't that—?"

The archbishop held up his palm in a display of impatience, even arrogance. "My actions are intended only to help the good father, not to hurt him in any way. It's a question of discipline, Mr. Dolan. And please don't lecture me on Church doctrine, sir. In a few years, with much prayer and reflection, I'm certain Father White will be ready to take up his clerical duties somewhere."

For the first time since Conor met him, Brendan appeared intimidated, meek even. He remained silent, as promised, but it was more than that. This was a new Brendan, or at least a different side to the man he respected so much. With all his non-conformance, his professed loss of faith, this was still a man very much in the grip of his Church, muted by a lifetime of fear and indoctrination. Had Brendan really lost his faith? Or was this rogue priest image simply an attempt to joust with the Church itself, his attempt to fight back and make it into something it would never become? Conor might never know. Still, he saw vulnerability in his friend for the first time, even fear. It filled Conor with a sense of determination.

Conor was not intimidated. He could see the consigliere from the corner of his eye, the well-placed fly in the room. The monsignor was folding his arms across a feeble chest. The conversation was becoming tiresome, Conor thought, and pointless. He removed the envelope from his breast pocket ceremoniously, holding it up for the bishop to see. It was the same envelope the police chief handed him in the flat.

The cleric rolled his eyes. "What have you there that you think will change my mind? You may hand it to Monsignor Henry."

"If you really want me to do that, I will, but let me tell you a short story first. I had a brother, Kevin, a Chicago policeman. His beat was the Southside Levee District. I came to Chicago to visit him, to get to know him, but I was told he had died. Well, I learned many disappointing things about my brother. He murdered people, destroyed lives, and ran through your entire playbook of sins, I guess. But there was one thing my brother couldn't tolerate.

"One night, he saw a very important man going into a house of debauchery. I'm talking real debauchery, Your Excellency, not fornication with adult women. My brother recognized the man and decided that, for once, he wouldn't walk away. He wouldn't surrender to the status quo. So he went inside and found the man…well, I think you know what he found. So he arrested the man and filed a report even though supervisors warned him it would ruin his career. But he filed that report anyway. Of course, the great man pulled strings and was released. The report was sealed and the entire matter quashed. So I would—"

The archbishop, head down, reached out his hand and interrupted. "Show me what you have."

He only looked at the report for a few seconds, then folded it and returned it to the envelope, a defeated man. "You may return to St. Michael's and resume your duties there, Father White, upon your solemn oath before God never to discuss or disclose the contents of that envelope."

"Of course, Your Excellency," Brendan said, a bit bewildered, maybe, but hardly clueless.

Conor could not resist. "Oh, there is one more item of business, Your Excellency, if we might impose on your generosity."

"Yes, Mr. Dolan?"

"Father White employs two domestic helpers at the parish, very reliable, hard-working ladies. I think a pay raise would be a wonderful gesture. Say, 20 percent?"

"Of course, Mr. Dolan. The monsignor will see to it. Good day, and I wish never to see you again, sir."

WINTER HAD DESCENDED UPON THE GREAT CITY BY THE LAKE IN all its miserable manifestations as the two friends stood happily waiting for a trolley at the world's busiest corner, State and Madison, at Christmas time, no less. It was a beautiful city despite its horrors, and Conor knew he would never leave. He still had not bought a new coat and now was paying the price. But there would be time for all that now, time for other things too.

"Where are we going?" Brendan asked. "We should do something to celebrate."

Conor laughed as his warm breath exploded into the freezing air. Ice was forming between his nose and his lip, and he wiped it away with an old coat sleeve. "Let's go to Murph's, share the good news with him and Dog. Then we might go somewhere for dinner."

"I have a good idea what was in that report, Conor. At least I understand the gist of it, but was it the archbishop himself in that brothel? I can hardly believe it."

"It doesn't matter anymore. Besides, technically you don't know what was in the envelope. You've never seen it, and I never told you. Accordingly, you have nothing to confess."

Brendan laughed loudly, then flashed a wicked smile.

Conor added, "So am I learning *the Chicago Way*?"

"Ye're my brightest student, Conor. Just tell me how you got that report."

"It's ironic, I know, but it came from my brother, Kevin."

The southbound State Street trolley was finally in sight. "Kevin?" Brendan asked. "From the grave?"

As they entered Murph's, Conor spotted the familiar figure of his young friend Lefty Hawk at the bar. The celebrated newsboy could not hide his delight at seeing him.

"Conor," he gushed, ignoring the priest. He pointed to the next barstool and said, "Sit. I'm buyin' you a beer to celebrate my new career." Finally acknowledging Brendan, he added, "You too, Fadda' Brendan. Bote a' you'z won't believe da news. I gotta new job."

"Well, let's hear all about it," said Conor, slapping him affectionately on the back. "I'm all ears."

As Murph arrived with a round of beers, Lefty proudly announced, "From now on, you'z can refer to me as Officer Hawk of the Shi-kaw-go Police. I'm a copper…well, as soon as I finish training. I just got da news from Boris da Heeler."

"Jezuz, Mary, and holy St. Joseph," Brendan exclaimed, making the sign of the cross.

Conor smiled, genuinely unaware of the news. O'Sullivan fulfilled his end of the bargain. "I'm happy for you, Lefty. You'll make a great cop. You know the city like the back of your hand. You're on a first-name basis with every professional criminal and juvenile delinquent in the city. More importantly, you're a good man. What about your brother?"

"Oh, Red is gonna be an Animal Control Officer. Ain't that the topper, Conor?"

The news was a perfect ending to a turbulent chapter in Conor's life. For the first time, the young lawyer felt as if he belonged here, and he wanted to play a role in the city's future with Lefty and Murph and Brendan and Maureen and the thousands of other good folks from around the world determined to tame this wild and wonderful city on the lake and on the take.

He held up his glass. "One last round, Murph, for my friend Officer Hawk." Turning directly to his companions, he added, "I have a feeling we'll be repeating this ritual over many years, my friends.

"Sláinte!"

About the Author

 Bob was raised in Chicago, enlisting in the Air Force in 1968. Following four years service as a Russian linguist in Security Service Command, a branch of the NSA, Bob attended DePaul University and The John Marshall Law School. With over thirty years experience as a criminal defense lawyer in Chicago, Bob brings a lifetime of understanding and experience to his novels. The author lives in the Chicago area.